Howard, Richard

Bonaparte's horsemen

BONAPARTE'S HORSEMEN

Also by Richard Howard

Bonaparte's Sons
Bonaparte's Invaders
Bonaparte's Conquerors
Bonaparte's Warriors
Bonaparte's Avengers

BONAPARTE'S HORSEMEN

RICHARD HOWARD

A *Time Warner* Book

First published in Great Britain in 2002
by Time Warner Books

This is a work of fiction.
Characters, organisations, situations and philosophies are either the product of the author's imagination or, if real, have been used fictitiously without any intent to describe or portray their actual conduct.

A CIP catalogue record for this book
is available from the British Library.

ISBN 0 316 85052 7

Typeset in Sabon by M Rules
Printed and bound in Great Britain
by Clays Ltd, St Ives plc

Time Warner Books UK
Brettenham House
Lancaster Place
London WC2E 7EN

www.TimeWarnerBooks.co.uk

Bonaparte's Horsemen

One

The breeze that swept through the confines of the pine forest ruffled the long brown hair of Alain Lausard. He brushed some strands from his face and pressed himself closer to the trunk of the tree behind which he was positioned. On either side of him, his companions also sought to melt into the shelter offered by the trees and thick undergrowth of the wood. Their dark green dragoon uniforms were something of an ally in this. The wool of their tunics and capes were made considerably darker by an accumulation of dirt and grime. Lausard was aware of the stench that he gave off but he was not alone in his lack of cleanliness. The sergeant could not remember the last time his uniform had been properly washed. He himself had yet to enjoy the simple pleasure of a good bath in warm water. During the last three weeks of the campaign, it had become virtually impossible to distinguish between the odour of unwashed clothes or the stink of the dirty bodies beneath them.

Every man in his squadron and, he suspected, every soldier in *La Grande Armée*, was suffering in a similar way. But at least the French army's discomfort at what had become such an unrelentingly unhygienic existence, was tempered by the fact that they had been victorious during their latest trial of arms. Triumphant beyond their wildest dreams. It had been barely six weeks since Lausard and one hundred and seventy thousand French troops had invaded Prussia and now, with December fast approaching, they were all dreaming fondly of an overall end to hostilities and the complete subjugation of a foe whose defeat had been comprehensive in the extreme. Thanks to the genius of the man Lausard and his companions called Emperor, Prussian military might had been effectively destroyed. Napoleon Bonaparte's mastery of tactics and warfare had, once and for all, exorcised the ghost of Frederick the Great. Prussia was a fallen giant and it was now up to Lausard, and men like him, to ensure that she did not rise again. To emphasise the ferocity of the victory. To reinforce their Emperor's assertion that France was the greatest power on mainland Europe. It was a claim embraced not just by Lausard and his companions but by their enemies too. A series of campaigns and major battles had seen Napoleon expand his power base to such an extent that few dared challenge him. *La Grande Armée* was the ultimate fighting machine and Lausard was proud to be a part of such a formidable organisation. Happy to carry out the orders of his Emperor and the Corsican's very able subordinates without question.

He edged forward slightly, careful not to step on the fallen twigs and branches that covered the floor of the forest with such proliferation. His dust-covered boots left imprints on the moss and lichens that grew in such abundance beneath his feet. He held his Charleville carbine in one powerful hand, the fifteen-inch bayonet attached to the end of the barrel. Lausard stooped slightly, making himself an even smaller target as he moved forward. He breathed slowly and evenly, attempting to disguise the exhaled breath that clouded on the chill breeze. Behind him, Karim drew the scimitar from the scabbard on his belt and followed the NCO. The Circassian was a powerfully built man but he still seemed to move with almost supernatural ease, barely, it seemed, putting any pressure on the forest floor. Like a ghost, he ducked from tree to tree, his eyes fixed ahead.

Lausard raised one hand and motioned to three more of his companions to move up with him. Rocheteau, Carbonne and Roussard did as they were instructed. The thief, the former executioner and the forger were also carrying their carbines at the ready. A little behind them came more dragoons, all on foot, all moving with the kind of practised ease and stealth that is only acquired by skilled fighting men over a long period of time.

Joubert, Bonet and Charvet. The fat man, the former schoolmaster and the boxer. Men who were as close to Lausard as the family he had seen die beneath the blade of the guillotine more than eleven years earlier. Individuals he had come to respect and to love as friends and comrades. Men who would die for him and who, in turn, he would happily give *his* life for.

Gaston, Moreau and Giresse were also close by. The trumpeter, the religious fanatic and the horse thief. Back on the road, guarding the horses, thirty or more yards through the dense wood, were Tigana, Tabor and Delacor. The horse expert, the man-mountain and the rapist. With them was Rostov, the Russian. All of them filthy dirty, stained with the blood of vanquished enemies and the mud of yet another conquered country but Lausard trusted them all with his life. He felt at one with them. A part of them. He himself, the son of an aristocratic family, was comfortable among murderers, thieves, rapists and fanatics because he knew how their minds worked. He had come to know during the last ten years. He had suffered as they had. Triumphed when they had. They accepted him unquestioningly. They respected his supreme skill with weapons, his brilliance on horseback and they admired his courage. A courage driven as much by an urge for atonement as by any love of his country or disregard for his own life. For, in Alain Lausard's mind, the only way he could ever be redeemed for allowing his family to die while he had lived was to find an honourable death on the battlefield. Whether that place be in Prussia, Italy, Moravia, the freezing and treacherous passes of the Alps or in the scorching deserts of Egypt. It mattered little to Lausard. He had fought in every one of those places but, as yet, death had forsaken him. He wondered how much longer it would continue to do so.

Karim moved ahead a little more rapidly now, ducking low as he emerged on to a stretch of ground that sloped away gently towards a shallow valley below. The terrain was also not as densely planted and, as it tilted away, it provided significantly less cover. The Circassian dropped to his knees then to his belly as he crawled along through the thick grass. Lausard watched him for a moment, his hand raised high in the air as a signal for his companions to hold their ground. Karim was making for an outcrop of bush-shrouded rock and, when he reached it, Lausard saw him rise slightly and peer down the slope. He turned to the sergeant and gestured him forward. Lausard tapped Rocheteau on the shoulder and both men scuttled in the direction of the Circassian, careful to keep their footing on the uneven ground. Both of them held their sword scabbards in one hand to prevent the three-foot-long metal sheaths from trailing along the damp, stony earth.

Still breathing evenly, Lausard and his companion dropped down beside Karim and gazed into the valley.

'How many of them do you think there are?' murmured Lausard, running his gaze over the scores of troops at the bottom of the slope.

Karim merely shrugged.

'A couple of hundred,' he answered. 'I can't be sure.'

Lausard scanned the valley and its inhabitants more closely.

There were Prussian troops of all ranks and arms in the muddled mass that sheltered at the bottom of the valley. Some wore the familiar dark blue tunic of Prussian infantry. Others sported the white uniform of their Saxon allies. There were a handful on horseback but most of the cavalry, some dressed in the normally resplendent attire of hussars, had been consigned to marching, like their battered companions. Few of the men had complete uniforms. Some wore their jackets open. Most had rips and tears in their tunics or trousers and many were without shoes or boots. Few, Lausard noted, carried muskets. Many more had discarded their packs. The animals that accompanied them were undernourished and the ribs of most horses were clearly visible beneath torn or blackened shabraques. Lausard could see that a number of men were riding horses that had quite clearly been used to haul artillery pieces. Some rode bareback. There was a small stream at the bottom of the valley and Lausard watched as men either washed quickly or collected water in battered canteens. Those with mounts were watering them, some kneeling beside the horses as they drank.

'They've posted no lookouts or sentries,' Rocheteau remarked.

'They're too concerned with running,' Lausard murmured.

'There don't appear to be many officers with them,' Karim observed.

'It wouldn't matter if King Frederick William himself was with them,' chuckled Lausard. 'They would still be as disorganised. I will venture that there *are* officers among them but they are as eager to reach safety as their men. Besides, retreating armies do not usually respond well to discipline.'

The three dragoons continued to gaze down at the impoverished gaggle of enemy troops before them, watching as some of the wounded were helped to their feet by hardier comrades.

'There are more than two hundred down there,' Lausard finally commented. 'Possibly even more over the next ridge.'

'What do we do?' Rocheteau wanted to know.

Lausard stroked his unshaven chin thoughtfully for a moment.

'Word has it that four thousand Prussian cavalry surrendered to less than seven hundred of our horsemen under General Milhaud at Pasewalk,' he murmured.

'What are you trying to say, Alain?' Rocheteau asked.

'The men before us are scarcely in a position to fight, are they?' said the sergeant. 'Karim, go back and fetch Lieutenant Royere. He should see this. Take the others with you.'

Again, ducking low to the ground, the Circassian scrambled to his feet and hurried back towards the enveloping safety of the thicker woods. Lausard kept his eyes on the mass of Prussian fugitives in the valley below, his gaze picking out more wounded here and there. Men were chewing on mouldy biscuits or stale bread, anything they could find to fill their empty bellies. Horses grazed the tough grass that grew on the slopes while their riders sat astride them looking exhausted. One officer, easily distinguishable by his silver and black waist sash, was moving among the more seriously wounded, occasionally checking on their condition. Lausard saw him shake his head over the figures of several men. Immediately, the others began to strip them of their clothes and what few belongings they still had.

'They're in a worse state than we are,' Rocheteau mused.

Lausard nodded almost imperceptibly.

'Why don't they just stop running?' Rocheteau said. 'Give up?' He shook his head. 'Men should know when they are defeated.'

'Would you, Rocheteau?' Lausard asked. 'Would I? If the positions were reversed would we be so eager to give up our freedom? Would we surrender our dignity so meekly? I think not.'

Lausard felt a rumbling beneath him, as if the earth itself was shaking. It was a sensation he recognised well, and it was followed a moment or two later by sounds that he also knew. The jingling of harnesses and the pounding of many hooves. He and Rocheteau turned to see several ranks of dragoons moving relatively easily through the woods, guiding their mounts around the pine trees and trampling the underbrush. At their head rode Lieutenant Royere and beside the officer was Karim. He led two horses by their reins. One, a powerful black animal, the other a smaller but no less robust brown and white mount. Ahead of the horses ran a huge black dog.

'I thought that black devil would want to come along,' chuckled Rocheteau. The dog ran up to him and licked at his hand. He stroked it roughly then pushed it to one side and swung himself into the saddle of the brown and white horse. Lausard also stroked his own mount then clambered aboard.

Lieutenant Royere looked down the gentle slope towards the Prussians and Saxons, his eyes surveying the terrain. He looked more concerned about the ground his men must cover than the numbers of enemy troops to their front.

'Open order, I think,' mused the officer. 'The trees appear to thin out completely towards the bottom of the slope. We will close ranks then if we have to. Your talent for finding the enemy is as infallible as this monster, Sergeant,' said Royere nodding in the direction of Erebus. The dog barked joyfully and ran back and forth in front of the slowly advancing horsemen.

'Draw swords,' Royere called and the relative silence was broken by the metallic hiss of blades being pulled from scabbards. 'Do you favour these odds, Rocheteau?' Royere looked at the corporal who grinned broadly.

'Thirty of *us* against two hundred Prussians, Lieutenant,' he chuckled. 'I'll give you even money.'

Royere raised his sword high into the air and waved it in the direction of the enemy.

The dragoons advanced, pulling on their horses' reins as they descended the slope, the horses careful to retain their footing on the frosty ground. They picked up speed slightly as they cleared the thicker outcrops of trees and bushes but never accelerated beyond a trot.

Lausard felt the cold air brushing his cheeks. The horsehair mane of his brass helmet trailed out behind him. He gripped the hilt of his three-foot-long sword more tightly and fixed his eyes upon the mass of Prussian and Saxon fugitives before him.

By now, many had heard the rumbling of hooves and were turning towards the French dragoons who were still advancing at the regulation two hundred and forty paces a minute. Lausard felt his heart beating a little faster and he waited for the first shots to be fired from the enemy. But none came. Even when the French had cleared the worst of the trees and were able to form into one solid unit, there was no response from the Prussians. Lausard could see many of the dark-coated men merely standing watching as the dragoons rode towards them. Then, as if an order had been given, the Prussians began to raise their arms in surrender. Those nearest the oncoming French were the first to react then the movement spread across the bottom of the valley and up the other slope until it seemed to Lausard that every enemy soldier had adopted an identical stance.

Lieutenant Royere raised his sword to halt his men and the dragoons brought their mounts to a halt, glancing around at the immobile forms of the Prussians.

'Who is in command here?' Royere demanded, the words spoken in perfect German.

Every sanguine face looked in his direction but no one answered. The men merely stood with their arms raised.

Lausard, less than twenty yards from his nearest opponents could now see just how pitiful a state they were in. A number were wounded but most seemed in reasonably good health but for the fact that they were so pale and hungry. Those in such condition certainly outnumbered the dragoons several to one. Should they choose to fight, it would be a bloody morning. But

Lausard had little fear of this collection of dispirited scarecrows that faced him. The sergeant patted his horse's neck to calm it. Erebus wandered towards the motionless enemy troops, sniffing the air cautiously.

'Which unit are you from?' Royere called again.

'Von Kleist regiment,' someone called.

'Alt-Larisch regiment,' shouted another.

'Regiments des Königs,' added a third.

From all over the valley floor and the slopes, men shouted the names of regiments they had been a part of. Formations that, Lausard could plainly see, had now ceased to exist in all but name.

Royere raised a hand to silence them.

'You are enemies of France,' he shouted, his voice echoing around the valley. 'Your country is defeated. Your king has fled. In his mercy, our gracious Emperor, Napoleon Bonaparte, extends to you the opportunity for honourable surrender without conditions. Your wounded will be cared for. You will not be mistreated. Accept these terms and you will live. Contest them and you will die like so many more of your countrymen already have. What is your answer?'

As one, the mass of fugitives in the valley made their way slowly towards the dragoons, arms still raised so there could be no mistake about the nature of their decision.

'Cowards,' sneered Delacor, watching them form into one huge ragged column.

'And what would you do in their place?' hissed Giresse. 'They are beaten and they know it.'

Delacor hawked loudly and spat in the direction of the defeated men.

'They surrender without firing a shot,' he snorted.

'That is just as well,' Roussard noted. 'We have fought enough battles already. There is no more need for loss of life.'

The enemy troops filed past and Lausard watched them impassively, glancing down to see just how many were without footwear. Many were walking on what looked like swollen lumps of bleeding meat. He could only guess at how long they had been trekking across their own country in a quest to escape the ever advancing French. The looks on the faces of many was not that of humiliation and despair but of relief that the chase was finally over. That they could finally find peace at the hands of their conquerors.

'A victory without death,' murmured Bonet. 'Would that all wars were fought this way.'

Lausard did not answer.

Men drew closer to the dancing yellow flames of the fire to warm themselves against the chill that had come with nightfall. Some were already beginning to doze, exhausted by the day's march. To Lausard and most of his companions, it seemed that they had been marching continually for the last two or three weeks. Constantly in pursuit of Prussian troops who had been driven to the point of despair by their defeat and subsequent harassment. Lausard had begun to wonder, upon hearing daily of more enemy capitulation from all over the theatre of war, if the entire Prussian army was intent on surrendering. Now, he sat alternately gazing into the flames of the fire and sharpening his sword with a stone he had retrieved from the frosty ground close by. The weather had remained almost unnaturally mild right up until the middle of November but, during the last three or four days, it had begun to assume the falling temperatures Lausard associated with the death of another year.

Charvet was standing beside a large metal pot dangling over the flames, stirring the contents with a bayonet. Every now and then, Gaston would add more vegetables. Mostly potatoes but the occasional carrot or turnip. Rice and oats were also mixed into the bubbling stew and Charvet sniffed the contents like some gourmet. Rostov looked on, smoke billowing from his pipe. Carbonne had removed one boot and was trying to repair a hole in the sole using pieces of felt he had cut from a dead Prussian's bicorn. Joubert sat with his metal plate in front of him, waiting for Charvet to dish up the food. The big man was chewing on a piece of stale bread he had taken from a Saxon prisoner but it did little to assuage his raging hunger. Tabor sat stroking Erebus and the dog lay contentedly beside him, its eyes half-closed, its nose twitching.

Rocheteau was cleaning his carbine. Sonnier was changing the flint in his. Delacor was sharpening the blade of his axe. Bonet was studiously counting his cartridges, replacing the wet ones. Those that were merely damp he placed at a safe distance from the fire and waited for the heat to dry the powder and paper. Once this was done, he returned them to his cartouche and sat back against his saddle. It was a familiar sight to Lausard. One he had seen in half a dozen different countries during the past ten years. The sights and sounds of a bivouac were commonplace to him and all his men. He continued sharpening his sword, occasionally running his thumb over the cutting edge.

Sonnier took a swig from the bottle of wine that was being handed round then passed it to Lausard.

'Lieutenant Royere said we captured three hundred and forty-six enemy troops this afternoon,' Gaston grinned.

Delacor clapped theatrically and held his companions' stare.

'Soon the entire Prussian army will be in our hands,' Giresse continued.

'Good,' Roussard intoned. 'Perhaps then we can go home. When the Prussians have all surrendered we can return to France.'

'You are dreaming,' said Delacor. 'Do you think that Bonaparte is going to stop now? We are already less than twenty miles from the borders of Poland.'

'Delacor is right,' Lausard offered. 'The Prussians may have been defeated but there are still other enemies to occupy Bonaparte. And if our Emperor is troubled by them, they will very shortly become *our* concern too.'

Some of the men chuckled.

'Which enemies?' Joubert wanted to know, rubbing his mountainous belly.

'The Russians,' Lausard told him. 'Why do you think we are still marching east? They have large numbers of troops in Poland.'

'One war finishes, another begins,' Roussard murmured. 'Are we *never* to find peace?'

'The only time *we* will find peace is when they lay us in the earth,' Delacor offered.

'I do not fear that day for it is the day I will see God,' Moreau offered, crossing himself.

'All you will see is the bottom of a mass grave,' Rocheteau snorted. 'There *is* no God. If there was, he would not allow the kind of suffering we have seen and experienced these past ten or more years.'

'Your blasphemy will not help you, come Judgement Day,' Moreau countered.

'How many of the Prussians do you think prayed to your God, Moreau?' Lausard wanted to know. 'And look where it got *them*.'

Again the men laughed.

'Perhaps they would have been better served offering their prayers to Allah, all praise to Him,' Karim interjected, inspecting a slight dent in the hilt of his scimitar. The wickedly sharp, curved blade glistened in the firelight.

'To a heathen God?' Moreau protested. 'A false idol.' Again he crossed himself.

'If I don't get some food soon, then *I* will be meeting God,' Joubert said, pushing his plate forward. 'How much longer are you going to cook that rabbit, Charvet?'

'Shut up, fat man,' snapped Delacor. 'You could go without food for six months and still not notice the difference. You have enough blubber to sustain you and half of the army.'

There was another loud outburst of laughter.

'That's another reason I do not believe in our taking prisoners,' Joubert said defiantly. 'The more prisoners that are taken, the more food must be set aside to feed them. Food that we ourselves need.'

'You have a point, Joubert,' Rocheteau offered. 'Our own men are starving and yet we give food to captured Prussians.'

'And what would you have us do with them?' Bonet wanted to know. 'Execute them?'

'Bullets are easier to come by than bread,' Rocheteau chuckled.

Lausard smiled, took one more swig from the bottle then passed it on.

Rostov accepted it gratefully.

'So, our next opponents are to be your countrymen,' Lausard said, looking at the Russian.

'Need we fear for your loyalty, Rostov?' Rocheteau laughed.

'I owe nothing to the Tsar or any of those Romanov bastards. It is because of them that I left Russia. Because of them that my family starved to death. When the time comes, you need have no fear of where *my* allegiance lies.' He passed the wine bottle to Giresse who rolled it between his hands then drank.

'Are we marching into Russia?' Tabor wanted to know.

'Of course not, you half-wit,' snapped Delacor. 'Not even Bonaparte would be mad enough to attack a country *that* size.'

'Men of genius can easily be mistaken for madmen,' Bonet offered.

'Then every man in this unit must be a genius,' Rocheteau grinned.

'But the sergeant said we are marching east,' Tabor persisted. 'Russia is in the east is it not?'

'We march to Poland,' Bonet said, patting his giant companion on the shoulder. 'Where we will be seen as liberators.'

'As we were in Egypt?' Lausard mused.

The men laughed once more.

'That hell-hole,' snapped Delacor. 'Surely Poland can be no worse than *that* infernal place.'

'Poland has been under Russian and Prussian domination for many years now,' the former schoolmaster continued. 'The Emperor will give them a chance to regain their national identity.'

'He comes as a liberator and leaves as a conqueror,' Lausard said flatly. 'He has done so before and he will do so again. He pays lip service to Polish nationalism while he swallows the country whole to expand the borders of his Empire.'

'The borders of the *French* Empire, Alain,' said Rocheteau wryly. 'Do you imply that the two are separate?'

'France and our Emperor,' Charvet offered. 'They are the same.'

'If you say so, Charvet,' the NCO conceded.

'I have never enjoyed the pleasures of a Polish woman, nor they I,' said Giresse, raising the wine bottle in salute. 'I drink to

Poland and her women and to those who *I* may liberate. I hope they are grateful.'

All around the blazing fire the men laughed.

Lausard wiped the blade of his sword with an oily cloth then slid the weapon carefully back into its scabbard. He wondered how long it would be before he would draw it again.

Two

Napoleon Bonaparte gazed in amusement at the statue of Frederick the Great that stood so proudly outside the palace in Berlin where the former Prussian king had once resided. The stone likeness in turn looked on blindly at the impeccably attired rows of French Imperial Guard drawn up before it. Big men in their traditional blue tunics and white breeches, sporting huge bearskins that made them look like giants. Red plumes blazed brilliantly on each bearskin and the brass front plates glinted almost as brightly as their fixed bayonets. On either side of them, mounted grenadiers sat astride black horses, their ranks as rigidly straight as those of their infantry comrades. Behind the infantry were more cavalry. Chasseurs in green dolmans and red pelisses, trimmed with yellow lace sporting brown kolpaks with bobbing red and green plumes. Guard dragoons in brass helmets with leopard-skin turbans also sported red plumes. Close by, most resplendent of all, were several ranks of Mamelukes dressed in their magnificent parade uniforms of red fez and white turban, light blue, red-edged waistcoats over dark green shirts and, most striking of all, their voluminous red breeches. They all rode the most magnificent Arab horses, many of them white.

The square that formed the frontage of the palace was crammed with the men of the Imperial Guard and the Corsican ran appraising eyes over them. He adjusted his bicorn and wandered back and forth in front of the statue of Frederick the Great as if willing the stone figure to see the stunning array of men before him. Men who had helped to destroy the armies of Frederick's country. Napoleon paused beneath the branches of the linden trees that grew near the statue and looked at those members of his staff who were present. General Jean Rapp had removed his bicorn and was running a hand through his hair. He murmured a few words to General Geraud Christophe Michel Duroc and the taller man nodded. Duroc was a powerfully built man with slightly protruberant eyes that gave him the appearance of being perpetually surprised. Like his colleagues, he was dressed in a magnificent blue uniform decorated heavily with gold lace and topped with a feather-trimmed black bicorn. Beside him stood General Armand Augustin Louis Caulaincourt, Master of the Horse and one of Napoleon's closest friends. He glanced down at his boots to ensure they were as sparklingly clean as he wished and saw his own reflection in the gleaming leather.

'A fine sight, eh, gentlemen?' said Napoleon, indicating the Imperial Guard troops.

'They honour you, sire,' Duroc offered. 'The finest troops in Europe commanded by the ablest man.'

'What do you think the Great Frederick would say if he could see the soldiers that conquered his country paraded before his palace?' Napoleon tapped the base of the statue with the flat of one hand.

The other men laughed.

'He would acknowledge their superiority, sire,' said Rapp, smiling. 'If a little grudgingly, I suspect.'

'That is one of my regrets,' the Corsican said softly. 'That I was never able to pit my own skills against those of such a fine leader on the field of battle. Those who succeeded him were an insult to his name.'

'This campaign was not won because of Prussian inadequacies, sire,' Marshal Jean Baptiste Bessiéres insisted. 'But because of our own superiority. Combined with *your* genius.'

Napoleon smiled.

'Thank you, my friend,' he said.

'I agree,' offered Marshal Louis Alexandre Berthier. The Chief of Staff stroked one cheek and glanced behind him at the palace.

'The Prussian army had not evolved beyond the tactics used in the time of Frederick the Great, sire. When we met them in battle it was like a meeting of the old and the new. The new will always triumph in such a case. As you always insist, an army must be adaptable. The Prussians were not. They suffered as a consequence.'

'They certainly did,' murmured Napoleon. 'Their armies are destroyed, their capital is in French hands. Of one hundred and sixty thousand of their troops who began the campaign, we have accounted for one hundred and twenty-five thousand, killed and captured.'

'Of the thirty-five thousand that remain, none has succeeded in crossing the Oder to link up with the Russians,' Rapp added triumphantly.

'And yet, despite that, there is still no end to the war,' Napoleon said flatly. 'King Frederick William would agree to an unconditional surrender immediately but he lacks the strength of those who advise him. His own queen insists that the war is not over. His Chief Minister, Hardenberg, has also convinced him that Prussia may yet negotiate a favourable peace. He blusters from the safety of Königsberg and refuses to accept the inevitable.'

'As long as the Tsar promises support, they will maintain their obstinacy, sire,' Berthier said. 'The promises of Russian intervention ensure that.'

'And, as ever, the English promise naval support and gold,' hissed the Corsican. 'Are that cursed island and its belligerent inhabitants sworn to oppose me at every turn?'

'The issue of the Berlin Decrees has done nothing to deter them, sire,' Caulaincourt offered. 'If anything, their nature has *increased* the aggressiveness of England's stance against us.'

'What other steps can I take against this nation of shopkeepers?' Napoleon snapped. 'The Decrees forbid all commerce and correspondence with the British Isles. British goods already stored in Europe are to be confiscated. Ports under our control have been closed to trade with the English. The British Isles are in a state of blockade.'

'The Decrees are admirable in essence, sire, but how can we be sure that they will be strictly adhered to?' Berthier said. 'You yourself have already had cause to admonish your own brother, the King of Holland, over the evasion of these regulations by his subjects.'

'Joseph is weak,' Napoleon snapped. 'I tell him constantly to bear down on the Dutch. He attaches too great a price to popularity. Before being good, one must be master.'

'The rumours of Austrian rearmament are also building, sire,' Duroc offered. 'It is a threat that we cannot afford to discount.'

'I realise that, Duroc,' declared the Emperor. 'Romanovs and Hapsburgs both beaten in battle during the last year and yet both continue to oppose me.'

'Perhaps the Austrians fear the same fate as their Prussian allies, sire,' Bessiéres said.

'That may be,' Napoleon said. 'But, for the time being, gentlemen, our thoughts should be occupied with the fact that we must, sooner or later, encounter and defeat the Russians. That confrontation, when it comes, will take place in Poland. I want the army in winter quarters, across the Vistula, as soon as possible. We are to be faced, it seems, with a winter war against those troublesome Muscovites and their boy ruler. I trust you have all packed your overcoats, gentlemen.'

The men laughed.

Napoleon had barely finished speaking when the entire square before him was filled with the staccato rattle of a hundred kettledrums. The sound rose on the cold air and reverberated in the ears of those who watched. Orders were shouted and, with almost mechanical precision, units of the Imperial Guard began marching back and forth in full view of their Emperor and his staff. Napoleon smiled to himself at such a magnificent show of force. He could see faces at the windows of buildings around the square and wondered what thoughts were going through the minds of those Prussians who now watched the faultless drilling of his most elite troops in the centre of their own captive capital. The noise of a thousand marching feet mingled with the clattering of many more horses' hooves and the deafening tattoo of drums to create one enormous cacophony of sound. For a full five minutes, Napoleon stood motionless, entranced by the faultless manoeuvrings of his Imperial Guard as they passed before him. Then, as if the spell had suddenly been broken, he turned to his watching staff once more.

'They are as immaculate in their appearance as in their conduct upon the battlefield,' he said, a slight smile upon his face. 'What enemy can hope to stand against men such as these?' The Corsican waved a hand in the direction of the Guard.

'The Russians, sire, you know, will try,' Duroc insisted.

'I have tried diplomacy,' Napoleon said. 'On every occasion, before every war, I have sought bloodless solutions to our problems. But, at every turn I am met by men who *want* war. Rulers who care so little for the fate of their subjects they are content to allow them to suffer at our hands. Men like the Tsar. Alexander has no compassion for those who serve him. He seeks only to expand a kingdom given to him by his father. A man ten times more able than the child he gave life to.' The Corsican clasped his hands behind his back and began pacing back and forth before the statue of Frederick the Great. 'Does he presume to think I treat the lives of my own men with such contempt? Does he not know that I would spare them what is to come if it were possible?'

'Alexander is badly advised, sire,' offered Berthier. 'His head is easily turned by those around him.'

Napoleon nodded.

'And I fear he will be unable to see sense before we meet him in battle,' murmured the Corsican. 'He has seen his allies destroyed and yet still he embraces an inevitable conflict. He seeks to send his armies against men who have already conquered half of Europe. Men who have already beaten his forces before, at Austerlitz. Did he learn nothing from such a humiliation? Well, so be it. He and his soldiers will suffer the same fate as all those who have gone before. He seeks to expand his kingdom, I fight to build an Empire fit for those who would follow me. The Tsar will learn the folly of resistance. I will destroy him as I have all others who have sought to oppose me. I will not rest until Poland and beyond is carpeted with the dead of those who wear the uniform of Mother Russia. Let us see how this boy ruler responds to such power.'

In the square before him, Napoleon's Imperial Guard continued to drill, the sound once again rising to deafening proportions.

THREE

As Lausard guided his horse slowly over the wooden bridge that spanned the Vistula river, he glanced over the parapet towards the dark, churning water that flowed beneath. Normally, with the onset of winter, the waterway would be swollen by seasonal rains, rising more than five or six inches above its usual depth. So far, there had been very little of the inclement weather that the sergeant had expected. Ever since *La Grande Armée* had invaded Prussia in early October the weather had been surprisingly pleasant. Now, over a month later, the temperatures remained surprisingly, and pleasingly, mild. Lausard removed his brass helmet and ran a hand through his long hair, gazing both up and down river. He knew that all along the length of this great waterway units of his fellow countrymen were crossing. Each with their own specific task and directive. Behind him, the men of his own squadron rode at a walk, some also peering at the river. Many, like himself, realised that once they reached the far bank they would be on Polish soil. Another country to conquer, Lausard mused. Fresh battles to be fought. He patted the neck of his horse and the animal tossed its head as if sharing the thoughts of its rider.

Erebus scampered about like some enormous black puppy, scurrying among the legs of horses or racing ahead, as if eager to reach the far bank and be away from the swiftly flowing river. Lausard saw Lieutenant Royere look down at the big black dog and smile. The officer was riding a few yards ahead of the squadron, apparently lost in thought. His uniform, like those of the men he led, was filthy. His shabraque was smeared with mud and gunpowder, his saddle dirty and in need of polishing. One stirrup was rusted. As he rode, his sword bumped against his boot, the constant clanking echoed by the men of the squadron who followed. All had been in the saddle for more than seven hours already that day, their progress as inexorable as the gathering banks of cloud that had been forming in the afternoon skies. They had seen no one during their advance. No locals. No fleeing Prussians. To Lausard it seemed as if this part of the world was deserted.

The ground had become increasingly sandy during the last ten miles and many of the horses were finding it uncomfortable coping with the more difficult terrain. Lausard's own mount, however, forged on seemingly effortlessly but he could sense that the animal was glad to be on the solidity of this wooden bridge, albeit even for a short time, in preference to roads that were degenerating with alarming rapidity. None was paved or ditched and, for the most part, only roughly hewn logs, laid end to end on either side of the thoroughfares, formed any kind of barrier against the somewhat marshy terrain on either side. Lausard glanced up at the sky once again and began to wonder what would happen should the heavens open, as they threatened to do. He jabbed his knees into his mount and guided his horse forward to join Lieutenant Royere.

'I think we saw more people when we were marching across the deserts in Egypt,' Lausard mused, gazing ahead to the open road and low hills.

Royere smiled.

'You are right. The population have *not* emerged to greet us as the liberators we are meant to be,' he chuckled.

'Unlike the Prussians. They welcomed us in the beginning then ended up hating us for taking their country.'

'I have always felt that an occupational hazard of soldiering is to incur the dislike of those one conquers, my friend.'

'Our talk is always of conquest and war,' Lausard said acidly. 'Were they the objectives of your revolution, Lieutenant?'

'It has been a long time since the word revolution was

popular. I sometimes wonder if anyone remembers the *true* reasons for what happened in France all those years ago.'

'Do *you*, Lieutenant? Can you still recall what made *you* follow the masses?'

'I was younger, Sergeant. We *all* were. I had ideals. I had visions of what France *should* be. I embraced the principles of the revolution; perhaps I still do. As you constantly remind me, my friend, I have little other than my idealism to cling to these days.'

Both men laughed amiably.

'And what did your idealism get you, Lieutenant?' Lausard wanted to know. 'An Emperor instead of a king. A change of regime, yes, but one consistent with the ideals of the revolution? I think not.'

'You are one of the few men I know who can make idealism sound distasteful, my friend,' smiled Royere. He sucked in a deep breath. 'You have a point though. One that I have considered many times since our Emperor assumed sole control of France. Is he better than the Bourbons he fought so vigorously to remove? I believe he is. He is also preferable to that herd of lawyers who once masqueraded as a government before we helped him force them out at swordpoint.'

'All we helped to do was replace one figurehead with another,' Lausard said flatly. 'We removed the Directory and replaced them with a dictator. Does that qualify as progress in a revolutionary sense?'

'The Emperor is loved by the people. He is one of them. In a way that a king could never be.'

'What does he have in common with those he rules? He lives in palaces just as those he purported to despise once did. He makes war against countries ruled by kings, then, when he has defeated them, he becomes their ruler, or hands them over to his brothers. He has created a *new* royal family. The only difference is that *his* crown is carried on the end of a bayonet.'

Royere nodded almost imperceptibly then glanced at Lausard.

'My support for the revolution was based on ideals,' he said. 'What about yours, Sergeant? Why did *you* embrace it?'

'I didn't,' Lausard said flatly. 'You forget, Lieutenant. Myself and many of those who fight alongside me were prisoners while you and those with higher aspirations were busy ferrying the upper classes to the guillotine. Prisoners of the very men you supported.'

'I supported no one. I agreed with the ideas and objectives of the revolution but I had no more feeling for men like Robespierre or Danton than you did yourself. I wanted to see all men in France free and equal. That was all.'

'Even if it meant the destruction of one entire class?'

Royere thought for a moment then nodded.

'I believe that the action taken against the upper classes was necessary for the betterment of France,' the officer said. 'Don't you?'

'Perhaps, Lieutenant,' Lausard murmured. 'If not for the revolution then I and some of my colleagues would still be rotting in prison cells now. If I have anything to thank it for it is that it gave me an opportunity to retain the self-respect I had lost. It gave me this uniform.' He pulled at the sleeve of his dark green jacket.

'Surely our Emperor gave you your self-respect,' Royere offered. 'You and thousands like you. Myself included. I am proud to be a part of this army. The Emperor has made many feel unbeatable. We have destroyed all opposition sent against us.'

'So far,' Lausard said quietly. 'But tell me, Lieutenant, if the fighting could stop tomorrow, would you welcome that?'

'What man in the army would not?'

'And when the fighting is over, what will become of us?'

'We will return to France. To our homes.'

'Those of us who have them.'

'I fear that it will be some time before any of us see France again, my friend. Our Emperor's ambition will ensure our continued absence.' Royere smiled.

'I am more inclined to think it will be our *permanent* absence,' Lausard added.

Both men laughed.

The NCO was the first to see the figures heading towards them. The riders crested a low ridge then guided their horses as quickly as they could along the poorly made road.

'Karim and Giresse,' Lausard murmured, watching as the dragoons drew nearer, their horses lathered. The animals were labouring as they hauled their riders over the difficult terrain. Both men finally reined in their mounts and saluted Royere.

'Anything to report?' the lieutenant asked.

'Nothing, Lieutenant,' Karim said, patting the neck of his horse. 'We saw neither man nor beast.'

'We rode for three miles,' Giresse added. 'This whole damned country is empty of people, animals or supplies. We are invading a wasteland. I hope the Emperor knows that.'

'And the roads become more difficult too,' Karim added. 'All are cut through sand or swamp with little to distinguish them from the rest of the countryside. It will be difficult to move quickly in these conditions.'

'Worse still for infantry,' Giresse added.

'Let us hope that the rain does not come too soon,' Lausard mused, gazing up once more at the banks of thick cloud gathering overhead. He had barely finished speaking when the first drops began to fall.

As one man, the dragoons reached for their tattered, reeking green cloaks and slipped them over their dirty uniforms, many muttering to themselves irritably as the rain began to pour down. Lausard himself fastened his own cloak and guided his horse on, marvelling at the ferocity of the downpour. The clouds seemed to have opened as if slit by some huge invisible knife. The rain hammered down so hard it stung the flesh of the men as they rode. With no breeze to temper its fury, the deluge came down like a sheet, battering the dragoons and their horses and drenching the barren countryside. Within minutes, puddles began to form on the road. Erebus growled and sought shelter beneath one of the horses, keeping pace with the larger animal as it walked.

'Another hour and this road will be a stream,' remarked Lausard, keeping his head tilted slightly down. The rain battering his brass helmet sounded like bullets singing off the metal.

'How close is the nearest village?' Royere wanted to know.

'A mile, perhaps closer,' Karim told him. 'But there is nothing there, Lieutenant. No food. Nothing.'

'I was thinking more of shelter than supplies,' the officer replied. 'Besides which, we are to receive both remounts and some new additions to the squadron very soon. I say we get out of this cursed rain and wait for them. We are more than ten miles ahead of our appointed position anyway. We have the time to spare. Let us see if, perhaps, this rain passes.'

Lausard looked up at the lowering banks of cloud.

'I wish I could share your optimism, Lieutenant,' he said flatly.

The downpour continued as the column of dragoons moved on.

The village of Szwajbek appeared as a small dot on the map that Bonet held. The former schoolmaster tapped at the rain-spattered paper with one forefinger and Tabor leaned forward in the saddle, looking first at the map then at the village itself. The structures that comprised this cluster of dwellings were roughly constructed of wood and straw and barely merited the relatively grandiose label of village. What had once passed for a main street was little more than a filthy stream coursing through the middle of the larger huts. The incessant rain dripped from the roofs. In many places, its ferocity had holed the flimsy canopies. Lausard glanced at the village and wondered how long it had been empty. Any footprints or signs of previous inhabition had been erased by the unceasing rain that, by now, had soaked the woollen cloaks of the dragoons. Every man could feel the added weight around his shoulders and seemed stooped in the saddle because of it. Most rode with their heads down, protecting their eyes from the stinging downpour. Roads already difficult had been transformed, in less than an hour, into quagmires. Lausard was certain that, if the rain continued throughout the night, the primitive thoroughfares would become almost impassable. And, throughout the journey into this waterlogged morass, the sergeant and his companions found their nostrils constantly assailed by the sulphurous stench of marsh gas that filtered through the air from the glutinous mud that formed the boundaries of the roads on either side of them. His own horse struggled to drag its hooves from the clinging mud, sinking, in places, as far as its fetlocks. Erebus too picked his way through the muck, barking irritably every now and then as he sought firm ground on which to flex his paws.

Lieutenant Royere urged his horse on into the village, glancing around at the filthy buildings.

'The horses will need cover too,' he murmured.

Rocheteau swung himself out of the saddle and wandered into the nearest hovel. He looked inside then turned to the officer.

'No more than three men and horses to each building, Lieutenant,' he called.

The officer nodded and the men immediately split up into threes, dismounting and leading their mounts inside the buildings as instructed, eager to be out of the pounding rain. Erebus padded into the hut behind Lausard who glanced around at the interior of the structure. The building was without windows. Only a small hole in the roof allowed smoke from the peat fires normally used by the inhabitants to escape. It was this same hole that was now allowing rain to gush in. The sergeant settled his horse close to those of Royere and Rocheteau; the animals shifted uncomfortably within the confines of the hut but they gradually became accustomed to the gloomy interior and contented themselves with pawing at the bare ground that formed the floor of the hut. Some charred pieces of wood lay in the centre of the room, the only reminder that a fire had once burned there. Lausard noticed a holed and battered pot lying nearby but, other than that, the hut, like the others in the village, was completely empty.

'The Poles obviously chose not to stay and greet their liberators,' mused Royere, digging in his portmanteau for something. He finally produced a handful of biscuits which he proceeded to distribute among himself and his two companions. Rocheteau scraped the mould from one of his then popped it into his mouth. 'I fear that even as fine a scavenger as you will find this country unyielding, Rocheteau,' Royere said, chewing on one of the biscuits.

'You may be right, Lieutenant,' the corporal agreed. 'I feel sure that the light cavalry will already have claimed whatever supplies were available. Damned peacocks.'

'They were two days ahead of us,' Lausard added. 'With a

combination of our own horsemen *and* the Russians, this entire country will be stripped clean.'

'Of what?' chuckled Rocheteau. 'What has it to offer?'

'Another conquest for Bonaparte,' Lausard said flatly. 'Another kingdom for him or a member of his family.'

'Or his marshals,' Rocheteau offered. 'They are as rich as kings now. With as many domains.'

'Bernadotte and Berthier are princes already,' Lausard said. 'Murat is a reigning Grand-Duke. Joseph Bonaparte is the king of Naples.' He looked at Royere. 'As I said to you, Lieutenant, Bonaparte is merely creating a new royal family to replace the one he helped remove. Now some will seek a kingdom here, in Poland.'

'I wish them well if the rest of the country is like this,' Royere smiled.

All three men laughed.

'Old Augereau will not be best pleased with a country he cannot pillage,' chuckled Rocheteau.

'If this rain continues, it will take more than one of his milk baths to soothe his rheumatism,' added Lausard, grinning.

'And Marshal Murat will have to ride around wrapped in oilskin, just in case some of this mud splashes his new boots,' laughed Rocheteau.

'Or his ostrich feathers,' murmured Lausard, chewing on another biscuit.

Again, the hut was filled with the sound of laughter.

'I am not sure whether your conversation would be classed as treason, my friends,' Royere offered with a smile.

'We only speak the truth, Lieutenant,' Lausard told him. 'Was that not one of the purposes of the revolution? For all men to be able to speak as they feel? Is it not one of Bonaparte's most fervent ideals? That of freedom? Of thought, action and speech. Surely that extends to his own soldiers?'

Royere nodded sagely and glanced up at the rain pouring through the hole in the roof.

Rocheteau suddenly slapped at the back of his neck and hissed in irritation. He pulled something from the nape of his neck and examined it between his thumb and forefinger.

'Fleas,' he said dismissively. He scratched beneath his armpit.

Lausard was soon copying him, raking fingers through his long hair.

'No decent roads. No supplies. No inhabitants. Just rain, mud and fleas,' he said quietly. 'I hope Bonaparte is happy with his new kingdom.'

Four

The sound of heavy boots on the marble floor of the corridor made Napoleon Bonaparte look up. He turned his back on the three secretaries to whom he had been dictating letters and faced the polished oak doors that led into the room. There was a knock and the Corsican waited a moment before calling to the visitor to enter. Marshal Berthier, with General Caulaincourt close behind him, strode into the room and saluted their Emperor.

'The Senate deputation from Paris is here, sire,' said Berthier.

Napoleon smiled.

'Show them in,' he said. 'They have travelled far to bring these congratulations.' The Emperor snapped his fingers and one of the secretaries poured glasses of wine with shaking hands, aware that the Corsican was watching him. Napoleon refilled his own glass from the jug of watered-down Chambertin and sipped at it as he waited for his visitors.

They filed in one at a time. Three men, all in their early forties, smartly but unostentatiously dressed. As one they bowed to the Corsican then accepted both the chairs and the wine he offered them. The secretaries left and Berthier closed the doors behind them. Napoleon perched on the edge of one of the desks and smiled at the three men before him. Berthier and Caulaincourt took up positions on either side of the desk, slightly behind their commander.

'I trust the journey from Paris to Berlin was not too taxing for you, gentlemen,' said the Emperor. 'As I'm sure you have seen, it is a magnificent city. A fitting prize.' He chuckled. 'I trust the gifts I sent back were received accordingly?'

The taller of the three men nodded and managed a smile as Napoleon continued.

'I could think of no more fitting tribute to this victory than to send back to France the sword of Frederick the Great himself together with his general's sash and the Ribbon of the Black Eagle. I hope that they were of at least some consolation to those who escaped the catastrophe of Rossbach.'

'The gifts were welcomed, sire, as was news of the victory and the subjugation of Prussia,' said the tall man.

'Though not met with the near delirium that engulfed Paris and the rest of the country after your victory at Austerlitz,' the second man offered tentatively.

Napoleon's smile vanished instantly.

'What I achieved here in Prussia was even more impressive, he snapped.

'But it has not brought peace, sire,' the tall man protested. 'Units of the Prussian army still remain and Russia now stands ready to throw her might against France.'

'Russia has already tasted defeat at my hands,' rasped the Corsican. 'And will do so again. France has nothing to fear from the Tsar and his armies.' The Corsican rose to his feet and began pacing back and forth in front of the three men. 'Did you travel so far to denigrate my achievements? Where are your congratulations? I have given France more victories. Is that not enough to satisfy you?'

'The whole country rejoices in your victory, sire, but the Senate dispatched us to reason with you and . . .'

Napoleon cut him short.

'The Senate only sits where it does because of me,' he hissed. 'Do they now presume to lecture me on the art of war?'

'The Senate hoped to persuade you to make peace,' said the first man, his voice losing some of its volume.

'Peace?' bellowed Napoleon. 'I have destroyed the Prussian army and the Senate speaks of peace. One hundred and sixty million francs, as well as supplies and requisitions, have already been bled from Prussia. The Grand Duke of Würzburg, Elector

Frederick of Saxony, and the Saxon princes have joined with me in the Confederation of the Rhine. All Prussian territories west of the Elbe, except Altmark, have been ceded to France and the Baltic ports have been closed to the English. Such is the extent of my conquest here. Yet still you speak of peace. Peace with Russia? I will make peace on my own terms and when *I* feel the time is right. Not when the Senate decides. My decision will be made for the greater good of France herself.'

'There is growing discontent within France, sire, about continued war,' another of the men offered. 'The public desire for peace surpasses even the gratification of pride.'

'So, what would you have me do?' Napoleon demanded. 'March my armies out of Prussia? Recall my troops from Poland? Would that satisfy your craven desire for peace?'

'Sending troops into Poland can only precipitate war with Russia, sire. The country does not wish for that. Many fear that your victory against Prussia was so complete that it may serve to make you intractable towards Russia. They see only the prospect of another long and arduous struggle. More wives will lose husbands, mothers will lose sons. Children will be deprived of fathers.'

'I will make peace with Russia only when the Tsar shows himself prepared to fight *with* me against the tyranny of England,' snarled the Corsican. 'When I first entered Berlin I found evidence of agreements between Prussia and the Tsar to fight against me. Even now, his forces march on Warsaw. If they gain that city, if they assume control of Poland, as they have in the past, then France's expansion is threatened. Is this what the Senate wish for?'

'The Senate, like the people of France, wish only for peace, sire,' offered another of the delegates.

'Even a peace detrimental to France herself?' said the Corsican angrily. 'You say that many fear the extent of my victory over Prussia. Why? Do they think I wage war for my own glory?'

There was a heavy silence in the room finally broken by one of the representatives.

'Sire, despite your triumphs here, France still finds herself confronted by four nations,' added the second delegate. 'Prussia will not make peace. The British remain adamant in their hostility. Russia is determined to continue the war and rumours of Austrian rearmament are rife.'

'I am aware of these developments,' snapped Napoleon. 'And plans have been instituted to deal with every eventuality. The Berlin Decrees that I issued against England will soon bring that most persistent enemy to its knees commercially. The Continental System will ensure that France grows stronger while England's trade routes are closed off.'

'But that is not happening, sire,' said the third delegate. 'Even now, there are those within France content to sell unofficial licences to merchants who would gladly trade with England. Your own Minister of Police is aware of this.'

'If Fouché is aware of it he should take measures to stop it,' snapped Napoleon angrily. 'Anyone dealing with English traders should be punished as strongly as the law can allow. How am I ever to defeat that troublesome nation if the businessmen of France will not support the sanctions I have initiated? They are governed by greed not by loyalty.'

'Of the fifty thousand cloaks you ordered for use in this coming winter campaign, many are being made with cloth and leather imported from England,' said the taller delegate. 'There is no other way, sire.'

Napoleon continued to pace back and forth, his brow furrowed.

'So,' he said quietly. 'You travelled all the way from Paris to inform me that my victories are not welcome and that my decrees are being ignored. You would have best saved yourselves a journey, gentlemen.'

'What are we to report to the Senate, sire?' the second delegate asked.

'You may report what you wish. I will fight Russia because I have to. I do not intend to be dictated to by a group of overfed politicians who are only in such a privileged position because *I* chose to put them there. Think about that on your way back to France. A France made stronger by *my* efforts, not by those of some whining "pekinese". I myself leave for Warsaw in a matter of days. I trust you will not pursue me to *that* city with your entreaties for surrender.' He turned his back on the delegates and walked to one of the large windows that overlooked the palace gardens. 'You may go. I have nothing more to say and *you* certainly have nothing else that I wish to hear.' The Corsican glanced at Caulaincourt. 'See these lawyers out,' he hissed. 'Then send in Rapp and Duroc.' Only when he heard the door close behind them did he turn slowly from the window. 'What must I do to earn their gratitude, Berthier?' said Napoleon quietly.

'Do you really need the gratitude of politicians, sire?' the Chief of Staff said.

Napoleon chuckled and shook his head.

'I do not need their gratitude, only their cooperation,' he said. 'And, if that is not forthcoming, I will remove them all. The army will support me and that is all that matters. Let us see how truculent these politicians remain with two hundred thousand bayonets pointing at their self-satisfied chests.' He crossed to one of the large desks on the far side of the room and looked down at the maps laid out there.

'Poland,' said Napoleon quietly. 'A country without an identity. Without a government. Without purpose.' He made an expansive gesture across the maps. 'Perhaps it is our destiny to restore that purpose.' The Corsican looked around at his subordinates. 'We come as deliverers, gentlemen. To a country that has been partitioned three times during the last thirty-five years. To a country that has lost its sense of worth.'

'The Tsar might disagree with you, sire,' said Duroc flatly.

The other men around the table laughed.

'And what of the Poles themselves?' Berthier wanted to know. 'Will they see us as deliverers or conquerors, sire?'

'They have already risen and driven out the Prussian administration,' Duroc offered. 'Surely that is a sign of their intentions and where their loyalties lie.'

'Their nobles are divided,' Napoleon said. 'Some, like Prince Radziwill, favour Prussian rule. Others seem more inclined to offer their support to the Tsar. Czartoryski has already advised the Tsar to proclaim himself king of Poland.'

'They fear reprisals in case of defeat, sire,' Caulaincourt

offered. 'Even Prince Poniatowski hesitates to commit himself one way or another. If the Russians win they are afraid of what will be done to them if they side with us. If we defeat the Russians then the Polish nobles fear that the emancipation of their serfs may bring them the same fate it brought the ruling classes of France during the revolution.'

'They want their independence, sire,' said Rapp. 'They see you as the man to provide it.'

Napoleon stroked his chin thoughtfully.

'And with their independence,' he said. 'They will encounter all the problems that come with government. And I doubt the Poles are capable of governing themselves. No. I do not see our invasion of Poland as a chance to restore a nation. They have allowed themselves to be partitioned. They have no public spirit. The nobles are too much; the people too little. It is a dead body to which life must be restored before anything can be made of it. I will make officers and soldiers of them first; afterwards I shall see. I will take Prussia's portion; I shall have Posen and Warsaw, but I will not touch Cracow, Galicia or Vilna. If the Polish state is to be revived then it will be as a vassal. One to provide troops to swell the ranks of *La Grande Armée*. How many men could we count on, Berthier?'

'It is estimated close to fifty thousand, sire,' said the Chief of Staff.

'What are the current positions of the two armies?' Napoleon asked, leaning closer to the maps that festooned the table.

'Marshal Davout is close to Warsaw, sire, and he has yet to meet any resistance,' Berthier announced. 'But we know that a force of Russians, at least fifty-six thousand strong, have moved eastward from Grodno. Their *exact* position is unknown at this moment.'

'Then our most pressing task is to prevent Bennigsen and his Russians from joining with Lestocq and his Prussian troops near Warsaw,' the Emperor mused. 'The west bank of the Vistula must be secured to provide winter quarters.'

'And when will you attack, sire?' Caulaincourt enquired. 'The terrain in Poland is poor. Not suited to moving troops with any speed.'

'I have no intention of fighting a winter war, if I can avoid it,' the Corsican announced. 'The main offensive will take place in the spring. When the ground has hardened and I can bring all my forces against the Russian bear.' He spoke the last two words with a note of disdain. 'What is their strength?'

'As far as we know from intelligence reports, sire, there are two armies,' Rapp interjected. 'The first under Bennigsen totals some forty-nine thousand infantry, eleven thousand cavalry and two hundred and seventy-six cannon. The second, under Marshal Buxhowden, comprises thirty-nine thousand infantry and seven thousand cavalry, supported by a further two hundred and sixteen guns. The two armies are under the overall command of Kamenskoi.'

'Ninety thousand men,' Napoleon mused. 'What of their reserves?'

'The Russian Imperial Guard, under the Grand Duke Constantine, are still in St Petersburg, sire,' said Duroc. 'General Michelson commands five divisions in Moldavia. Four more divisions are stationed in Russia under Count Apraxim. Another hundred thousand men at least.'

'And then there are the Cossacks, sire,' Rapp offered.

'Undisciplined rabble,' said Napoleon dismissively.

'But some of the finest light cavalry in the world, Sire,' Rapp insisted. 'Their commander, Platov, is a very able man. He has an almost mystical hold over his men.'

'What are their numbers?'

'Thirty thousand, perhaps more.'

'And our own strength?'

'Close to two hundred thousand,' Duroc informed him. 'Of those, thirty-six thousand are cavalry, most of them newly mounted.'

'If this struggle develops as I foresee, we will need more troops,' the Corsican said, staring down at the maps.

'Eighty thousand conscripts are already beginning to reach the army, sire,' Caulaincourt said. 'Swiss, Dutch and Spanish troops numbering thirty-five thousand will also reach here within the month, as will the eight cavalry regiments you ordered transferred from the Army of Italy.'

Napoleon nodded.

'I fear we may need them all, in time,' he said. 'Those cursed Muscovites seem to breed with the rapidity of flies. What they lack in expertise, they more than compensate for in numbers.'

The other men laughed.

'Much blood will be spilled, gentlemen,' Napoleon said. 'But, when the time comes, I trust that most of it will be Russian.'

FIVE

Lausard had never seen rain like it. Never before had he encountered weather so unrelentingly ferocious. It was as if the dark clouds that heaved perpetually over the barren landscape had been torn by huge invisible hands. Ripped apart and discarded. The torrents were unceasing in their severity and fury. The rain had been battering the countryside, without pause, for more than four days. Night and day had virtually become one, so thick were the banks of cloud that clogged the sky. Leaves that had fallen from trees, pieces of broken branch, discarded equipment and lost belongings were all trapped in the sucking mud like fossils in a tar pit. Men and horses could barely move through the glutinous ooze that made the rudimentary roads all but impassable. Lausard urged his exhausted mount on and looked around him at flat, featureless countryside that had become nothing more than one enormous, all-consuming swamp. The rain had transformed streams into rivers and Lausard was beginning to wonder if even the trees that dotted the landscape might eventually sink into the mire. Pack animals and cavalry mounts sank to their bellies in some places, drawn down by the sucking filth. Many of the dragoons had dismounted in order to relieve their mounts of the added weight, but they found themselves knee-deep in slurry. Some were unable to move. Others, Tabor included, had gripped the tails of their horses and were relying on the animals to drag them clear of the murderous grip of the mud. It clung to them like a reeking hand, determined not to allow them to escape its grasp. Lausard and his men had struggled past countless cannon and limbers, all helpless in the almost primeval ooze. Their crews could only sit on the soaking wooden carriages and watch as their companions struggled past, every man spattered from head to foot in the mud, horse droppings and filth that constituted a road. Puddles that had formed in the mud overflowed as yet more rain continued to beat down, adding to the appalling discomfort the men were already encountering.

Lausard watched as several light infantry fought their way along the road. Without exception, the men had rope lashed around their feet, securing their shoes to their ankles. Despite this, the sergeant saw several of the men stopping to dig into the mud to retrieve footwear tugged free by the ever present ooze. Some infantry were marching without shoes or boots, their muskets slung across their shoulders in a vain effort to protect the firing mechanisms from the wet. All muskets were wrapped in oilskin. The dragoons themselves had their own Charleville carbines encased in the protective material. Flints and cartridges had also been similarly bound wherever possible.

At the side of the road, men were sitting hopelessly in the mud, completely exhausted by their constant struggle against it. Officers and NCOs, as weary as their men, made no attempt to bully or cajole their subordinates into continued advance. Lausard saw a young captain of the 93rd regiment of Line infantry, head bowed and shako in his hand, weeping softly. All around him his men either fought their way through the mud or simply sat at the roadside, shattered by their efforts to continue. Many had discarded their equipment, including their packs. Indeed, the full length of the road was littered with equipment of all kinds. Every step was a battle. A strength-sapping confrontation with nature in which there could be only one winner. Some of the men were wrapped in cloaks, others in blankets or discarded shabraques. Anything to give them a little extra cover from the driving rain, but it was useless. The never ending torrent had soaked everything long ago. Lausard wondered, if the rain ever stopped, how long it was going to take to dry out all his clothes and equipment. But, as he glanced again up at the sky, he decided that there was a distinct possibility that the downpour simply would *never* cease. Perhaps the rain would fall for so long that the whole of Poland would be immersed beneath a flood of biblical proportions. As he glanced around at the sallow faces of his companions and the other struggling French troops, he wondered if many would *prefer* that fate for this country they sought to conquer.

Lausard's horse stumbled and pitched forward. He pulled on the reins, trying to keep the animal upright as it whinnied helplessly and floundered in a puddle deep enough to drown a child. It took all of Lausard's expertise to remain in the saddle as the horse tried to gain a hold in the sucking mud. Great geysers of brown slime and water erupted into the air as it brought its hooves down hard on the constantly shifting road. Lausard wiped mud from his face and patted the animal's soaking neck. Its mane was already plastered to its coat and it was panting heavily, struggling to keep going on the treacherous surface. He waited a moment longer then swung himself out of the saddle.

Stepping down into the mud, he was immediately engulfed up to his knees. Some of the rancid water spilled over the top of his boot cuffs and filled the leather but Lausard was already so drenched he barely noticed this additional discomfort. He gripped the bay's bridle and led it on, walking a couple of steps ahead, heaving his own feet free of the enveloping mud with almost superhuman effort. Beside him, Rocheteau was leading his own horse. As were Lieutenants Royere and Gaston. The trumpeter's red tunic looked almost pink, the colour virtually washed out of it. His red shabraque was also losing its dye, which, dripping from the corners of the saddle cloth, looked uncomfortably like blood.

'At the first opportunity, we rest,' said Royere, raising his voice slightly to make himself heard above the pelting rain. 'I fear more for the wellbeing of the horses than I do for ourselves.'

'If there were some supplies to be had in this godforsaken country at least we could feed them,' Rocheteau grunted.

'Whatever there is has been removed by the peasants or ruined by the weather,' Lausard offered. He glanced at Royere. 'Didn't you say we were to receive remounts, Lieutenant?'

The officer nodded.

'Fresh horses and fresh troops to replace those lost during the last campaign,' he said, trudging along.

'They'll all be dead of pneumonia before they reach us,' Lausard said. 'Men *and* horses.'

'Where are the remounts coming from, Lieutenant?' Rocheteau wanted to know.

'From a depot at Potsdam,' Royere told him. 'The victory over the Prussians gave us something of a windfall as far as fresh mounts go. More than fifty-three Prussian squadrons surrendered their horses.'

'I hear that the commander of the depot is something of a tyrant,' Gaston interjected.

'General Bourcier is not known for his even temper, I grant you,' Royere smiled. 'But perhaps his concern for the mounts that leave his care is well founded. For every trooper killed, three or four horses perish. Many of them from neglect and bad care.'

'Remember, Lieutenant,' Lausard said, the faintest hint of reproach in his voice, 'it was your revolution that abolished the royal breeding studs back in '99. Forty thousand animals a year is a lot of horse flesh to lose. The fact that our Emperor insists on five as the minimum age for a cavalry horse does nothing to help our situation in the short term. We may all be riding Arab or Spanish stallions in five years' time but, while we wait, we are forced to rely on the mounts of other nations.'

Royere could only nod in resigned agreement.

'There are never enough *vétérinaires* in the field,' Gaston suggested. 'I knew a man who graduated from the Ecole hippiatrique at Alfort and he said that he could never hope to advance beyond sergeant. The chief vet at the Niort remount depot receives only one hundred and twenty francs a month, and out of that he must keep not just himself but fifteen hundred horses too.'

'Where is this man now?' Royere asked.

'He was killed at Saalfeld, earlier this year.'

Moreau, riding close by, crossed himself.

'He may think himself lucky,' Rocheteau grunted, almost

falling over as he stepped in a puddle that reached his knees. He shot out a hand and grabbed the stirrup of his horse, keeping himself upright. 'Damn this country, *and* its stinking weather, to hell.'

Lausard looked behind him at the column of dragoons following, dragging themselves and their mounts through the mud. Saddle sore, exhausted almost beyond endurance, hungry and soaked to the skin, they looked like a squadron of corpses as they battled their way onwards. And, as ever, the rain continued to hammer down.

Lausard found that, with a combination of the onrushing winter and the perpetually dark skies, night came with almost inordinate speed. He glanced at his pocket watch and saw that it was almost five p.m. and yet, despite the relatively early hour, the dusk was descending like a gloomy blanket. Within thirty minutes, the entire countryside would be in darkness. He had no idea whether a halt would be called to the advance or if, as had happened already during the march, the dragoons would be required to continue with their inexorable progress throughout the blackness. As he pushed his watch back into his tunic pocket he glanced up at the sky and almost smiled.

'The rain is stopping,' he proclaimed.

Other men in the column had noticed and a burble of conversation began to spread among the sodden dragoons. The fact that the continuous downpour appeared, at last, to be ending was a relief but the men knew that they would still have to deal with its legacy. The roads, such as they were, would remain virtually impassable for the foreseeable future. It would require several days of scorching sunshine to dry out such a waterlogged landscape and, because of the time of year, Lausard and his companions knew this was not to be. Away to the east, the sky was relatively clear of cloud and a strong, crisp wind had sprung up. Lausard shivered as he rode, pulling his soaking cape even more tightly around him but feeling little benefit from the drenched material. Ahead, the ground rose sharply and the sergeant could see a clutch of all too familiar mud and straw houses clinging to the slope just ahead of a small wood.

'We'll camp there for the night,' Lieutenant Royere announced, gesturing to the village. 'Sergeant, take two of your men and reconnoitre the woods beyond. Check for supplies. For any enemy activity. Or any sign of the local inhabitants.'

Lausard raised an eyebrow and nodded. He called Karim and Sonnier to him and the three of them urged their mounts on through the clinging mud, up the slope and towards the scattering of buildings. The ground was a little easier for the horses to traverse because, Lausard reasoned, the worst of the rain would have run down the slope into the shallow valley below. The NCO was grateful for the chance to reach higher ground. Throughout the march he had been struck by the flatness of the countryside, a feature that made the effects of the incessant rain even more acute. The road was still little more than an extended mud slick but the horses carried their riders on with assurance, finally emerging among the roughly built houses that passed for a village.

'It's getting colder,' murmured Sonnier, shivering.

'Good,' Lausard said. 'If there is a frost tonight, it might harden the ground enough to make it more passable tomorrow.'

'Anything is preferable to the rain,' added Karim.

'Check the woods, I'll take a look around here,' the sergeant said, waiting a moment as his two companions rode off into the enveloping trees. Sonnier slid his Charleville from the boot on his saddle and stripped the oilskin from it. Karim touched the hilt of his sabre.

Lausard dismounted, tied his reins to a tree stump and wandered in the direction of the nearest house. The door was open and he stepped inside. There was a clay stove in the centre of the room, some filthy straw around it and pieces of torn material that looked like the remnants of a blanket. He knelt down and was about to pick it up when he saw that it was alive with fleas. The sergeant found a couple of buckets, one filled with rancid water, the other with rotting peat. He moved out of the building to the next. It was the same in every one. Each of the dwellings looked as if it had been abandoned several days earlier. What little the peasants possessed they had taken with them. That included livestock, bread, beer and anything else that might pass as provisions for the advancing French. The only thing that the Poles had left behind were potatoes. There were more in a sack in another of the houses Lausard entered. He checked inside the sack and saw that many were rotten, but there were enough to make something that might pass for a meal. He took off his helmet and ran a hand through his hair.

'Alain.'

The sound of his name sent him hurrying outside again.

Sonnier was sitting astride his horse, his carbine gripped in one fist.

'Where's Karim?' Lausard wanted to know.

'Checking the rest of the wood,' Sonnier told him. 'There's cover there and something else.' A slight smile creased Sonnier's face. 'Something those miserable Polish bastards couldn't carry away.'

'What is it?'

'Two dead pigs. Cut up properly, they will make good eating if we can find any wood dry enough to make a fire.'

Lausard smiled.

'Any sign of Russians?' he wanted to know.

Sonnier shook his head.

'There are footprints in the wood but Karim says they probably belonged to the peasants who lived here.'

'The Russians were not foolish enough to linger too long in such an unforgiving country,' Lausard mused.

'Neither, I trust, will we,' Sonnier said.

'We will remain here or wherever else we are ordered for as long as Bonaparte decides, you know that, Sonnier. Now ride back and tell the lieutenant it is safe to bring the rest of the squadron forward.'

Sonnier nodded and guided his horse down the slope towards the remainder of the dragoons. Lausard watched him go then turned back towards the thick wood. Karim emerged a moment later, his horse panting heavily as it bore him across the clay-like soil.

'There is barely room to drive a cannon through that wood,' exclaimed the Circassian. 'And beyond it, yet more of this same infernal countryside.'

'You must long for the warmth of your homeland, Karim,' Lausard observed.

'Don't you wish you were home too, Alain?'

Lausard glanced up at the unforgiving sky then turned his back on the Circassian.

'I have no home,' he said flatly. 'All that I am resides within this uniform now. It has been so for longer than I can remember and that is how it will remain.'

'And when the war is over? Where will you return to then?'

'We have no guarantees any of us will see either an end of this war or any others.'

Karim nodded almost imperceptibly.

'If Allah, all praise to Him, decrees,' the Circassian noted. 'Then it may come to pass.'

'Allah has nothing to do with it, my friend. Only Bonaparte can decide *our* fate.'

Six

The night brought with it a frost that, to Lausard and his companions, seemed to penetrate their very bones. They sat huddled in small groups, still wrapped in the sodden cloaks that they had worn for so long. Despite the spluttering fires that the men had lit, the cold dug freezing needles into every inch of their exposed flesh. Horses, too, despite being covered with blankets, stood shivering in the rapidly falling temperatures. Lausard glanced around him at the men of his squadron. They had built fires from fallen branches and now sat around the smoky pyres, seemingly oblivious to the clouds of thick, noxious smoke that billowed from the damp wood. Some had moved so close to the flames it seemed they would be engulfed but it was a necessary risk in order to draw any warmth whatsoever from the embers. As the sergeant watched, Tabor dragged a huge branch from a fallen tree towards the fire then stepped back as Delacor set about it with his axe, feeding pieces into the meagre flames. Some of the other squadron members had sought refuge in the gathering of huts and thick smoke was billowing from those too. Lausard and his companions had realised that the buildings gave no more protection against the elements than the dense forest itself and chosen to bivouac two hundred yards or so into the mass of trees.

In a large pot hanging over the fire was a mess of muddy brown water, some potatoes and pieces of pork. The remains of the two dead pigs they had found earlier had been hacked up into manageable lumps and forced into the pot but one carcass had been partially rotten and was considered inedible by Rocheteau and several of the others. That had immediately been claimed by several other dragoons who seemed willing to ignore the putrefaction and were, even now, busily cooking portions of the dead pig on makeshift spits over another smoky fire. Even Erebus had seemed uninterested in the rotten flesh. The great black dog lay on the frosty ground close to Gaston, occasionally raising its large head to sniff the aromas coming from the cooking pot. Charvet had retrieved half a bottle of schnapps from his portmanteau and emptied it into their own concoction in a desperate effort both to give it some flavour and to kill any germs that might be lurking in the foul-coloured mixture, but as he sipped at the stew with a small spoon he winced slightly in Lausard's direction. The NCO merely shrugged. He and his companions at least had *something* to eat. Most of the other dragoons had been reduced to consuming their last meagre rations of biscuits, most of which had gone mouldy during the march. Rocheteau and Gaston had both shared small bottles of wine but each man was limited to three swigs each, such was the shortage of liquor.

Karim and Tigana were inspecting the horses, walking among the skittish mounts. The animals were as hungry as their riders and there was precious little to give them. Half a sack of oats had been found in one of the huts but it was a pathetic amount with which to try and satisfy horses that were already starving. A number were gnawing at the moss and lichens that grew on the frosty floor of the forest. Others had been reduced to chewing at the bark on fallen branches or, in the worst cases, on the trunks of trees themselves.

'Half of these horses will be dead within the week,' Tigana observed, running his hand along the flanks of a black mount. 'I can feel the ribs of most.'

'That black devil has more meat on him than most of the horses,' Karim added, nodding in the direction of Erebus. The dog growled low in its throat as Gaston stroked it.

'If they die we can eat them,' Joubert offered. 'At least then *we* might survive.'

'Survive for what, fat man?' Delacor snapped. 'So that we can die before the cannon of the Russians? Or on their bayonets or swords? It isn't much of a choice, is it?'

'We might all be sucked down into the mud in this stinking country or die of hunger before we have the *chance* to fight,' said Roussard.

'We've been hungry before and survived,' Bonet observed, running a hand over his rumbling belly.

'I can put up with the hunger,' Rocheteau added. 'It's this weather that I can't stand. Rain. Frost. More rain. Surely the snow cannot be far away.'

A chorus of murmured agreement rippled around the other dragoons.

'How cold does it get in this country?' Tabor wanted to know.

'As cold as Russia?' Sonnier mused.

'Nowhere is as cold as Russia,' Rostov confirmed. 'I've seen winters where the snow reached my waist. Where a man dare not cry for fear that the tears would freeze in his eyes and blind him.'

'Do not presume you have seen the last of such occurrences, my friend,' Lausard murmured. 'If temperatures continue to fall in the way they are doing, we may yet experience those conditions *here*.'

'If it freezes tonight, what then?' Tabor asked, rubbing his hands together and shuffling nearer the fire.

'The ground will harden slightly,' Lausard told him. 'It *may* help our passage. I don't know. After frost, I can only assume, will come snow, as Rocheteau said. For as long as it lie on the ground we will be able to advance. If the snow then thaws . . .' He allowed the sentence to trail off.

'Or the rain might come again,' Rocheteau interjected.

There were more grumbles from around the fire.

'If the roads are impassable to wheeled vehicles then are we to fight the Russians without the benefit of artillery support?' mused Sonnier.

'If we do we will be slaughtered,' Roussard said, gazing into the flames.

'Movement will be as difficult for the Russians as it is for us,' Lausard said. 'They face the same problems we do.'

'But they have the benefit of being in front of us, Alain,' Rocheteau reminded him. 'With the opportunity to pillage this damned country of what little it has to offer before we can even get close.'

'Are the Poles on the Russians' side, or ours?' Tabor wanted to know.

'They are supporting the Russians, you half-wit,' snapped Delacor. 'Why do you think they are always hiding from us? Abandoning these hovels they call villages before we arrive and taking any food or livestock with them. They are in league with the forces of the Tsar. They have no wish to become another of Bonaparte's conquests.'

'They have no love for the Russians,' Bonet observed. 'Russia has shown them little mercy during the last thirty or forty years. If we fail against the Russians then the Poles would once again be at the mercy of the Tsar.'

'So you believe,' Delacor said dismissively.

'When the fighting begins we will discover where their allegiance lies,' Lausard muttered.

Charvet gave the pot of brown stew a final stir then began ladling it into the metal bowls that the men presented to him. Some of them ate without benefit of spoons or forks, anxious to dip their hands in the watery gravy to help stave off the increasingly biting chill that seemed to permeate every part of their bodies. The steam rising from the stew mingled with the smoke from the fires and the clouding breath of each man as he exhaled. Lausard took his own helping and began picking at the pieces of meat.

'When you've finished, Delacor, you and Rostov relieve Giresse and Moreau,' said the sergeant. 'They'll freeze to death if they're left on guard duty for too long without some warmth.'

'Let Moreau pray to his God for warmth,' Delacor snapped irritably.

Lausard eyed the other man silently for a moment, his stare locked on the dragoon.

After a moment or two, Delacor nodded and dropped his gaze. He concentrated on his food and did not allow his eyes to catch those of Lausard again.

As the men ate, almost unconsciously, they huddled closer together and drew nearer to the sputtering flames of the fire. The cold, if anything, was increasing. Clothes soaked by days of rain felt as if they were freezing on the men, the frost digging into the wool and leather of their uniforms. Lausard accepted his own three swigs of wine then passed the bottle on. He noticed that Delacor and Rostov had finished eating. The Russian was already on his feet, reaching for his carbine. Delacor joined him a moment later and they trudged off through the woods to relieve their companions.

'No one wants to stray too far from the fire tonight,' Rocheteau commented.

'Do you blame them?' Lausard answered.

Moments later, two more figures could be seen making their way through the woods towards the other dragoons. Lausard could see that it was Giresse and Moreau. As the men drew closer, the sergeant saw that both were covered in what appeared to be a thin white sheen of frost. The icy weather had touched the men as surely as it had spread across the ground. Tainting them as if it was some freezing contagion. Small particles of frost fell from Moreau's cape as he drew nearer to the fire, his body shivering. He gratefully accepted some of the steaming broth from Charvet and began to eat hungrily. Giresse put out a hand to stop him.

'I thought you were supposed to thank God for all that you received before consuming it,' Giresse smiled.

'God understands my need for sustenance,' Moreau mumbled through a mouthful of meat and potato. 'He will forgive me this once.'

The other men seated around the fire laughed. It was a sound that had become alien to them during the last few tortuous days of the march and many other members of the squadron looked around from their own camp fires, wondering what could possibly elicit an outpouring of joy in such murderously uncomfortable conditions.

'Anything moving out there?' Lausard asked as the two men sat down close to him.

'Wolves,' Giresse answered. 'We heard them. No other

creature would be so insane as to venture forth in conditions such as these.'

'They must be hungry if they are willing to come so close to the camp,' murmured Bonet.

'Even wolves will find meagre pickings in such a place as this,' said Carbonne.

'They could be after the horses,' Tigana muttered.

'Or us,' Lausard intoned.

'We should give Joubert to them,' chuckled Rocheteau. 'He would feed the whole pack.'

There was more laughter.

Joubert looked on indignantly and licked the bottom of his plate in a desperate effort to consume every last drop of the watery broth. Tabor pushed several more pieces of wood into the dying flames in a desperate effort to keep the fire going. It sputtered for a moment but then began to glow more brightly. The flames danced more vigorously and the men attempted to warm themselves around it. Lausard got to his feet. The feel of wet and freezing cold material clinging to him was almost intolerable.

'Be careful you do not end up as dinner for wolves, Alain,' Rocheteau called.

The sergeant turned and looked at him.

'They only have an appetite for corporals,' he smiled and wandered off away from the fire, in the direction of the small cluster of buildings on the edge of the wood. As he walked he passed other groups of dragoons, similarly wet, cold and miserable, huddled around their own fires. Some were trying in vain to snatch some sleep but it was virtually impossible in such appalling conditions. Despite the ferocity of the rain during the last few days, Lausard noticed that several patches of ground were already beginning to firm up due to the severity of the frost. If temperatures continued to fall during the night, as he suspected, then perhaps the troops of *La Grande Armée* would indeed find their advance a little easier come the dawn.

A number of the men he passed glanced in his direction and many nodded a greeting which Lausard returned. He was a well-recognised figure within the squadron, not least for the fact that he was one of the few men who still wore his hair long. He had not, unlike most of his colleagues, succumbed to the fashion for short locks, encouraged by the Emperor himself. He had little desire to conform, despite his allegiance to the army. As Lausard walked he glanced around at the other soaking wet, freezing cold men of his squadron. He wondered, as he had often done before, what thoughts were going through *their* heads. Were they thinking of home? Of loved ones, unseen for so long and possibly never to be seen again? Or were some wondering why they were in this place? Up to their ankles in mud, speckled with frost. Hungry, thirsty and desperately in need of shelter and a good night's sleep. He wondered how many resented Bonaparte for their plight. It was, after all, the Corsican's orders that had brought them to this place. Lausard had no doubt that more instructions would follow that would lead them onward across the wooded, rain-soaked, freezing plains of Poland finally to clash with the troops of Mother Russia. For many of the men around him, Lausard knew that life held the promise of little else but more misery. Beyond that, they had death to look forward to. At the hands of the elements or the enemy. Yet still these men, many of whom he had fought with across different continents for more than ten years now, marched and battled without question. There were those among them who would doubt the wisdom of what they were being asked to do. Many more who loathed their present predicament. But all obeyed the orders they were given. All were prepared to suffer whatever horrors were sent against them in the name of their Emperor. Lausard wondered what drove them. Patriotic fervour? Idealism? Or, like himself, were some of them only truly alive when on the battlefield? The flame of life, he had found, burned with even more incandescent luminosity when faced with the possibility that it might be snuffed out.

As for himself, Lausard followed orders because he was a soldier. He felt a swell of self-congratulation at the thought of the word. Twelve years earlier he had been a criminal. A common thief, like so many of those he now called friends. Bonaparte and the army had given him back at least some of his self-belief and pride. What it would never return to him was the loss of his family and of his position in society. One that he had held before the revolution. What thoughts would pass through the minds of the men around him, he wondered, if they knew that this long-haired sergeant had once been a member of the aristocracy they all purported to despise? It was a question he had pondered before and would doubtless do so again. Several other men huddled around a dimly glowing fire nodded in his direction as he passed and Lausard returned the gesture again. He was among the dirty huts that passed for a village now but those inside were benefiting little from the shelter. The frost jabbed its icy needles into every nook and cranny. It came like an inexorable flood of cold and no one could escape its touch. Sentries walked back and forth to prevent themselves from being frozen to the spot. Every now and then, Lausard could see men glancing in the direction of the thick woods, alerted in the solitude by the sounds of movement. More than one of the sentries shouldered his carbine, as if to draw a bead on the source of the sound only for it to die on the icy stillness.

'Russians?' one man murmured aloud.

'Wolves,' Lausard told him. 'Their hunger draws them close.'

'They will find little to eat here,' another voice added and Lausard turned to see Lieutenant Royere standing close to the door of one of the huts.

Lausard nodded a greeting.

'Another of your late night strolls, my friend?' the officer enquired.

'I savour time spent alone, Lieutenant. Something, you will appreciate, that is not always easy to do when one is part of an army.'

Royere smiled and nodded.

'Very true,' he said. 'Do you not find that solitude sometimes brings with it unwanted thoughts?'

'It is a small price to pay. Will you join me, Lieutenant?'

'I find it as difficult to sleep as you, my friend. Thank you. I would appreciate that.'

The two men moved slowly through the village, Lausard occasionally glancing in through open doors to see men huddled around the clay stoves in the centre of the buildings. Dense smoke was belching from most of them and he wondered how the men inside were able to breathe; but, he reasoned, to most a few lungfuls of reeking air were preferable to the ravages of the frost that had now gripped the land as tightly as an unforgiving fist.

'One of my men has a thermometer,' Royere observed, his breath clouding the air. 'He took it from a dead engineer. He tells me we are experiencing fifteen degrees of frost tonight.'

'That does not surprise me. Surely death itself cannot be much colder than this.'

'I hope none of us ever discovers the truth of that, Sergeant.'

'You said one of *your* men, Lieutenant,' Lausard smiled. 'Are thoughts of advancement the thoughts that come to *you* in the darkness?'

Royere grinned.

'Doesn't every man crave advancement in life, my friend?' the officer said.

'Some do not need gold braid on their uniforms to achieve it, Lieutenant. I have never thought of you as a man who is more concerned with his stirrups being bronze than steel.'

Again Royere smiled, pulling up the dirty scarf he wore to cover the lower part of his unshaven face.

'And what do you wish for, my friend?' he asked, his voice now slightly muffled.

'At the moment, a good meal, a dry uniform and a bed with crisp clean sheets would be enough, Lieutenant,' Lausard told him. 'And I am sure that every other man in *La Grande Armée* would share those wishes.'

'When and where will we ever dry our boots, I wonder? Warsaw? Königsberg? Vienna? Or does our Emperor intend that our march east should take us even further?'

'To Russia itself? Perhaps we will not dry our boots until we reach Moscow.'

'Who can say how the mind of such a man as the Emperor works? He is a genius, of that I have no doubt, even if his methods are sometimes questionable.'

'They say that there is a thin line between genius and madness. If he walks that line let us hope his balance is good. For, whichever way he chooses to step, *we* will be the instruments of his desires. We have fought through olive groves, vineyards, wheat fields and deserts for Bonaparte. Now he sends us into a country that is little more than a wooded swamp. And with what objective, Lieutenant? The same as ever. Conquest. If there is one man in *La Grande Armée* who craves advancement more than any other it is Bonaparte himself.'

The two men walked in silence for a moment longer until Lausard put out an arm to halt the officer.

'Listen,' he said quietly.

Off to the west there was the unmistakable sound of movement. Of what seemed, in the blackness, to be a sizable body of men.

'Have we been encircled by the Russians?' Royere mused as the sound grew louder.

'Riders,' shouted a sentry, his voice cutting through the icy stillness.

Lausard and Royere hurried in the direction of the sound, the sergeant almost unconsciously touching the hilt of his sword as he ran. The three-foot scabbard bumped against his thigh, the weapon rattling slightly inside it. The two sentries were both holding their carbines across their chests but, as figures became visible in the gloom, one drew the butt into his shoulder, ready to fire if necessary.

'Halt,' shouted Royere and the leading horsemen slowed their mounts. 'Identify yourselves.'

'*Vive l'Empereur*,' shouted one of the men.

'We are looking for your commanding officer,' called another. 'We have ridden from Bielshun, a depot on the banks of the river Ukra.'

Royere and Lausard took a step forward, both men squinting into the darkness.

'They're wearing dragoon uniforms, Lieutenant,' Lausard said quietly. 'I think our new blood has finally arrived.'

Seven

'Seven men. Are these the reinforcements we were promised?' Lieutenant Royere took a deep breath, held it a moment then exhaled, the air clouding around his face as he spoke.

'We were told that we were to report to our units as soon as possible, sir,' said one of the dragoons. 'We were assured that others would follow.'

'Thank you,' Royere said flatly. 'And don't call me sir,' he added as an afterthought.

Rocheteau pulled up the collar of his cape to hide a grin.

'I entrust these men to you and your companions, sergeant,' said the officer, glancing at Lausard. 'I can think of no one better equipped to acquaint them with what is required of them and what they may expect from this campaign.' He saluted then walked back in the direction of the village, his boots crunching on the heavily frosted ground.

Lausard looked at the seven dragoons, all of whom seemed to have moved closer to the fire. Without exception they looked pale and drawn. Each one of them exhausted and cold. They ranged in age from late teens to mid-forties. Like Lausard and his men, they were filthy. Grimed with the mud of Poland's sub-standard roads and unforgiving terrain. Chilled to the bone by the frost and soaked by the rain that had only recently abated. They stood in a ragged line, aware of the appraising glances that met them from the dragoons nearby. Erebus wandered back and forth behind the men, occasionally stopping to sniff at them until he returned to Gaston who began stroking the great black dog.

'It might be best to start with your names,' said Lausard, nodding in the direction of the first man.

'Varcon,' said the trooper. 'I used to work as a guard at the asylum at Charenton.'

'The madhouse?' Rocheteau grunted. 'You've come to the right place.'

Some of the others huddled around the fire laughed.

'I understand the Marquis de Sade was a prisoner there,' Bonet said, his interest aroused. 'Did you ever have occasion to speak with him?'

'I knew him well,' Varcon answered. 'We often spoke about . . .'

'Never mind the chatter,' snapped Delacor. 'There'll be time for that later.'

'You,' Lausard said to the second man.

'Gormier. I volunteered.'

'I would respectfully suggest that you volunteer for nothing from this point on,' Lausard told him and again there was laughter from the other men.

'Volunteered for what?' Roussard wanted to know. 'To get killed?'

'I felt it was my duty to fight for my country and for the Emperor,' Gormier answered. 'What better reason would a man have to offer his life than for his homeland?'

The third man stepped forward and met Lausard's gaze.

'My name is Collard,' he announced. 'I was a coachman. For six years I served a family of aristocrats in Bayonne. When they were executed I stole some of their money and fled to Spain. When the money ran out I returned to France.'

'How long did you live in Spain?' Lausard wanted to know.

'Ten years,' Collard said. 'From '95 until last year.'

'You should have stayed there,' Giresse said. 'I hear that Spanish women are particularly forthcoming.' He grinned.

'You,' Lausard said to the fourth man.

He was by far the youngest of the group. Lausard guessed he had yet to reach his twentieth birthday. He was a slight, almost uncomfortably thin individual with smooth, sunken cheeks that looked as if they had yet to feel the touch of a razor.

'My name is Delbene,' he said, his voice low.

'They are sending us babies now,' Delacor sneered. 'He's even younger than you, Gaston.'

'Where are you from?' Lausard asked.

'Just outside Paris,' the younger man replied, shuffling awkwardly from one foot to the other. 'My father was a priest.'

'It seems you have a friend, Your Holiness,' Delacor said, nudging Moreau. 'This boy is practically related to your God through his father.'

Moreau crossed himself.

'I have no love for God or for my father,' Delbene snapped, his voice catching. 'If either of them had cared about me, they would have spared me this.'

'Are you a conscript?' Rocheteau wanted to know.

'Do you think I would have volunteered? I wanted no part of this war, or the army.'

Lausard raised one eyebrow.

'There are many like you, Delbene,' he said. 'You will learn quickly that choice is something of a luxury in these times.'

'I heard that the Emperor had called up the conscripts of 1807 a year early to boost the numbers of the army,' Bonet interjected.

'So it would seem,' Lausard answered, his gaze still on Delbene. 'Let us hope they do not all share the attitude of our new companion.'

'You mean they might not *want* to fight?' said Rocheteau, feigning surprise.

The other men around the camp fire laughed.

'Not all of us share Delbene's reluctance to fight,' said the fifth man, stepping forward. 'My name is Laubardemont. I too was conscripted. I was assigned to the artillery originally but I requested a transfer to the cavalry.'

'Why?' Lausard wanted to know.

'I wish to fight the enemies of France face to face,' said the younger man. 'To look into the eyes of those who would challenge her and the Emperor.'

'Death can strike as easily from the sky as it can from three feet away,' Lausard mused. 'A cannonball or a sword. What is the difference? During a battle, artillerymen often come face to face with the enemy. Do you care so little for your life that you would gallop to your death astride a horse? Do your feet not carry you quickly enough?'

'I have no intention of dying, Sergeant,' Laubardemont said flatly. 'On foot *or* on horseback.'

Lausard smiled thinly then nodded towards the next man.

'Baumar,' he said, clearing his throat. 'I was a poacher. The gendarmes arrested me. The magistrate told me that I could either join the army or be imprisoned.'

'I think I would have rather gone to prison,' Roussard offered.

'A man after our own hearts,' chuckled Rocheteau. 'A criminal.'

The others laughed. Some clapped.

Baumar looked puzzled.

'Many of us were in the same position as you,' Lausard told him. 'When the Directory were in power, many of us were ordered to join the army. We were offered the guillotine or army life. It was easier to choose this uniform.'

It was Baumar's turn to smile.

'And you,' the NCO continued, nodding in the direction of the last man. He was a powerfully built individual with the thickest moustache Lausard had ever seen. He could only guess at the last time the man had shaved but the moustache itself looked impervious to even the sharpest razor.

'My name is Kruger,' he said and the men all noted the harsh accent that coloured his words. 'Ernst Kruger. I am Bavarian.'

'You are on the wrong side, my friend,' Rocheteau said flatly. 'Thousands of your compatriots are already massing, ready to fight with the Russians *against* us. What is a Prussian doing in the French army?'

'I have no allegiance to Frederick William,' Kruger rasped. 'Not any longer. I fought *against* you at Saalfeld and Auerstadt, I do not deny that.'

'So why, two months later, do you wear the uniform of your conquerors?' Lausard asked.

'I fought for Prussia because I believed in my country,' Kruger continued. 'I believed that I was right to resist invaders like yourselves. But while I was gone, while I protected my homeland, my family starved. Then, when the fighting was over, my farm was destroyed. Not by the French, but by my own people. Thousands of them, fleeing in defeat and yet they still had time to kill my son because he resisted. They still had time to rape and murder my wife. My *own* people. Those who fight with Lestocq now are as much my enemies as you were this summer.'

'How do we know we can trust him?' Delacor said, looking at Lausard. 'He could be a spy for all we know.'

'Would he have told us these things if he was a spy?' Lausard murmured. 'I do not think so. Rostov is a Russian and yet you trust him. Where is the difference?'

'I agree,' Rocheteau said. 'He has lost those close to him as have many of us. If he wears our uniform then I am prepared to accept him as one of us.'

There were murmurs of approval from around the camp fire.

'As long as you remember,' Lausard said, his gaze never leaving Kruger, 'that your duty now is to us, this squadron. This regiment. Fulfil your responsibilities or I will personally gut you like a fish.'

Kruger nodded and smiled.

'You are all welcome,' Lausard continued. 'We would offer you food and wine but those are luxuries we do not possess in abundance. All we *can* offer you is saddle sores, hunger, cold and exhaustion. They are gifts we are *overly* blessed with.'

'And don't forget the fleas,' added Rocheteau.

'Or the mud,' Carbonne offered.

'You see,' Lausard continued. 'We have much to share with you.'

The other men laughed.

'So, I suppose we are to assume that none of you has any supplies you could distribute among your new comrades,' Joubert asked hopefully, rubbing his mountainous belly.

Rocheteau nudged the big man hard in the ribs.

'We heard that the Emperor had taken certain measures to increase morale,' Varcon offered. 'Every man in the army is to be given a pay bonus. The commissariat equipment is to be doubled. Every man will be issued with a new shirt, sleeping bag and boots.'

'So, when we all march to our deaths before the Russian cannon, we will be well paid, well fed, warm and well dressed,' Rocheteau said cryptically.

'More pay, more food,' snapped Delacor. 'We have heard these rumours too. We hear promises every day but few of them ever come to pass.'

'The only promise that is kept to us is that we will fight,' Sonnier added. 'And fight we do.'

'And when we fight we win,' Rocheteau reminded him.

Gaston pulled his sodden cloak more tightly around him and continued to stroke Erebus, ruffling the fur of the great black dog as it lay beside him on the freezing mud.

'What else have you heard on your travels?' Lausard wanted to know.

'That the Russians continue to retire before us,' said Gormier.

'They are planning something,' Delacor hissed. 'Luring us into a trap. Enticing us on to ground of their own choosing before they fight.'

'Four army corps are advancing across Poland as we speak,' Varcon added. Marshal Murat is already in Warsaw. The Emperor will join him soon.'

'Rumours,' Delacor said dismissively.

'If the weather stays as it has been, the roads will remain impassable to wheeled vehicles, to artillery,' Rostov said. 'The Emperor may as well stay in Berlin. This war will be over before he has time to pull his boots from the mud.'

'Were the roads you travelled bad?' Lausard asked. 'The ground is like clay. We are lucky to cover seven miles a day.'

'Our journey has been difficult,' said Laubardemont.

'Well, don't expect it to get any easier,' sneered Delacor.

'General Duroc's coach overturned the other day,' the former artilleryman continued. 'Word is that he broke his collarbone.'

'He's lucky,' said Roussard. 'An injury like that will ensure he is confined to hospital. There will be no confrontations with the Russians for *him*.'

An uneasy silence descended over the men, finally broken by Collard.

'Why were we assigned to this squadron?' he wanted to know.

'Because we take heavier casualties than most,' Lausard told him flatly. 'You are now, gentlemen, among the more expendable of Bonaparte's horsemen.'

Some of the other dragoons smiled with something akin to pride.

'We are usually part of the advance guard,' the NCO continued. 'Chosen for duties that others are spared. Presented with tasks befitting our former status. Many of us were criminals before we were soldiers. It seems we are never to be allowed to forget that.' There was something approaching anger in the sergeant's voice and a number of his colleagues were not slow to catch the intonation. Rocheteau and Bonet, in particular, glanced in his direction as he spoke.

'What of your officers?' Baumar wanted to know.

'We lost our captain at Saalfeld,' Lausard said. 'He was wounded. We haven't heard from him since he was taken to hospital more than two months ago.'

'Larrey's butchers have probably sent him home for burial by now,' Delacor grunted.

'He was a good man,' Lausard continued. 'And so is Lieutenant Royere. We never have need to challenge or doubt their judgement and, as we obey them, they obey their own superiors. That is all the army asks of any of you. To complete your orders when they are given. I can't guarantee that all of you will live. We might *all* die tomorrow. It is up to Bonaparte, the Russians or the weather to decide our fate.'

'And when our time comes, God will judge us,' Moreau said, crossing himself. 'I hope that none of us is found wanting.'

'Allah, all praise to Him, will welcome me into paradise when the time is right,' Karim added.

'As you will see,' Lausard said, looking at the newest additions to the squadron. 'There are those among us who still believe in a power higher than Bonaparte himself.'

Some of the other dragoons laughed.

'And you, Sergeant?' asked Varcon. 'What do you believe in?'

'In this,' said Lausard and he gently patted the hilt of his sword. 'The only God I trust *my* life to is the God of sharpened steel.'

'Or the God of the musket ball,' echoed Sonnier, smiling.

'What about the God of the bayonet?' said Giresse.

'Or the axe?' Delacor added.

'Don't forget the knife,' Rocheteau grinned, sliding the blade from his right boot cuff. 'In my hands, this blade is as much a deity as any of the other weapons you have mentioned.'

The other dragoons laughed.

'Try and get some sleep,' Lausard said, his words directed to all the men around him but mainly towards the newcomers. 'It isn't easy, I know, but no one can be sure what dawn will bring.'

Even as he spoke, the first gleaming flake of snow fell gently on to the freezing ground beside him.

EIGHT

Napoleon Bonaparte gazed from one window of the state room in which he stood, his eyes scanning the hordes of people crammed into the square before the palace that he had made his headquarters. Two lines of Imperial Guard grenadiers had been formed across the entrance to the building. Behind them was a set of iron railings fully twelve feet tall. They formed another protective wall in addition to the fifteen-inch bayonets that sparkled atop the Charleville muskets of the grenadiers. A wide paved area, adorned with half a dozen statues, led to the main entrance of the palace and there were more guardsmen there, drawn up in three ranks, their long blue cloaks wrapped around them to keep out the chill. In addition, several dozen mounted chausseurs, their red pelisses fastened over their green dolman jackets, also guided their mounts back and forth just ahead of the infantry. The plumes on their fur kolpacks waved and danced every time the wind blew. It cut across the open square like an invisible blade, causing men to shiver where they stood or rode. The breath of horses and men clouded in the night air and the sheen of ice on the stonework made the troopers guide their mounts even more carefully, for fear that the animals might slip on the treacherous ground.

Napoleon guessed that there were anything between two and three thousand civilians jammed into the area ahead of the double ranks of his most loyal soldiers. Men, women and children, some waving lighted torches, shouted his name and cheered even though they could not see him watching from the window. The Corsican shivered slightly and looked back in the direction of the roaring fire that was blazing away in the huge marble fireplace behind him. Despite the leaping flames, there was still a distinct chill and the Emperor rubbed his hands together slowly, his gaze still drawn to the heaving mass of Polish civilians shouting his name.

'Warsaw in December or Paris in April,' murmured Napoleon. 'Given the choice, Berthier, which would you choose?'

The Chief of Staff looked up from the orders he was scribbling and smiled.

'I think you know the answer to that, sire,' he said quietly. 'To be honest, I fear the entire army would gladly choose that option if it were offered.'

'With the exception of my brother-in-law, I suspect.'

'If Marshal Murat finds something enchanting about this land then he has seen something that the rest of us have not within this wasteland of mud, ice and swamp.'

'I think he sees a kingdom for himself. He feels at home here. I hear that the Poles greeted him with the exuberance normally reserved for a king when he arrived in the city. Prince Poniatowski presented him with the sword of Stephen Bathóry. I suspect he sees that as an omen. That he too will one day rule here.'

'The population have emerged in their thousands to greet *you*, sire. And at such a late hour. They recognise you as their true deliverer. Marshal Murat dreams, my lord, just as every man dreams.'

'Dreams I accept. Even dreams of ruling kingdoms.' The Corsican smiled. 'And meanwhile, Davout and Bernadotte continue to scowl at each other. Ney dreams of glory. Augereau takes to his bed with rheumatism. Soult says nothing and Lannes warns me that he distrusts the Poles. I sometimes wonder if I have marshals of France under my command or squabbling, selfish children dressed in gold lace and ostrich feathers.'

'The campaign has been hard on everyone, sire, yourself included. When men have little to cheer them, they seek diversion. Be it in complaint, agitation or conflict.'

'My marshals squabble while my army protests. They have no food. Only foul beer to drink. The bad weather grows worse by the day and, when they finally find shelter, they are forced to share billets with cows and pigs. Reports reach me daily of breaches in discipline. Davout has hanged as many deserters as we have rope. As you say, Berthier, it has not been easy this past month, but I will not see the army I created fall apart because of some bad roads and lack of provisions. Bands of deserters follow the army like vultures after a kill. They take what few supplies this country has to offer. The last thing we need is conflict within the army. It has taken me ten years to make *La Grande Armée* the most effective fighting machine in the world. I will not allow that work to be eroded by renegades.'

'One victory and all that will be forgotten, sire,' Berthier offered. 'All the petty squabbling. All the complaints. Even the cursed weather.'

'Difficult to gain victory over a foe more concerned with running than standing and fighting, Berthier.'

'They cannot run for ever, sire. Our men move faster. We march more quickly. We are more flexible.'

'On good ground, yes. But not on this mud heap.'

The Emperor returned to his vigil at the window, his brow furrowed slightly. A silence descended, finally broken by the Corsican. 'I was thinking about my wife,' he said, distractedly. 'Not a day passes without her entering my thoughts.'

'That is only natural, sire. She is your Empress. Your love. I ache to see the beauty of my own love, my Madame di Visconti. I think of her alone, hundreds of miles from where I too sleep alone, and it cuts me to the very soul.'

'I wonder if I occupy as significant a part of Josephine's heart as she does mine.' He leaned forward, pressing his forehead to the cold glass, looking beyond the square full of rejoicing Poles as if he wished his gaze could travel all the way to Paris to rest upon the woman he loved.

Berthier looked at his superior for a moment, surprised at the melancholy tone of his voice. He lowered his gaze and picked up his quill once more, preparing to continue with his work. Napoleon suddenly spun round and walked briskly across to the fire where he rocked back and forth on his heels, warming his hands.

'Enough of this fatuous romanticism,' he said dismissively. 'We are soldiers, are we not? Soldiers above all else. For now, our only concern is this campaign and what is happening here. Not the fortunes of those hundreds of miles away.' There was a steely look in his eyes. He wandered away from the fire towards a large table that was festooned with maps. Berthier got to his feet and joined him, glancing down at the symbols and arrows that had been scrawled across the pieces of paper. Several small blocks of wood, each marked with a number, had already been placed on the largest map. Napoleon picked up one of the blocks and weighed it carefully, first in one hand then the other as if trying to ascertain its weight. After a moment or two he banged it down on to the map.

'Pultusk,' he said, indicating where he had placed the block of wood. 'The place where the Russian communications cross the river Narew. Bennigsen has been reinforced to the north of that town but I would assume, judging by his conduct so far in this campaign, that it is still his intention to retire.'

'If that is the case, sire, could we not be forgiven for thinking that he may be retiring towards ground of his own choosing before he accepts battle? If indeed he ever does.'

'Murat already has orders to sever the Pultusk–Königsberg highway and engage the enemy advance guard. I trust he will show restraint if it is called for. After all he has thirty thousand of my cavalry under his command.'

'With the support of just thirty light guns and no infantry, sire.'

'I am aware of that, Berthier. The Russians moved beyond the marching range of our infantry when they evacuated Pultusk.' The Corsican stroked his chin thoughtfully, his ever alert gaze moving over the map with incredible speed. 'Murat will accept or refuse battle, depending upon the circumstances. As for the rest of the army, Davout is to occupy Sierock.'

Berthier began scribbling, his quill scratching across the paper in the stillness of the room. He barely looked up, content instead to listen as Napoleon dictated.

'I wish Augereau to halt at Zakroczin and Wyszogrod,' the Corsican continued. 'Once there, he is to draw supplies from Plonsk and Blonie. Soult will continue to move towards Plonsk.

I want Lannes to assemble his forces before Warsaw.' Napoleon walked around the map, occasionally stopping to study portions of it. 'If my assumption is correct, and the Russians still intend to retire then the best way to cut off their lines of communication is to concentrate our forces toward the river Narew.' He stroked one cheek with his index finger. 'The Fourth, Seventh, Third and Fifth Corps are to move north from the Vistula and seize Pultusk. Simultaneously, the Sixth and First Corps are to move forward from Thorn to Bielshun then on to Soldau and Mlava. Such a movement will deny the Russians a northerly line of retreat and prevent them making contact with Lestocq and his Prussians. Soult's corps will link the two wings of the army. I have no doubt that these movements will lead to a major battle on 21 or 22 December. A victory will be a fine Christmas present, will it not?'

Berthier continued to scribble down the orders.

Napoleon walked slowly across to the fire then back towards the window. He could see the hordes of Poles still celebrating in the square beyond.

'What do they expect of me, Berthier?' he mused. 'What makes these peasants so delighted by my arrival?'

'They see in you a saviour, sire. A man to restore their very nationality.'

'They seek the reconstitution of their kingdom. They see, in me, a restorer of nobility and monarchy.' He laughed humourlessly. 'How little they understand me. They wish for their national identity to be returned while all *I* wish for is for my army to occupy cantonments for the remainder of the winter. The Poles and I, it would seem, are not united in our desires. Were they to know that, I fear their welcome would be less extravagant.'

'But you intend them to fight alongside *La Grande Armée*, sire,' the Chief of Staff said.

'I have every reason to believe that they will make fine soldiers and they will provide much needed reinforcements when the fighting begins. Prince Poniatowski and General Dombrowski, in particular, have shown themselves to be very able commanders. Did I myself not help Dombrowski to raise a Polish legion back in '97? He and his men fought with great valour. They have done so in most of my campaigns since then. Even now, he has close to thirty thousand men concentrated at Posen, ready to support *La Grande Armée*. But my opinion of the Poles as troops and my views on the future of their nation are as different as the white knight to the black bishop.'

'Poniatowski says that you have given the Poles the chance to fight the Russians under Polish banners,' Berthier offered. 'For that alone, sire, you may expect their unwavering support.'

'They will serve a purpose. Nothing more,' the Corsican said flatly.

Napoleon continued to gaze out of the window, while the only sounds within the room were the scratching of Berthier's quill and the crackle of the burning logs in the fireplace. In the square beyond the palace, the residents of Warsaw continued to rejoice.

Nine

Lausard wiped a hand across his face to clear his vision. The snow that had been falling for most of the night had increased both in severity and density. Driven by a biting wind, it raged like a white tornado, driving frozen flakes against exposed flesh and stinging like glistening shrapnel. Ahead of him, the sergeant saw a riderless horse stumbling through the blizzard, its reins hanging limply from its bit, its girth strap so loose that the saddle it bore on its bowed back was virtually slipping off. The animal walked with faltering steps over ground now hardened to the consistency of steel. The snow was already to its forelocks and each step seemed to cause the animal pain. Where its rider was Lausard could only guess. Dead in the snow further back along with hundreds of other French troops, he reasoned. It was difficult to make out which regiment the animal and its rider had belonged to because both the shabraque that covered the saddle and the regimental number displayed on the portmanteau were covered with thick snow. It was difficult enough to make out regimental colours. The sergeant guessed, from the pointed edges of the saddle-cloth, that the horse had belonged to a hussar. He watched it for a moment longer as it picked its way across the rutted, frozen terrain then, with a pitiful whinny, the horse collapsed into the snow and lay still. Immediately, snow began to cover it. Lausard wondered how many more men and animals lay hidden beneath the white shroud of snow that was covering the land so quickly.

The sergeant reached up with a shaking hand and pulled the scarf he wore, more tightly around his nose and mouth. He bowed his head slightly as he and his companions rode on slowly into the very mouth of the snowstorm. The other thing that struck Lausard was the stillness. Despite the fact that the road was clogged with mounted troops, there was very little noise. The snow acted as a gigantic, freezing muffler, capable of cutting out even the loudest sounds. Lausard heard none of the noises he had become so familiar with over the past ten years. The usual clatter of hooves was swallowed up by the fallen snow. Even the jingling of harnesses and the metallic rattle of so many swords bumping against riders' boot cuffs and thighs was absent. None of the men spoke either. Each seemed more concerned with guiding his mount on through the blizzard, terrified that the animal might, at any moment, simply collapse from cold and hunger.

From the slate grey sky, the snow continued to fall so densely that visibility was already down to a hundred yards. Of the patrols sent ahead earlier that morning, the snow had already covered their tracks. Some had returned but others had merely disappeared in the white wasteland, perhaps, Lausard reasoned, lost and disorientated in the murderous snowscape. Unable to re-establish their directions in such a wilderness. On all sides of them, the dragoons saw the ever present forests of pine trees thrusting up into the dull heavens. Roads that had, days earlier, been impassable because of the deep mud, were now equally as difficult to traverse because of the depth of the snow. Lausard knew that conditions would now become worse whichever course the weather took. Should the snow continue to fall with such density, then movement would be slowed to a crawl once again. Troops following would be faced with a trek through treacherous slush created by the passage of so many feet and hooves and, should a thaw set in, the entire army would be bogged down once more in the oozing, clinging mud they had encountered upon first entering this most inhospitable of countries. Whatever happened, Lausard and his companions knew that the passage of *La Grande Armée* would continue to be slow, difficult, costly and painful.

The NCO gripped his reins more tightly, partly to urge his horse forward but also to ensure that he still had some feeling in his fingers. He also continuously flexed his toes inside his boots, anxious that they too were not already frozen off. The cold was seeping through his entire body as surely as if someone had filled his veins with iced water. He shuddered in the saddle, his horse tossing its head mournfully as it too struggled to see through the ever growing blizzard.

He wiped snow from his eyes once again and saw an infantryman sitting by the roadside. Lausard guessed the man was in his early twenties although it was difficult to be certain because of his haggard appearance. He was watching the passing troops as if he was seated on some sun-drenched hill reviewing those who passed before him. The man was dressed in just his blue tunic and white breeches. His boots were missing despite the fact that his gaiters were buttoned from ankle to knee. The flesh of his feet was almost as blue as his tunic. The rest of his uniform was spattered with mud. His shako lay in the snow beside him, as did his pack. As Lausard watched, the infantryman carefully loaded his Charleville as ably as he could with shaking hands then turned it so that the barrel was in his mouth. With infinite care, he slipped one frost-bitten toe through the trigger guard then pressed down. There was a muffled, almost silent pop as the weapon went off, drilling the lead ball into the infantryman's skull. He fell sideways, blood from his splintered skull spreading across the snow. A cloud of condensation began to rise from the steaming fluid like ethereal mist. Lausard exhaled wearily. Moreau crossed himself. Rocheteau immediately swung himself out of the saddle and hurried, as best he could, over to the fallen infantryman. He stepped over the body and went straight for the man's pack, rummaging through it quickly. He pulled out the contents, spilling them on the blood-drenched snow. A razor. Some needle and thread and a small round object that the corporal recognised as a potato. It was already beginning to sprout shoots but he nonetheless stuffed it into his pocket and ambled back to where his companions were still making their tortuous way along the road. He swung himself into the saddle and rode on, patting his horse's neck as it stumbled in the snow. The animal whinnied protestingly but continued on its way, head lowered to escape the worst of the blizzard. Rocheteau looked across at the corpse, wondering if he should have taken the dead man's jacket or shirt too. He could always have wrapped them around himself if the temperature dropped further.

'You realise you could be hanged for what you just did?' said Laubardemont, his voice muffled by the upraised collar of his cloak.

'If every man who scavenged for food was hanged the army would number less than a hundred by next week,' snapped Rocheteau. 'If I had found a bottle of vodka in that man's pack would you have refused your share of it? I think not.'

Laubardemont considered the question then turned away from the corporal and rode on.

'If this weather continues then the army may well cease to exist entirely,' Bonet offered, his voice almost lost on the howling wind.

No one answered. Every ounce of strength was being used to battle through the snow. Every word that remained unspoken seemed to preserve what little heat the cavalrymen retained within their ravaged bodies. Gaston rode with Erebus perched on the front of his saddle. The great black dog was wrapped in a discarded cloak with just its head poking out. Gaston kept one arm around the animal both to prevent it falling and also in an attempt to draw some meagre warmth from its body. The large grey horse the trumpeter rode seemed relatively untroubled by the extra weight and battled through the snow taking huge steps with its powerful legs.

'Where the hell are we anyway?' Delacor wanted to know.

'Approaching a town called Pultusk,' Bonet told him.

'A town?' Delacor said dismissively. 'We have seen three huts together described as villages before now. How large is this town?'

Bonet could only shrug.

'It appears on the map I have,' said the former schoolmaster. 'But I have no idea of its size.'

'Large enough to carry supplies, I hope,' Joubert intoned.

'The damned Poles will have run off with every last morsel,' snapped Delacor. 'You know that. Just as they have everywhere else we've passed through.'

'How far away are we?' Lausard asked.

'Less than twenty miles,' Bonet told him.

'It could take three days to cover that distance in weather like this,' the sergeant muttered.

'The patrol should have returned by now,' Lieutenant Royere remarked. 'They should be able to give us more information.'

'If they haven't been smothered by the snow or frozen to death,' Roussard grunted.

'Perhaps they've finally run into the Russians,' Rocheteau mused. 'I heard that Cossack patrols had been sighted to the north. If their cavalry are around then the army can't be far away.'

'They are reckoned to be particularly fine horsemen, aren't they, Rostov?' Giresse asked.

'Some say the Cossacks are the finest light cavalry in Europe,' the Russian said. 'But they are ill-disciplined and unreliable without strong officers.'

'But a threat nevertheless,' Lausard murmured.

Rostov nodded.

'And they know how to operate in conditions such as these,' he added. 'They will look upon this weather as an ally. Not a curse, as we do.'

'You see what you have to look forward to?' Delacor snapped, turning to look at Varcon and Gormier. 'If the weather or hunger don't get you then the Cossacks will.'

'We will be ready when the time comes to fight them,' Varcon said proudly. 'Just as you will.'

Delacor regarded the men irritably for a moment then returned his gaze to the snow~blasted landscape ahead. The road curved slightly through a particularly thick outcrop of forest and the dragoons were thankful that the trees acted as something of a shield against the biting wind, albeit for fleeting moments. The snow that was piled up on the remainder of the road was not quite so deep within the woods and the dragoons found their horses better able to cope with the icy ground. However, despite the slight respite from the onslaught of the snow and wind, the cold intensified.

Lausard glanced around at his companions and saw that, almost without exception, they were shivering as they rode. He himself patted the neck of his horse as the animal snorted dispiritedly. His movements felt stiff and wooden, as if the numbing cold had already penetrated his joints and dulled their effectiveness. Beneath his cloak, he wore his woollen tunic, two shirts and a scarf. He sported a pair of long johns beneath his breeches, two pairs of socks and, under his thick leather gauntlets, his hands were wrapped in strips of material cut from the pelisse of a dead hussar but still he suffered from the merciless temperatures. Many of his companions also wore additional pieces of uniform acquired from the many corpses that had dotted the countryside through which they had passed. But, as with Lausard, it seemed that no amount of clothing could fully protect them from cold that threatened to freeze the blood in their veins. The sergeant looked to his right and left, gazing into the woods, wishing that the men could just stop, hack down several of the pines and ignite them into one, massive, warming bonfire. The ground sloped upwards slightly on either side of the rudimentary road that led towards Pultusk and, in places, the woods were less dense. Bushes, covered with snow, looked like huge balls of wadding, squeezed together and dropped by giant, disinterested hands.

It was close to one of these bushes that Lausard spotted the footprints.

'Lieutenant, look,' he snapped, jabbing a finger towards the tracks.

Royere glanced in the direction indicated and narrowed his eyes, both against the wind and also to take in what Lausard was showing him.

'Let's get a better look,' the officer said and snapped his reins, guiding his horse towards the indentations in the freezing white carpet covering the earth. Lausard, Karim and Rocheteau followed and all four of the men finally brought their mounts to a halt close to the tracks.

'They must be recent,' Lausard remarked, swinging himself

from the saddle and kneeling down beside the marks. 'The snow would have covered them otherwise.'

Karim also clambered down and wandered a few more yards into the woods, his eyes fixed on the jumble of tracks in the snow.

'Russians?' Royere mused.

Rocheteau slid his Charleville from its boot on his saddle and held it across his chest, eyes scanning the woods.

'These don't look like boot tracks,' Karim said, touching the nearest footprint with one gloved hand. 'There's no indentation where the heel would be.'

'Then who made them?' Lausard asked, his own gaze still riveted to the tracks.

Karim could only shake his head.

'Sergeant, take five men and follow the tracks for two hundred yards into the trees,' Royere ordered. 'Return to the column if you find nothing. If you discover anything of value then send a rider back to fetch me and some more men.'

Erebus suddenly came lumbering through the snow. The big black dog sniffed at the tracks, barked loudly once or twice then padded off into the trees, nose to the disturbed snow. Karim followed closely, one hand resting on the hilt of his scimitar.

'Varcon, Kruger, Moreau and Rostov,' shouted Lausard, gesturing towards the woods. 'With me. Now.'

The four men whose names had been called hurried to join Lausard and Karim. They dismounted. Varcon and Moreau pulled their carbines free and checked the firing mechanisms. Rostov chose a pistol from his twin holsters.

'Kruger, watch the horses,' said Lausard. 'The rest of you, come with me.'

Slowly, picking their way over uneven, snow-covered and icy ground, the men moved deeper into the all-enveloping woods. They moved in single file, no more than five paces apart. Varcon looked back and saw that the column of dragoons on the makeshift road were now all but invisible behind the screen of trees. The silence that had been prominent before now became almost intolerable. Lausard felt as if it were a tangible force, crushing in on his ears. He narrowed his eyes against the gleaming brilliance of the snow and trudged on. The only sound he could hear clearly was the low panting of Erebus as the black dog continued to follow the tracks. Even as they walked, the still falling snow was filling the tracks, making them indistinct in places. Another thirty minutes and there would be no evidence that they had ever been there.

Lausard increased his pace, drawing closer to Erebus. The dog had reached a slight incline and it paused there, glancing down into even more thickly wooded land. There was barely room for the men to move through the dense trees, but the rapidly disappearing tracks led down the reverse slope and Lausard urged his companions onwards as they followed the imprints. They were less than a hundred yards from the crest of the low ridge when the NCO spotted a thin plume of smoke rising into the slate-grey sky. Invisible from the other side of the ridge and masked by the trees, it was rising from a thicket away to their left. Lausard raised his hand to halt the men, tapped his sword hilt then pointed in the direction of the smoke. Varcon and Moreau gripped their carbines more tightly, holding them across their chests. Lausard gently drew his sword, the metal sliding effortlessly and silently from the steel scabbard. Rostov eased back the hammer on his pistol as he advanced, protecting the flint and pan from the falling snow with the palm of one hand. Erebus prepared to scamper on ahead but Lausard caught the great black dog by the thick fur around its neck and held it back. Ducking low, all four of the dragoons moved closer to the still-rising smoke.

The tracks were more numerous now. They were not just in a single line but spread out over a much wider area. Karim tapped Lausard's shoulder and pointed with the tip of his wickedly curved scimitar. A pile of kindling had been gathered. Close to it was an empty iron pot. The dragoons moved closer. Lausard heard an unmistakable sound. It was the squealing of a pig. He raised his eyebrows and looked at the other men. They were less than twenty yards from the thin plume of smoke now. Lausard heard another sound that he was sure was the lowing of cattle.

Erebus suddenly pulled free of his grip and hurtled down the slope barking furiously.

'Damn that black devil,' hissed Rostov, raising his pistol.

Varcon swung his carbine up to his shoulder, his hands shaking slightly.

'Wait,' snapped Lausard.

Erebus was still barking.

The dragoons heard words being spoken. The language was alien to Lausard. He looked across at Rostov as if for confirmation of the origin of the words.

'It's Polish,' the Russian told him.

Lausard saw a tall, thin man dressed in a long brown overcoat come into view. It was as if he had materialised from within one of the thick tree trunks. It took Lausard a moment to realise that the man had in fact emerged from what was a well-concealed cave entrance.

'Stand still,' shouted Lausard, pointing at the man who instantly froze where he stood, a look of horror on his face. He remained motionless for only seconds then made to dart back into the cave. 'Tell him to stay where he is or he'll be shot,' the sergeant rasped.

Rostov barked out some words in Russian and the man stopped in his tracks once again.

By now, the dragoons were at the mouth of the cave. Lausard could see the thin plume of smoke rising from within it. He could also see other figures moving inside the stony retreat.

'Tell the others to come out,' he told Rostov and the Russian repeated the instruction.

Erebus stopped barking and contented himself with prowling back and forth close to the cave entrance, watching as three other figures cautiously emerged: two men in their thirties and a third figure, wrapped in a huge fur coat complete with hood. It took Lausard a moment to realise that it was a woman. She moved close to the man in the long brown coat and stood with her head bowed. She was gently turning something over in her fingers. Moreau stepped forward and peered more closely at it.

The woman closed her hand around the small object, jealously guarding it. Moreau moved nearer, reaching out towards her, gesturing for her to show him the thing she held so tightly. She merely shook her head then glanced at the tall man who nodded gently. The woman opened her hand and displayed what lay in her palm. It was a gold Star of David, barely the size of Moreau's thumbnail. The dragoon nodded and reached inside his shirt, pulling out a small crucifix. He held it between his thumb and forefinger, allowing the woman to study it for a moment before he slipped it back inside his clothes.

'They are Jews,' Moreau proclaimed.

'Ask them what they're doing here,' Lausard told Rostov.

The Russian repeated the question and then, after some nervous chatter from the man in the brown coat, relayed the answer to Lausard.

'He says they live in these woods now,' Rostov translated. 'They fled from Pultusk when the Russians occupied it. As Moreau says, they are Jews. They say that the Russians have no love for them or their kind. Many had their property taken. Many were abused. They fled.'

'Ask him how long ago the Russians came to the town,' Lausard said. 'And if they still remain there.'

There was more nervous chatter from the man in the brown coat.

'He says that he and some of his people left the town two days ago,' Rostov said. 'As far as he knows, many of the Russians left too. They marched south-west, towards the Ukra river but there are still many in the vicinity.'

The Jew in the brown coat spoke again.

'He says his name is Elias,' Rostov translated. 'The woman is his wife, Marla. The other two are Penkowski and Zarnatin. Everything they own is inside that cave.'

Lausard walked towards the cave entrance. He could still hear the sound of livestock coming from within. The smell from inside was rank and the sergeant wrinkled his nose as he stepped into the dark recess. Several pigs and cows were roaming free in the cave, competing for space with chickens that squawked and flapped as the dragoon walked among them. The stench of animal excrement was curiously potent within the damp confines. A marked contrast to the clean, fresh smell that came with the snow. A small fire was burning, the smoke escaping through a hole in the cave roof. It was that which the dragoons had first spotted. Over the fire, a small metal pot had been suspended. Lausard glanced around as he heard footsteps behind him. In the gloom, he could just make out Varcon's features. The dragoon knelt beside the pot and stirred the contents. He lifted the spoon and sipped at the bubbling soup. It was watery, with a faint flavour of potato. There were several bundles laid around the fire, some were quite obviously clothes. Varcon began pulling at the others, scattering the meagre contents over the cave floor.

'Leave them,' snapped Lausard.

'But there may be food here, Sergeant,' Varcon protested.

Lausard bent and picked up a small locket that had fallen from one of the bundles.

'Food?' he rasped. 'I see none. Do you? But, if you want *this*, then take it. And anything else they call their own.' He glared at Varcon, pushing the locket into his face.

The dragoon shook his head, stepping aside as Lausard strode back out into the open.

'Five chickens, two cows, three pigs,' Lausard said. 'Tell them we will take three of the chickens, one cow, one pig and any eggs and flour they may have. The rest they can keep for themselves.'

Rostov relayed the instructions. The tall Jew bowed his head and managed a smile; then he spoke quietly.

'He thanks us for leaving them something,' said Rostov. 'He says we are more merciful than the Russians.'

'Let us see if he still holds that opinion when the rest of the army come through here,' Lausard said flatly, turning to walk away.

The next voice was soft and Lausard realised that the woman had uttered a few words.

'What did she say?' he wanted to know.

Rostov paused for a moment.

'She wants to know if we are taking the food for our celebration,' he said.

'What celebration?' Lausard asked.

'My God. How could we have forgotten?' Moreau said, crossing himself. 'Has war even robbed us of our memories? Today is the day our saviour was born. December the twenty-fifth.'

'Christmas day,' murmured Rostov. 'I hadn't realised.'

'And on this day, He has seen fit to bless us with the gifts we need more than anything else,' Moreau smiled. 'Food.'

'These gifts are not from your God or His son,' Lausard hissed. 'But rather from those who crucified the one you call saviour. The Jews.' Lausard turned and headed off up the slope, before turning briefly. 'Merry Christmas,' he said quietly.

Ten

The dense and impenetrable smoke from dozens of fires rose into the air and hung like some choking man-made cloud over the camp that had been established by the Imperial Guard grenadiers. Most of the wood that was being used was damp, hence the noxious fumes that belched from the fires. There was no shortage of trees in Poland; the soldiers of *La Grande Armée* had marched across countryside dense with pines and oaks but the recent searing frosts had made some trunks impervious to even the sharpest of axes. Where trees could not be felled, the buildings of the town of Lopaczin had been demolished and their timbers smashed into the kindling that now formed the centre of the camp fires. Wheat sheaves, stored in farm buildings, had also been used to help start the much needed fires. It had also been scattered on the muddy ground to make the passage of the grenadiers and, more importantly, their commander in chief, easier.

They moved around their fires, huddled close together for the most part, still wrapped in their long blue overcoats, cooking their meagre supplies, smoking, and cleaning their equipment. A small detachment of chasseurs, their pelisses fastened against the biting cold, led their horses to the barns that had been set aside as cover for the mounts. Horse grenadiers also wandered back and forth, their huge bearskins nodding as they walked, the red plumes that adorned them stirred by the wind. Some artillerymen, sweating despite the freezing temperatures, were sliding planks of wood beneath the wheels of an eight-pounder.

If the thaw continued as it had done for most of that afternoon, the cannon would not be too deeply immersed in the clinging mud so as to prevent its movement the following morning. Other blue-uniformed gunners were completing the same procedure with the carriage that pulled the gun and also the caisson that served it. So far during the campaign, double and even treble teams of horses had sometimes proved unable to haul the heavier cannon across countryside that was often little more than sticky clay. The thaw, if it continued, would ensure that their passage remained difficult, if not impossible. Cannon discarded in the mud merely sank deeper until the frost finally trapped them in the earth as surely as a wasp in amber. All that could be done then was to wait for the thaw to come again and try to drag the gun clear.

Napoleon Bonaparte walked slowly through the hordes of elite troops, nodding greetings, accepting cheers and occasionally stopping to speak to the men who made up his personal bodyguard. With him walked Marshal Berthier, General Jean Rapp, General Geraud Christophe Michel Duroc and Jean Dominique Larrey. Each of the men moved with some difficulty through the freezing mud, occasionally stopping to haul themselves free of its sticky embrace. Napoleon himself almost overbalanced but Larrey shot out a hand to steady the Corsican who looked at his Chief Surgeon and smiled.

'You almost had another casualty to treat, my friend,' he said, making his way towards the disused barn that passed for his headquarters.

'I and my surgeons have already treated more men for frostbite than we have for wounds, sire,' Larrey said. 'Combined with the lack of good food and water and the constant changes of temperature, I am surprised that there is a single man in the entire army fit enough to carry a musket.'

'Ever the soldier's friend, Larrey,' smiled the Corsican. 'You underestimate the hardiness of our troops. Whatever deprivations they suffer now are not new to them.'

'I beg to differ, sire,' Larrey insisted. 'They have been through cold, I agree. They have suffered the opposite extreme while in the heat of Egypt but never before have they suffered so miserably, so *constantly*. There is no respite from this infernal weather or these damnable conditions.'

'I have to agree, sire,' Rapp added. 'This country is the most godforsaken part of the world any of us has had the misfortune to encounter. The terrain is the worst for cavalry I have ever seen.'

'Then spare a thought for the infantry,' Napoleon said. 'They slog through the mud using only their own strength. At least the cavalry have horses to carry them.'

'Horses that are as desperate as their riders for food and shelter, sire,' Rapp continued. 'When this campaign began, our men were mounted on the finest horses in Europe. Now they bestride animals more fitted to prowling farmyards. You can count the ribs on every one of them. Those that can still walk.'

'It is the roads that are crippling us, sire,' Duroc added. 'They are not best suited to an army accustomed to moving with speed and purpose such as *La Grande Armée*. Would it not be worth considering assigning the punishment companies to the task of making the roads more serviceable, Your Highness? At least the more important of the routes to be used by our troops.'

Napoleon nodded sagely.

'Bourienne tells me in his correspondence from Hamburg that the letters he receives are nothing but a succession of complaints about the bad state of the roads,' the Corsican confirmed. 'And yet, what am I supposed to do? I am not in the position of being able to command the weather. Would that I was. Nor am I responsible for the reprehensible state of this country's thoroughfares.'

'That is true, sire,' Duroc admitted. 'But the combination of the two is causing problems none of us could have imagined.'

'There is no need to tell me, Duroc,' snapped the Corsican. 'I myself travelled from Warsaw in a peasant's cart. I am well aware of the difficulties posed by this country, its climate, its roads *and* its people. Reports reach me daily of the apathy of the Poles themselves. For a people so desperate to have their national identity restored they seem to be doing precious little to aid those engaged in that task. They run from our troops. They will not share their supplies.' He saluted the tall grenadiers guarding either side of his headquarters as he entered, removing his hat and moving towards the fire that had been built in the centre of the building. A sergeant of the guard, charged with tending the fire, tore the top from a cartridge and sprinkled some gunpowder on the leaping flames to ensure that they continued to burn. He then saluted and left the officers alone inside the building.

'The only people in the country who have anything are the Jews,' said Rapp. 'They follow the army, charging exorbitant prices for substandard foods they have prepared. Salt fish and inferior bread. Short-weight loaves. Flour mixed with everything from hair powder to sand and bread that is underbaked because the wood has been stolen from the stoves to make fires. They are parasites, exploiting the needs of men they know are starving. Unfortunately, they are also the only ones who speak any kind of language that can be understood.'

'The troops say that one needs to know only four words of Polish,' Berthier mused. '"*Kleba?*", "*Niema*", "*Vota?*" and "*Sana.*" "Some bread?" "There is none." "Any water?" and "We will go and fetch it."'

The other officers laughed. Napoleon was unimpressed.

'At the moment I have more pressing concerns,' he snapped. 'Namely the Russian army.' The Corsican poured himself a glass of Chambertin and sipped at it as he walked to another table inside the barn that was, as ever, strewn with maps. Each one was marked with pins or small wooden blocks. Every one an indicator of the positions of bodies of troops, both French and Russian. 'It seems they have finally stopped running.'

'I think that was proved by the difficulty Marshal Davout encountered crossing the Narew,' said Berthier. 'He lost fourteen hundred men forcing a passage over the river at Tscharnovo. Marshal Bernadotte's men also encountered and engaged a Prussian force at Bielshun. It would seem that the two allies are in close proximity, sire. But, due to the efforts of Marshal Ney, they are unable to keep their lines of communication open.'

'How many men does Lestocq have under his command?' asked Napoleon.

'Around six thousand, sire,' Berthier said. 'But they are not in a position to link up with the Russians at the moment. Intelligence indicates that they are completely severed from the Russian right and are marching away from it in the direction of Königsberg. The forces of Marshals Ney, Bessiéres and Bernadotte are between them.'

'What of the remainder of *La Grande Armée*?' the Emperor asked, his eyes scanning the maps.

'As you ordered, sire, Marshal Davout is marching directly on Streshegozin to support Marshal Lannes who is currently at Pultusk,' the Chief of Staff said, jabbing his finger at various places on the map. 'Marshal Augereau has occupied Novemiasto. His advance guard have reached Bondkowo.'

'And Soult's corps?' Napoleon interjected.

'They have occupied Sochoczin,' Berthier informed his Emperor. 'He has light cavalry support at Oirzen. Marshal Murat and the cavalry reserve is also in that vicinity. The rest of the army face the Russians towards Golymin and Pultusk.'

'Has there been any news from Lannes as to the strength and dispositions of the enemy?' the Corsican wanted to know.

'There are reckoned to be in excess of thirty-five thousand Russian troops facing him, sire,' said Berthier. 'Supported by forty guns. Marshal Lannes has, at present, twenty thousand men under his command.'

Napoleon smiled.

'Lannes will favour those odds,' he chuckled.

'He may favour the odds, sire,' murmured Rapp, 'but he will not favour the conditions.'

'The weather works against the Russians as much as it does ourselves,' Napoleon snapped dismissively. 'They march, camp and fight on the same terrain and in the same conditions. Why should *we* be more susceptible to the vagaries of winter than they?'

The other officers remained silent. Larrey warmed himself by the fire. Its crackling filled the stillness. Duroc glanced at the maps, as did Rapp and Berthier. Napoleon sipped his wine and looked at his companions.

'Why do you all harbour such doubts as to the outcome of this campaign?' he asked finally. 'For ten years now we have known nothing but triumph and yet still all I hear is indecision and foreboding. None of you attained your ranks with thoughts of that nature. Why do you entertain them now?'

'Have you never had doubts yourself, sire?' Rapp wanted to know.

'I believe in my own abilities. I trust those I command and I gladly put my life and the fate of France in the hands of my soldiers,' Napoleon said. 'It has been that way ever since I was given command of the Army of Italy back in '96. I do not doubt any of you, why do you doubt me?'

'We do not doubt you, sire,' Duroc explained. 'But what soldier does not entertain *some* misgivings on the eve of battle? What kind of man is free of fear when death could strike him at any minute of the day or night?'

'And this campaign has been different, sire,' Rapp continued. 'Our soldiers are less satisfied. They showed a lively distaste to crossing the Vistula. Misery, the winter, the bad weather, have all imbued them with an extreme aversion for this country. If we had been *fighting* our way across Poland it might have been a different matter, but we have been *chasing* the Russians. Nothing more. No more than ten thousand men have been committed to any one battle as yet and we have been marching for more than two months.'

'That may well change come the dawn,' Napoleon said. 'And when it does and the fields are strewn with dead and the hospitals crammed with wounded, will you all be happier then?' There was a note of defiance in his voice. 'Will the troops be less vociferous in their condemnation of this land once they have buried some of their companions?' He drained his glass then refilled it from the jug on the table.

Another heavy silence descended over the officers gathered within the barn. It was broken by the Emperor himself. He cleared his throat and gazed at one of the maps.

'What of the Russian positions?' he said finally.

'Bennigsen is with the divisions of Sedmaratzki and Osterman Tolstoi,' the Chief of Staff told him. 'They are in and around Pultusk, as are parts of the divisions commanded by Sacken and Gallitzin. The remainder of Gallitzin's division is retiring in the direction of Golymin, twelve miles north-west of Pultusk. Word has it that Marshal Kamenskoi has given orders for artillery to be abandoned if it slows their progress.'

'He is either supremely competent or extremely stupid,' Napoleon smiled.

'I fear the years are catching up with him, sire,' Duroc interjected. 'He is approaching his seventy-sixth year. His mind is not as sharp as it was.'

'Word has it that he has a tendency to rashness or indecision and he is known for his violent temper,' Berthier added.

'Never a good trait in a commanding officer,' Napoleon grinned. 'Bennigsen too is of senior years, is he not?'

'He is sixty-one, sire,' Berthier announced. 'He is a capable commander of cavalry but his skills as a field commander are limited. The more junior generals such as Prince Bagration and Barclay de Tolly seem to show the most promise.'

'What of the other Russian commanders?' Napoleon asked.

'Marshal Buxhowden is a courageous man but he has little to offer other than his valour,' Berthier said. 'His conduct at Austerlitz was irreproachable, as you may remember, sire. But his grasp of battlefield command, like Bennigsen's, is suspect.'

'Where are the forces under *his* command?' Duroc asked.

'Doctorov's division is on the road through Golymin to Makow,' the Chief of Staff declared. 'The troops of Essen and Anrepp are at Popowo on the Bug. Intelligence says that they are preparing to retire to Rozan and Ostrolenka.'

Napoleon nodded slowly.

'Men of courage but no imagination,' he murmured. 'A little like their own troops.'

'As regards the infantry, sire, I would agree,' Rapp said. 'They are poorly uniformed, badly armed and rarely paid. The vast majority are uneducated and subservient to even the most ridiculous orders given by their officers. But their bravery is unquestionable. The Russian cavalry, on the other hand, is easily the equal of our own. Well mounted and well organised. The Cossacks, although it pains me to say it, are possibly even superior to our own light cavalry.'

'Their artillery are also of a very high order, sire,' Duroc added. 'There are plenty of guns, three-, six- and twelve-pounders. The horse teams are well organised and the gunners more than proficient.'

'We will see,' Napoleon muttered. 'Do not overlook the capabilities of our own troops.'

'No one doubts the abilities of *La Grande Armée*, sire,' Duroc intoned. 'But they have been through much these past few months. Even the finest fighting men have limits beyond which they cannot be pushed.'

'One victory,' snapped the Corsican. 'That is all that is needed. All thoughts of hunger, discomfort and bad weather will be forgotten when our troops stand victorious on the battlefield. We have beaten the Russians before and we will do it again.' Napoleon turned away from the maps and gazed into the leaping flames of the fire. Outside, the biting wind was growing in ferocity. The timbers of the barn creaked ominously and Duroc looked up more than once as if fearing that the entire structure was going to come crashing down at any moment. Larrey pulled his cloak more tightly around him and glanced at his pocket watch.

'If I might be excused, sire,' he murmured. 'My concern is not with strategy and tactics. I have men to attend to and the hour grows late.'

'Indeed,' Napoleon said, nodding in the direction of the Chief Surgeon. 'On this Christmas day, let your gifts to them be your expertise and your brilliance.'

Larrey left the barn, the wind howling momentarily as the door was opened. The flames of the fire wavered slightly.

'Where would we all be now on this Holy day if the demands of war were not made upon us?' the Corsican mused, gazing into the flames. 'With our wives, lovers and families?' He glanced at each of the remaining men in turn. 'Embraced by the warmth of those we love, instead of being smothered by the grip of the foulest weather and conditions one can imagine?'

The subordinates remained silent, content merely to gaze into the fire as their superior had. Lost in their own thoughts, they seemed incapable of providing Napoleon with an answer.

'You may return to your quarters, gentlemen,' the Corsican

said finally. 'Today much of the world gave thanks for the birth of God's son. By this time tomorrow night, there may well be families in France and Russia who are mourning the *loss* of sons.' He raised his glass in salute and watched as his generals filed out of the barn. The wind howled around the building. Napoleon continued to stare into the flames of the fire.

ELEVEN

The snow was stained with blood for several yards around where Baumar, Tigana and Gaston worked. In the freezing night, condensation rose like an ethereal shroud from the hot life fluid that soaked into the earth and mud and coloured the sprinkling of white flakes. Lausard and some of the other dragoons watched as the animals were butchered. Hacked into manageable portions that were to be strapped to the saddle of a riderless horse. The animal's rider had perished in the freezing temperatures, his body left unburied in the winter mud along with so many of his comrades. With prudent use, the meat from the cow, the pig and the three chickens might last a week and, Lausard reasoned, in a land so devoid of sustenance for a scavenging army, those few meals that the dead livestock provided could mean the difference between life and death for himself and his companions. Rocheteau and Giresse were quickly and expertly cutting strips of the cowhide into lengths of about eighteen inches. With the fat still attached, they could be wound around the arms or legs of some dragoons as further protection against the incredible cold. No one seemed to mind the stench. All the men were in a similarly dishevelled and filthy condition. The odour of rancid fat was a minor addition to the plethora of smells already rising from the troops. Lausard himself was aware of his own stench, made more pungent by the crispness of the air. Every odour was more acute, it seemed. Not least the enticing aroma of the stew that Charvet was cooking in a large metal pot over a spluttering fire. Lausard wandered over to the bubbling pot and looked in. He had watched as pieces of pork, beef and chicken had been added to the concoction. His own mouth had begun to water when Charvet had added two pig's kidneys and some slices of cow's liver too. The remainder of the offal had been wrapped in pieces of gauze, packed with lumps of ice hacked from a frozen stream and bound in a discarded shabraque. The entire precious bundle had then been secured to the back of a riderless horse. Lausard guessed that the ice would last two or three days in the murderous temperatures.

All the men sat close to the fire, both for the warmth but also to be near to the glorious smell coming from the cooking food. None knew when they would eat such a hearty meal again and their hideous deprivations, if not forgotten, were at least pushed to the back of their minds by the promise of the culinary delight to come. Joubert, Tabor and Delbene sat with their metal plates at the ready, watching the cooking pot. Joubert rubbed his stomach as it growled protestingly. Another pot of water had been suspended above the fire and Varcon had sprinkled a handful of coffee grounds into it. He had had them in his pocket for more than three weeks but the other men were unconcerned. Stew and coffee was a repast to be savoured.

'We should give thanks to God for this meal we are about to eat,' said Moreau, crossing himself.

'Give thanks to those Jews we took the food from,' Rocheteau said, wrapping several lengths of hide around his hands.

Some of the other men laughed.

'Who would have thought that we'd end up eating a Christmas dinner in the middle of *this* miserable place?' chuckled Carbonne.

'Christmas,' Bonet mused. 'A time for gifts and rejoicing. What gift would you choose if you had the choice, Alain?'

Lausard shrugged.

'An end to this cursed weather,' he said flatly.

'Not to be with your family on this day?'

'I have no family,' Lausard told him sharply. 'What about you, schoolmaster, what would *you* choose?'

'I would appreciate the chance to read again,' said Bonet. 'I have seen nothing but army proclamations lately. I have not even had the pleasure of seeing a newspaper. It has been too long since I enjoyed the simple pleasures of a book. Perhaps, Varcon, one written by the Marquis de Sade.'

Bonet and Varcon laughed.

'I doubt it,' Varcon said. 'His writings were banned by the Emperor, I believe. We were told to remove anything from his cell with which he could produce his literature. He was allowed no quills, no paper. When they were taken he wrote on linen with red wine. After that he wrote in blood on the very walls themselves.'

'Who is this man of whom you speak?' Kruger wanted to know.

'He was a nobleman,' Bonet said. 'Imprisoned in an asylum because of the nature of his writings. They were thought blasphemous. He was damned by the Church and the authorities. Dismissed as a madman.'

'What kind of things did he write?' Tabor wanted to know.

'Vile, unpleasant things,' Bonet continued. 'Tales of debauchery such as had never been known before. Tales of sexual perversion and deviance.'

'If I had met him I would have been able to furnish him with some ideas,' Giresse smiled. 'And any of the women who had the pleasure of knowing me would have told tales of my prowess that would have astounded him.'

The other dragoons laughed.

'Did you ever read any of his work, Bonet?' Lausard wanted to know.

'I saw one in Paris once, but I never had the chance to read more than a few pages of it. Anyone found in possession of his works was usually arrested. The same applied to those who printed and distributed his material.'

'And quite rightly,' snapped Moreau. 'His writing sounds like an affront to God.' He crossed himself.

'I think his writing was an affront to *everyone* in some way,' Lausard grinned. 'And yet he was merely exercising one of the rights embodied in the philosophy of the revolution. That all men are not only equal but that they have the right to speak as they wish. In freedom. Bonaparte created a country and a regime then twisted it to suit his own ends.'

'And we helped him create that country,' Rocheteau offered. 'And his regime. We were there when he drove the lawyers from their offices, Alain. Are we not as much to blame?'

'We were following orders as soldiers are expected to do,' Lausard said. 'The outcome of those orders and their repercussions are beyond our control. Perhaps just as some men's thoughts are beyond *their* control. Wouldn't you agree, Varcon?'

'I always found the Marquis to be a reasonable man, although he was obviously insane,' Varcon added. 'No healthy mind would have the capability of imagining the horrors and depravities that *he* enjoyed and found so easy to visualise.'

'Then perhaps *we* are all insane, too,' Lausard offered. 'Who would be capable of imagining some of the things that *we* have seen and experienced these past ten years?'

There were murmurs of assent from around the fire.

'Gormier is insane,' chuckled Delacor. 'He *volunteered* to join the army.'

'I felt it was my duty,' Gormier answered. 'Where is the insanity in wanting to serve one's country and one's Emperor?'

'Just look around you,' Lausard said. 'Is this what you expected?'

'I don't know *what* I expected,' Gormier confessed.

'Expect more hardship followed by death,' Roussard grunted. 'That is all the army has to offer us.'

Rocheteau slapped him on the back and shook his head.

'With Charvet cooking our food, they also offer us meals that even the Emperor and his staff would be honoured to eat,' said the corporal, sticking his nose close to the pot and inhaling the rich, succulent aromas rising from within.

'I agree,' Tabor chuckled, clapping his hands.

'Stop this torture,' groaned Joubert. 'Feed us before we waste away.'

Charvet tasted the stew and nodded that it was ready. Plates were thrust towards him and he began to fill them one at a time. The men ate ravenously as each was served. Lausard waited until his companions had received their share before claiming his own.

'Make sure there is some of that left for Karim, Laubardemont and Sonnier,' the sergeant snapped. 'They will have earned it by the time they return from patrol.' He looked up and saw Lieutenant Royere ambling through the camp. Lausard beckoned the officer over. 'Join us, Lieutenant,' he said.

Royere sniffed the stew deeply and licked his lips.

'If there is enough I would be most grateful,' he said. 'Thank you, my friend.' He wrapped his cloak more tightly around himself and squatted down on the wet, icy ground. Charvet filled Royere's plate and smiled as he watched the officer savour his share.

'If you were as fine a soldier as you are a cook, Charvet,' said Royere, 'the Emperor need send only you against the Russians to ensure victory.'

The other dragoons laughed.

'I asked Sergeant Lausard what he would want as a gift on this Christmas day, Lieutenant,' Bonet continued. 'What about you? If you could have anything. What would it be?'

'That is a difficult question,' said the officer. 'A home. Perhaps a wife. An end to this war once and for all.'

'An end to *this* war or to all wars?' Lausard wanted to know.

'To *all* wars. Be they military, political, theological or philosophical.'

'In short, an end to conflict?' Lausard elucidated.

'If such a thing were possible. But I do not delude myself that such an eventuality will ever come to pass. Conflict seems to be the driving force behind mankind.' Royere smiled. 'Certainly behind our Emperor and his thinking.'

'I would wish for a different woman for every night of the year,' Giresse chuckled. 'And another for the daylight hours,' he added as an afterthought.

The men laughed.

'I would wish for an endless supply of food, cooked by the finest chefs in the world,' Joubert offered, shovelling some meat into his mouth.

'I would be happy with a small farm and enough land to work for the rest of my days,' Rostov said.

'And I would wish for the finest rifle in the world,' said

Baumar, grinning. 'Then, with it, I would come on to your land and poach all the game running free there.'

There was more laughter.

Not for the first time in his life as a soldier, Lausard thought how much more easily men with full bellies were amused than those who were starving. He watched as Joubert licked the last of the stew from his plate, anxious not to miss a single morsel.

'I would wish for the largest and best stocked stables in France,' Tigana offered. 'Where only the finest horses would be bred and cared for.' The big Gascon grinned broadly.

'What about you, Kruger?' Lausard wanted to know. 'What would you wish for?'

'He would wish he was fighting with his countrymen against us, instead of masquerading as someone who sympathises with our struggle against the Tsar and his forces,' said Delacor dismissively.

'I told you,' rasped Kruger. 'I have no allegiance to my country anymore. Not to Prussia or to the Muscovites. If I were to wish for *anything*, it would be revenge against those who murdered my family.'

Delacor hawked loudly and spat in the direction of the Bavarian.

'So you say,' he chided. 'Are we supposed to believe that? Do you think any of us cares about what became of your family? Or about what you think and believe? You fought against us in Prussia. That makes you an enemy and it always will.'

Kruger got to his feet and took a step towards Delacor who rose to meet him.

Lausard and Rocheteau stepped between them.

'Sit down,' Lausard said quietly. He locked stares with Delacor for a moment. 'Both of you.'

They hesitated a moment then did as he instructed.

'You take *his* side against one of your own countrymen?' snapped Delacor.

'As long as he wears that uniform, he is as much one of us as you are,' the sergeant said. Then he turned and looked at Royere. 'An end to conflict, Lieutenant? I think not.'

All heads turned as the sound of horses' hooves filtered

through the snow-flecked air. Lausard squinted through the sickly yellow light of a dozen camp fires and saw three horsemen guiding their sweating mounts through the clinging mud. The first of them was Karim. The Circassian was easily discernible despite being spattered from head to foot in mud and filth, something that made him look identical to every other man in the unit. His posture in the saddle, the ease with which he coaxed his mount across the treacherous landscape, together with the curved scabbard that housed his scimitar, made him instantly recognisable. Behind him rode Laubardemont and Sonnier. All three men looked exhausted, their faces made paler by the freezing temperatures. Tigana and Tabor rose to their feet and took the reins of their horses as they dismounted and hurried across to the fire where they began to warm themselves. All three were shaking. Charvet hastily ladled some stew on to their plates and passed them the gloriously hot mixture. The men devoured it quickly.

'Did you see any Russians?' Royere wanted to know.

'They have sentries posted on several roads approaching Pultusk itself,' Karim said, wiping his mouth with the back of his hand.

'Others in the woods around the town,' Laubardemont echoed. 'We saw *them* but they didn't see *us*.'

'What of the terrain?' Lausard interjected.

'The greater part of the town lies in the low ground,' Karim said. 'It is intersected by a branch of the river.'

'The river itself runs from north to south,' Sonnier offered. 'Parts of it are frozen. We saw ice floating in other places.'

'There is a road that runs alongside the river,' Karim continued. 'The ground rises steeply upwards from the bank.'

'Bonet, get your map,' Lausard urged.

The former schoolmaster hurried across to his horse and pulled the map from his portmanteau. He spread it out on the icy ground close to the fire. Rocheteau weighted the four corners with small stones that he picked up and the dragoons cast appraising eyes over the map.

'The road runs from Streshegozin to Golymin,' said Royere, running a finger of his gloved hand over the outline of the route. 'The area all around seems to be heavily wooded.'

'Difficult for cavalry and infantry to move in with any speed,' Lausard mused. 'Especially in these conditions.'

'We saw Russian artillery lining that road,' Laubardemont said. 'More than twenty guns. It was difficult to see exactly how many.'

'Beyond Pultusk itself,' Royere said, scanning the map. 'The village of Mosin and more woods.'

'There is a deep ravine beyond the Golymin road,' Karim said. 'It is invisible when approached from the front. The main Russian strength seems to be there, hidden by the ravine and by forests.'

'Plateaux, ravines and forests,' Lausard remarked. 'Not much open ground to speak of.'

'That may be just as well,' Rocheteau said. 'At least there may be some measure of cover for us if we are forced to advance.'

'I see no other way,' Royere commented. 'The Russians occupy the best ground. They are not going to forsake such advantageous defensive positions to make an attack. They will sit and wait.'

'Just as *we* must,' Lausard murmured. 'Until we are ordered forward.'

'To our deaths?' Roussard said acidly.

'Only God knows that,' Moreau said, crossing himself.

'I will put my trust in Allah, all praise to Him,' Karim added.

'This will be your first battle, won't it?' Lausard said, looking at Delbene.

The younger man nodded.

'Then hope it is not your last,' Roussard added.

'It might be the last for all of us,' the sergeant continued. 'Only time will tell.'

Bonet rolled up the map, then wandered back to his horse and stuffed it into his portmanteau. As he returned to the fire he felt the first flakes of snow on his unshaven face. Within minutes, the crystal flecks were pouring from the scudding clouds like white cinders. Many of the dragoons cursed, their fury intensifying as the snow rapidly turned to hail, hammering down like translucent grapeshot as it spun off the icy mud, dampening the camp fires around which the men sought solace and warmth. Clouds of thick smoke began to rise into the air as the fires died. Lausard could hear the whinnying of horses, frightened by the vicious downpour. The hail was so intense that it sang off his brass helmet with a high-pitched whine and more than one man felt its stinging impact on his face as he glanced skyward. Many of the dragoons moved closer to the relative protection of the trees around them, anxious to be out of the hailstorm. Lausard and his companions found positions on the icy ground and drew their cloaks more tightly around them as the hail continued to pound the earth.

Lausard awoke with a start and instantly began to shiver. He blinked hard and rubbed his eyes, surprised, not by his sudden wakefulness, but more by the fact that he had managed to fall asleep so easily and so quickly in the first place. Sleep was not something that came to Alain Lausard easily and, when it did come, it usually brought unwanted dreams and memories. Recollections of distant and better times. Of a different way of life. Of those he had loved, now lost forever except in the sanctuary of his own mind.

The NCO rubbed his face with one gloved hand and glanced around him. A number of his colleagues were still asleep. Joubert was snoring loudly, curled into a foetal position at the base of a tree, his soaking wet cloak wrapped around him like a dead leaf. Rocheteau was dozing too, his chin resting on his broad chest. Some of the others had found comfort in the oblivion of sleep but, for the most part, the other members of the squadron had found, as they had so many times during the present campaign, that sleep was impossible in such appalling conditions. Lausard had found that, if tired enough, men could sleep just about anywhere. In extremes of heat or cold or the most inhospitable of conditions. But the constant changes in the nature of the weather in Poland had disturbed the sleep patterns of even those most determined to retreat into oblivion when the chance came.

The sergeant clambered to his feet, stepping over the figure of Gaston. The trumpeter stirred slightly and Erebus, lying next to him, growled deep in his throat. The dog too was having difficulty sleeping. The hail that had been falling earlier had been replaced by rain. The incessant, sheet-like rain that the men had come to know only too well. For as long as he could remember now, Lausard and his men had been at the mercy of weather that changed with dizzying speed from one extreme to the other. Rain became hail, only to be replaced by snow that fell thickly then thawed as quickly as it had carpeted the ground. And, with the night came achingly cold frosts, hardening the ground to an iron consistency, only to melt hours later and leave the earth like a morass. It was as unpredictable as it was uncomfortable. Lausard exhaled deeply as he made his way across to where his horse was tethered, his boots sinking to the calves in the sludge. He checked on the animal, feeding it a couple of handfuls of grain from his palm then he trudged off in the direction of the dragoon sentries. The men were stationed about a hundred yards from the main camp, completely invisible within the stifling confines of the woods and further shielded by a downpour that made visibility everywhere bad. Lausard approached with a stealth born of experience and, despite the foul sucking noises his boots made in the clinging mud, the two dragoons standing miserably in the downpour, carbines clutched tightly to their chests, seemed not to hear him.

'How goes it?' he said.

Collard spun round, raising the Charleville to his shoulder. He squinted down the sight at the sergeant for a moment then lowered the weapon again.

Tigana nodded in the sergeant's direction then wiped rain from his face.

'Anything moving?' Lausard wanted to know.

'Plenty,' Tigana told him. 'We can hear the Russians but we can't see them. For the last hour we've heard men and horses moving into position.'

'Advancing?'

Tigana shook his head.

'Probably building fortifications,' the big Gascon said.

'I believe it is something of a pastime where the Russian soldier is concerned,' Lausard smiled.

Tigana also chuckled.

Collard merely looked at the two men blankly.

'Word has it that Marshal Lannes and his two divisions are approaching,' Lausard said.

'So there *will* be a battle tomorrow?' Tigana mused.

Lausard nodded and looked up at the pitch-black sky.

'In rain, hail or snow,' he murmured. 'Whatever the conditions it won't be easy.'

'Nothing is easy in this damned country,' Collard snapped.

'It may not have the climate of Spain, I grant you that,' said Lausard. 'Perhaps you should have stolen more than you did from your former employer. If you had, you could still be enjoying the sun now.'

Tigana chuckled.

Collard regarded Lausard silently for a moment, his eyes narrowed slightly.

'What I took I had a right to take,' he said finally. 'That aristocratic bastard I worked for all those years had done nothing to deserve his money. I merely liberated it on behalf of the revolution.'

'You liberated it for yourself,' said Tigana. 'You gave none back to the cause for which the whole country was fighting. You contributed none in the name of freedom.'

'I attained freedom for myself,' Collard smirked. 'Is that not enough?'

'Was your employer a poor master?' Lausard wanted to know. 'Did he or his family treat you badly?'

'What difference does that make?' snapped Collard. 'He was an aristocrat. An enemy of the state. All of those bastards who went to the guillotine deserved their fate. None of them cared for those in their service. All that interested them was their own wealth and wellbeing. They lived like kings while those who worked on their estates starved. What the hell would *you* know about the aristocracy anyway?'

Lausard shrugged almost imperceptibly, wondering what Collard's reaction would be if he suspected that the sergeant himself had been born and raised among France's privileged classes. He had often wondered how the men whom he had called comrades and even friends these past twelve years would have regarded him if they knew the true nature of his origins. Would they have despised him and all he had stood for? Shunned him as an outcast? Regarded him as a relic of a time and way of life that had been swept aside by a wave of revolutionary hysteria and snuffed out by the blade of the guillotine? Or was that feeling one that also belonged to the days of the Terror? With Bonaparte himself creating a new aristocracy among his family and his marshals, perhaps the ideals that had brought death to Lausard's family and condemned *him* to a life as a common criminal were now as irrelevant and forgotten as dust in the wind. Would he be accepted now, should he choose to reveal his past? Perhaps he would now be judged on his achievements as a soldier and not on his upbringing. It was a dilemma he felt he would wrestle with for as long as he continued to live. Exactly how long *that* would be no one, including himself, had any idea.

'Sergeant,' Tigana said quietly, his voice practically inaudible in the pouring rain. 'When are we to attack?'

Lausard could only shake his head.

'Marshal Lannes will wait until first light, I would think,' said the NCO. 'His infantry will find it difficult to reach these positions much before dawn anyway. They have trouble marching more than a mile in every hour.' He pulled his watch from his pocket and glanced at it. 'There are still more than four hours before the new day breaks. Then we will see.'

He looked up at the black sky. The rain washed his already wet face as it continued to pour from the swollen clouds.

Twelve

The cannonball arced across the grey sky, spat from the muzzle of one of the Russian six-pounders arrayed in front of the woods that masked the approaches to Pultusk. Lausard, sitting astride his horse, followed its trajectory, watching as the solid lead projectile curved across the heavens then dipped sharply. It fell among the lines of blue-clad French infantry struggling across the sea of mud into which the land had been transformed. The ball fell to earth a few feet ahead of the eagle bearer of the 64th Line infantry. It hit the morass, ripped into the earth and sent a geyser of reeking mud and dirty water spewing five or six feet into the air. Some of the clay-like muck spattered the already filthy infantrymen but they marched on, trying as best they could to drag themselves through the mud with any semblance of order. Officers and NCOs shouted commands, demanding that they keep their shape despite the slippery and almost impassable nature of the terrain. Lausard saw the flag beneath the eagle fluttering in the breeze as the men continued to advance. Close by where he sat, the guidon of his own regiment waved and danced in the breeze. The red, white and blue oiled silk material cut into its familiar swallowtail pattern. Above it, on the staff, stood the fourteen-inch-high bronze eagle. It seemed to sparkle despite the fact that the day was dull and dreary and no sun had managed to penetrate the thick banks of cloud hanging over Pultusk and its surrounding forests. There was a hint of snow in the air and Lausard pulled his scarf more tightly around his mouth and chin as he felt the wind growing in intensity too.

His horse whinnied and pawed the ground, sending up gouts of liquid mud. The sergeant patted its neck to calm it and watched as several more Russian cannonballs went hurtling across the open stretch of ground where the French infantry were advancing.

Several hundred bodies were already scattered over the mud and, in many places, the dark brown of the pulverised earth had been stained crimson. Lausard could see bandsmen scuttling back and forth over the slippery ground, hauling the wounded clear of the advancing infantry. Some were lifted into small tumbril-like carts drawn by a pair of horses, but the others were simply carried bodily by the bandsmen. Some casualties took four men to move them, others two. Some unfortunates could be borne away by a single man.

Medical staff, their medium blue tunics with distinctive black or red velvet facings, hidden beneath long cloaks, also moved among the wounded, heedless, it seemed, of the cannonballs that could just as easily claim *their* lives as those of the men they were supposed to tend. Lausard saw two of these medics kneeling close to a private whose leg had been severed by roundshot just above the knee. One of the medics looked down at the shattered remains of the limb and shook his head, before hurrying off to cast his expert eye over other wounded; the first man simply lifted the injured private, as one would lift a child, and carried him towards one of the several carts labouring back and forth through the sucking mud. That task completed, the man turned and began picking his way over other fallen troops. He was examining a writhing drummer boy when a cannonball caught him in the back and tore a hole in him large enough to place two hands. Pieces of shattered bone, internal organs and other viscera sprayed on to the mud and the wounded drummer boy. The medic slumped forward into the ooze, his body twitching slightly as the muscles gave up their hold on life.

From their position on the left of the French line, the dragoons, who had sat immobile for most of the day, could hear gunfire coming from the forests that masked Pultusk. More than once, they had been ordered to dismount and stand beside their horses. The animals were, without exception, thin and weak and any respite from the burden of carrying their riders was welcomed. Now, as Lausard watched Lieutenant Royere riding slowly back and forth before the lines of green-clad horsemen, he wondered whether the order was to be given again or whether he and his companions were finally to be allowed to advance. Royere pulled his telescope from inside his cloak and pressed it to his eye, sweeping it back and forth across the battlefield. Lausard held out his hand and Rocheteau passed him his own glass. The sergeant, like his commanding officer, surveyed the scene before him. Smoke was rising in thick plumes over the trees in the direction of Pultusk. Some of it, he knew, came from thousands of muskets. The rest, he assumed, from the burning buildings of the town itself. Russian artillerymen, sweating despite the cold, could be seen loading and reloading their pieces, keeping up a constant fire against the advancing French infantry. A curtain of noxious black smoke hung in front of the guns and, with each discharge, it grew more dense. Lausard could also see the brightly coloured uniforms of some French hussars beyond a ridge off to the north. They were struggling through the mud on their exhausted mounts, moving at little more than a walk, sabres drawn but held to their shoulders. A moment later, they disappeared behind more thick woods. Lausard handed the telescope back to Rocheteau and exhaled deeply.

'Why is it that in battles the fighting always seems to be happening elsewhere?' Rocheteau remarked.

'Be thankful for that, my friend,' Lausard grinned. 'Are you so eager to be within range of the Russians?'

'Anything would be better than sitting here like tailors' dummies,' the corporal told him.

'I agree,' Delacor added. 'How long has it been now?'

Lausard consulted his pocket watch.

'More than three hours,' he remarked. 'The first of the infantry went forward at about eleven this morning.'

'And we've heard nothing since. The battle could have been lost for all we know,' Delacor said irritably. 'If they leave the fighting up to the dog-faces then what hope is there of victory?'

'It's difficult terrain for cavalry,' Bonet mused. 'Karim said that the approaches to Pultusk itself were masked by woods. We couldn't manoeuvre effectively in such—'

'Don't tell me what we could or couldn't do, schoolmaster,' snapped Delacor, cutting his companion short.

'We could fight on foot,' Rocheteau offered.

'We will do nothing until we are so ordered,' Lausard said, scratching one unshaven cheek with his index finger.

Erebus padded back and forth in the mud, occasionally barking in the direction of the Russian positions.

'Turn *that* black devil loose on them,' Delacor said, nodding in the direction of the huge canine. 'He would do more damage than the infantry.'

Some of the other men laughed.

Lausard glanced in the direction of Lieutenant Royere and saw the officer still peering through his telescope, as impatient as those under his command to receive some information about the progress of the battle and, more pointedly, to discover if he and the dragoons lined up behind him were to take a part in it. Lausard wondered if the swiftly moving grey horse thundering across the slippery mud bearing a blue uniformed aide-de-camp might well provide the answers they all sought. The ADC was holding something in his hand that fluttered in the wind and, as he drew nearer, he shouted something loudly. Royere turned in his direction.

'*Vive l'Empereur*,' bellowed the ADC and reined in his mount, patting the lathered animal's neck. He handed the orders to Royere who scanned them and nodded.

'Orders at last?' Rocheteau mused, chewing on a piece of tobacco.

Lausard said nothing but merely kept his gaze fixed on the aide who saluted Royere then turned his horse and galloped off in the direction of Pultusk. A moment later, the lieutenant guided his own horse across the front of the leading line of dragoons. He paused, stood in the stirrups and waved his hand back and forth above his head, as if to attract the attention of the men before him. Behind him, the Russian cannon continued to fire. French infantry continued to advance, those at least who were not blasted to atoms by the roundshot ploughing through their ranks.

'The regiment will advance, trumpeter,' Royere shouted. 'Walk, march.'

Gaston pressed the brass instrument to his lips and blasted out the opening notes of the advance. As one, the dragoons put spurs to their mounts or snapped their reins, whichever it took to urge their horses forward in the mud. Beneath their hooves, the ground quickly became reeking brown liquid, A number of the animals slipped in the morass but their riders expertly kept them on their feet. Lausard himself patted the neck of his mount as it sank to its fetlocks in a puddle of rancid water. The animal whinnied protestingly then forged on. Despite the difficulty of the terrain, the dragoons managed to keep their lines relatively straight. Lausard, in particular, glanced to his right and left to check but years of drill and experience in battle had transformed those around him into some of the finest cavalrymen in Europe. Almost without thinking, the dragoons advanced in lines as straight as if they had been on a parade ground. They moved inexorably forward at the regulation one hundred and twenty paces a minute.

Lausard could feel the wind growing stronger and now, as they neared the outer reaches of the woods, he could smell the stench of gunpowder as the smoke rolled towards them from the Russian artillery positioned among the trees. Beyond them, towards Pultusk itself, the sound of musket fire intensified and, judging from the amount of smoke rising into the air now, Lausard assumed that some of the buildings of the town were ablaze. He felt his heart begin to thud more rapidly against his ribs. The adrenalin that coursed through his veins before every conflict heightened his senses. He could see colours more vividly. He could pick out sounds with greater clarity and even smells seemed more easily recognisable. The stink of wet leather, of soaking clothes, of horse droppings and stagnant water all fused together to create a smell he had come to know so well during his years as a soldier. All around him, he knew, his comrades were experiencing the same thing. He saw Moreau cross himself. Karim was sitting high in the saddle, his eyes scanning the woods. Every now and then, the Circassian would unconsciously touch the hilt of his scimitar. Delacor reached back towards his portmanteau and ran an index finger along the handle of the axe hidden there. Rocheteau leaned down and touched the hilt of the knife that jutted from his boot cuff. Lausard could see the faces of Varcon and Delbene from where he rode. Both were set in hard lines. Delbene, in particular, looked pale, his eyes narrowed against the ever increasing wind. Kruger swallowed hard and urged his horse on through a particularly deep puddle, whispering something in its upraised ear.

Lausard guessed that there was a little over five hundred yards between the dragoons and the Russian artillery on the outskirts of the wood. However, the sergeant was surprised that the enemy gunners had yet to swing some of their pieces in the direction of the advancing French cavalry. They seemed content to pour roundshot into the lines of blue-clad infantry, still heaving themselves through the mud to the front of the thickly planted trees.

'To the right,' shouted Royere and Lausard, mildly puzzled by the order, guided his horse in the direction he was instructed. The officer murmured something to Gaston and the trumpeter blasted out the familiar notes instructing the dragoons to form column. They did so seamlessly and, following Royere and their own fluttering guidon, they turned in the direction of the rutted mud slick that had once passed for a road. It ran parallel with the woods towards which the French infantry were still advancing and Lausard was fairly sure that the dragoons would be invisible to the Russian batteries once they had moved fifty or sixty yards down the road. The slippery route was barely wide enough to take four horses moving abreast and the column contracted even more to allow every mount access and also to avoid contact with the trees that grew so densely on either side of the thoroughfare. Despite being surrounded by woods, the sounds of battle coming from the direction of Pultusk were still loud in the ears of the cavalrymen. Lausard glanced to his right and left, watching for any movement in the trees. Like his companions, he had no idea as to the exact positions of the Russian troops although the fact that French infantry were advancing towards woods protected by cannon would seem to indicate that their main strength was off to the north, around the town itself.

Within the confines of the thickly growing pine trees, the sound of hundreds of horse harnesses mingled with the whinnying of already tired animals, the sucking sounds made by the oozing mud and the occasional curses of dragoons as they struggled to guide their mounts on over the treacherous terrain. As the column moved further along the road, more of the men began to look anxiously around them. Erebus moved with relative ease along the edge of the road, darting in and out of the trees, stopping occasionally to sniff the air. Lausard glanced frequently at the big dog, watching its reactions.

'What the hell is going on?' Rocheteau murmured. 'Some kind of outflanking manoeuvre?'

'If the Russians know we're coming and they catch us in a crossfire it'll just be a matter of counting our dead,' added Bonet.

Lausard nodded almost imperceptibly and glanced ahead in the direction of Royere. The officer was also looking to either side, as uneasy as his men about the terrain. Less than fifty yards ahead, the ground sloped upwards. A gentle incline at first that gradually steepened. The crest was also heavily wooded and it was impossible to see what lay beyond the summit. Lausard felt the wind whipping more keenly about him and he pulled the dirty scarf he wore more tightly around his lower face. His horse neighed protestingly as the column continued to advance. The sergeant noticed that the trees to the right of the road were thinning slightly. He wondered if there would be more open ground beyond the rise.

He was still wondering when Erebus dashed ahead of the column and began barking frenziedly.

Sonnier slid his carbine from the boot on his saddle and thumbed back the hammer. Lausard felt his own heart thumping harder against his ribs.

Another sound suddenly filled the men's ears. The rumble of hooves mingled with an assortment of oaths and shouted curses. Erebus turned and ran back towards the column, slipping in the mud.

The first wave of Cossacks swept over the incline, swords, lances and muskets brandished above their heads. For fleeting seconds, it looked to Lausard as though a race of centaurs had crested the ridge. Wild-eyed riders borne by swift and hardy little ponies that seemed to have no problem negotiating the sticky mud. They swept over the ridge in what seemed to be one ill-disciplined horde, their horses straining their heads as if eager to reach the dragoons. Mud flew up into the air beneath their churning hooves and the whole mass, crammed into the narrow stretch of road, bore down on the dragoons like an incoming wave upon a shore.

'Front two ranks fire from the saddle,' shouted Lieutenant Royere, himself pulling both pistols from their holsters beneath his shabraque.

Twenty or thirty dragoons, working with almost mechanical precision, dragged their carbines free and swung them to their shoulders. Lausard pulled the weapon in tight to absorb the recoil he knew would come when he fired. Already, the Cossacks were less than twenty yards from the dragoons, still screaming their oaths. Two or three fired their long rifles at the steady lines of dragoons but none of the bullets found a target.

'Fire,' roared Royere and the carbines were discharged as one. A great cloud of sulphurous smoke filled the air, momentarily blinding the men and the sound of weapons deafened them. Lausard heard screams from both horses and men and, through a gap in the smoke, he saw dozens of the Cossacks hit the ground. Several horses collided and brought down others. But those behind rode on, over the bodies of their fallen comrades. The sergeant barely had time to pull his sword free of its scabbard before the Cossacks crashed into the waiting dragoons. Despite the fact that the Cossacks had the element of surprise in their favour, they were still smaller men on smaller horses and the sheer power of the French dragoons was telling as the two sets of cavalry first crashed together. Lausard struck madly to his left and right, cut one Cossack across the face and another through the shoulder. The blow almost severed the man's arm and he pitched sideways from his saddle, landing heavily in the mud. To his left one of the Cossacks lowered his twelve-foot-long lance and drove it into the stomach of a dragoon. The wickedly pointed pole penetrated with ease, tore its way through the dragoon and erupted from his back. As he fell from the saddle, the lance was pulled from the Cossack's hand but he instantly drew a sabre and began slashing at the Frenchmen near him. Karim met his first downward stroke, parried it then struck backhanded at the man, cutting his throat from ear to ear with an effortless flick of his scimitar. Sonnier used the butt of his carbine to deflect the thrust of another lance then swung the Charleville like a club, smashing it into the temple of his foe. Erebus dashed across and seized the fallen Cossack by the throat, tearing madly at him. He shook him like a rabbit as he tried feebly to fight back. Gaston pulled a pistol from his holster and shot another Cossack point-blank in the face.

Dozens of the Russian cavalry sped into the trees, only to emerge further down the column where they drove into the dragoons again. Lausard turned his horse and saw several dragoons speared or shot. He saw more of the French cavalry dismount, some using their saddles as rests as they fired their carbines at their attackers. Baumar shot one of the Cossacks down, reloaded with lightning speed and blasted another from the saddle. Beside him, Sonnier worked with similar speed and accuracy. Tabor fired one round then used his bayonet against another Cossack. The big man avoided a sword blow then skewered his opponent in the chest with the fifteen-inch bayonet, tugging hard to rip it free of the ribs between which it had become jammed. Varcon struck out with his sword and caught a large Cossack across the face, shaving off part of his left eyebrow. The man shrieked but hit back with his own sword. He cut Varcon's right forearm just below the elbow, but the Frenchman quickly transferred his sword to the other hand and caught the Russian a powerful backhand blow that almost hacked his head from his body. The Cossack toppled over backwards into the mud. Lausard saw more dragoons speared as he and Rocheteau, still fighting from the saddle, urged their mounts towards the relative safety of the woods. Delbene ducked beneath the thrust of a lance but his sword stroke missed its target and the Cossack following ran his lance into Delbene's horse. The animal shrieked in pain and fell sideways, spilling Delbene into the mud. He spun round, looking for cover among the seething mass of men and horses, aware that more Cossacks were bearing down on him. He saw Kruger spur towards him, sword in one hand and pistol in the other. The Bavarian shot down one man and drove his sword point into the chest of the next. Delbene snatched at the flailing reins of one of the Cossacks' horses and swung himself into the saddle. It reared wildly but he managed to keep control of it and glanced across at Kruger who merely nodded before turning his attention to more of the oncoming Cossacks.

The road, and the area on either side of it, was becoming clogged with the bodies of both men and horses. Riderless mounts were also charging madly back and forth. Lausard could see that most of the muddy ruts in the road were now filled with crimson. The morass itself was taking on a deep red hue. The coppery stench of blood was now as noticeable as the smell of horse droppings and gunpowder. Burning cartridge papers fell with a small hiss on to the sodden ground and were extinguished immediately by the rain-drenched mud. The condensation from freshly spilled blood rose in small clouds from dead and wounded men and horses. Lausard saw a horse hit the ground, the front two feet of a lance embedded in its neck. A dragoon sheltering behind its carcass was struck down by the same Cossack who had speared the horse. Lausard shook his head in disbelief as he saw that the Cossack was carrying a bow and arrow. He watched the Russian position the pointed shaft against the draw string, pull it back and let fly. The arrow caught the dragoon in the chest and he toppled backwards, clutching the wooden shaft. Only now did the sergeant notice that many other Cossacks were also equipped with the same primitive but very effective weapons. Another dragoon was hit in the face, the shaft puncturing his cheek. Arrows flew through the air with incredible speed, hitting both men and horses. Lausard reloaded his carbine and shot one of the bowmen from the saddle. More arrows thudded into the trees where he and Rocheteau sheltered. One of them nicked the sergeant's arm and he hissed in pain as the point cut through his tunic, scraping the flesh of his left bicep. Another shaft thudded into the cuff of Rocheteau's boot with such an impact that the corporal felt his leg give out beneath him and he dropped to the ground. Lausard looked down anxiously but Rocheteau tugged the shaft free and held it up to show that it had caused no damage.

'What manner of men are these?' snarled the corporal as

Rostov joined them, his sword stained with blood. The Russian was breathing heavily and there was blood on his left thigh.

'They are Kalmucks,' he said. 'Magnificent riders. They come from the Crimea.'

'But they're using bows and arrows,' snapped Rocheteau, brandishing the shaft he had pulled from his boot accusingly at his companion. 'They fight with weapons from antiquity.'

'In their homeland they use them to hunt,' Rostov explained.

Even as he spoke, two more of the steel-tipped shafts thudded into the ground close by the dragoons. Another hit the pommel of Rostov's saddle. His horse reared wildly as the impact shuddered through it but the animal was unhurt. Rostov grabbed its reins to steady it.

There was another burst of carbine fire from several dragoons who had taken refuge in the woods on the far side of the road. The volley brought down a dozen more Cossacks and also, due to the melee that was still raging within the confines of the trees, one or two Frenchmen. Lausard saw them hit the ground. One began crawling towards the woods, the other lay still on his back, sightless eyes gazing at the sky. Lausard heard several loud shouts in Russian and saw the Cossacks wheeling their horses. They rode away with the same speed and fury with which they had attacked. In less than a minute, the Russian horsemen had disappeared over the ridge or deep into the woods, apparently finding no difficulty guiding their lean ponies among the trees. Several shots were fired after them but most of the .50 calibre lead balls either thudded into tree trunks or screamed harmlessly away in the cold air. Lausard led his horse back out on to the road, glancing at the carnage around him. At the dead and wounded of both sides spread out on the freezing mud. There were dropped and discarded weapons scattered across the ground and hundreds of arrow shafts either embedded in it or lying on the surface. He stopped and knelt, picking one up and hefting it before him.

'Savages,' murmured Rocheteau, wandering on to the road beside him. He snapped one of the arrow shafts in two and tossed it contemptuously aside before kneeling by the body of a dead Cossack and rifling through his brown overcoat. The corporal smiled when he found half a bottle of vodka in one of the man's deep pockets. He slipped it into his own jacket, gazed down at the thick fur that had been used to trim the Cossack's garment then began tugging that free too, ignoring the blood that had stained it. The result of two sword wounds to the stomach and chest. All along the road, other dragoons were also hastily stripping any pieces of warm clothing from the dead Russians, some slipping it on immediately while others stuffed their acquisitions hastily into their portmanteaux or secured them to their saddles.

Dozens of horses from both sides had been killed or wounded in the brief exchange and Lausard noted that a number of the dragoons were in the process of removing their saddles from their own dead mounts and replacing them on captured Russian horses. Some of the ponies did not take too well to the intrusion and reared violently but most were subdued by a hard cuff across the muzzle. Some of the dragoons did not even bother removing the rudimentary saddles used by the Cossacks; they merely strapped their own portmanteaux across the rumps of the animals and swung themselves into the saddles, shortening or lengthening the stirrup leathers as necessary. Nearby, one of the regimental farriers was moving among the wounded horses, checking those most seriously injured. Any beyond help were dispatched immediately by a pistol shot to the head. Lausard saw one animal, its front legs broken just above the fetlocks, lifting its head almost imploringly as the farrier approached. It neighed pitifully as the farrier gripped its muzzle and pressed the barrel of the pistol to its head. The loud bang reverberated through the thick woods, soon to be joined by many more. And, all the time, the sounds of battle rose into the rapidly darkening sky as the struggle around Pultusk itself continued. Lausard swung himself into the saddle and glanced at the heavens. Another hour and darkness would have descended completely.

THIRTEEN

Napoleon Bonaparte glanced around him at the small wooden building that served as his temporary headquarters. It was a spartan dwelling, possessing only the most rudimentary necessities. A wooden table and chairs stood in one corner, the remaining furniture having been broken up and used as kindling for the fire that now burned in the small hearth. There was a large wooden crucifix above the fire and the Corsican allowed his gaze to linger upon it. For fleeting seconds he wondered if it should be added to the blaze to create more heat.

'I wonder if the priest who once lived in this house would resent our presence?' he murmured. 'Would he, do you think, find it ironic that we stand here now discussing how many of his flock are, this very night, in the presence of his God?' Napoleon sipped his glass of Chambertin then pulled his thick grey woollen greatcoat more tightly around him. Despite the fire, the bone-chilling cold of the night seemed to penetrate even those most protected from it.

'Those who died today, sire, were not a part of *this* priest's flock,' Berthier said flatly. 'They were from a hundred different towns and villages all across France. Those who would have sought spiritual guidance from the man who fled this place had long ago left Pultusk before we ever reached it. Only those in our homeland will feel regret for the dead out there.' He gestured towards the door of the building, a movement designed to encompass the lands beyond. The freezing mud where French troops had fought and died hours earlier.

'There will be many Muscovite families who will also grieve in the coming days when they hear the news of the battles that took place today,' General Rapp added.

'Enough,' Napoleon said, with an air of finality. 'Other matters are more pressing upon us now than the destination of those souls lost today.' He began sifting through a pile of papers spread across the table in front of him. 'Casualty lists. Reports. Requisitions. Complaints. Some sense must be made of this as it must be of what happened here today.'

'Marshal Lannes reports casualties close to seven thousand, sire,' Rapp said, warming himself beside the fire. 'Dead, wounded and captured.'

'Where is Lannes now?' the Corsican asked without looking up.

'He and his men are camped a mile or so beyond Pultusk, sire,' Berthier said. 'They were in no state to pursue the Russians.'

'Lannes underestimated the size of the force opposing him,' Napoleon muttered.

'He was misled as to the strength of Bennigsen's army, sire,' Rapp continued. 'Our intelligence was negligent in that respect.'

'He fought forty thousand Russians with half that number of his own troops and still succeeded in forcing them to withdraw,' the Corsican snapped. 'How many casualties did he inflict? Five thousand? Let them slap *that* news on the walls of Moscow.'

Rapp shifted uncomfortably then glanced at Berthier who met his gaze evenly.

'What of the other battle at Golymin?' the Emperor continued.

'Initial reports indicate losses of around one thousand to the corps of Marshal Davout and Marshal Augereau, sire,' said the Chief of Staff. 'The Russians are retreating from Golymin too. It would appear that a general withdrawal has been ordered.'

'They must stand and give battle eventually,' said Napoleon. 'These conflicts today were skirmishes compared to what must come.' He jabbed a finger at the map. 'Kamenskoi will turn and fight here, at Makov.'

'How can you be sure, sire?' Rapp wanted to know.

'His rear headquarters are already established at Rozan on the banks of the Narew. If he stands at Makov he can choose his position. He can fight with the river Orzyc to his front. Gaining bridgeheads before fortified positions will be difficult for us, the Russians know that. Makov is a strong position. Kamenskoi will not have been slow in noting that fact.'

'Marshal Murat's cavalry have, as you ordered, sire, already been instructed to harass Buxhowden's men as they make their way to the bridges at Makov,' Berthier interjected.

'What of the other corps?' Napoleon said.

'Compliant with your orders, sire, the cavalry of Marshal Bernadotte and Marshal Bessiéres will head for Ostrolenka to cut off any possible line of Russian retreat. Marshal Ney will ensure that Lestocq and his Prussians do not link up with the enemy in the centre around Neidenburg and, once Marshal Lannes' men are suitably rested, they will pursue Bennigsen along the right bank of the Narew.'

'The only problem continues to be the weather, sire,' Rapp added. 'As you are aware, the state of the roads makes rapid pursuit almost an impossibility. It is inconceivable that our own forces will catch up with the enemy unless Kamenskoi decides to stand and fight.'

For long moments Napoleon said nothing then he finally looked up from the maps and pieces of paper before him and gazed first at Rapp then Berthier.

'I have never met an enemy I was afraid of,' he breathed. 'Never encountered one I could not defeat. But there is one adversary which defies me. One over which I have no control. As you say, Rapp, the weather is our most formidable foe in this campaign. I fear I must consider the possibility of ending a pursuit that has barely begun. My instincts tell me that unless the Russians can be brought to decisive battle within the next three days, it would seem prudent to enter winter quarters until the worst of this cursed weather has passed.' He reached for several of the communications on the table. 'Desertions are rife. Some units have lost 40 per cent of their men. They maraud through the countryside looking for food, unconcerned with anything but the fullness of their bellies. My own marshals are stealing supplies from one another.' He sucked in a deep breath. 'This army, usually so disciplined, is being corroded like steel in rain.'

'The men have put up with much since the campaign began, sire,' Rapp offered. 'The lack of supplies, this damnable weather and the conditions under which they have been forced to march and fight . . .'

'I am aware of the hardships they have faced,' Napoleon snapped, cutting him short. 'Have we not all suffered? Is there a man in this army, be his rank private or marshal, who has not endured the most intolerable deprivations these past weeks?'

'Then perhaps your suggestion to enter winter quarters would be advisable, sire,' Berthier added. 'Every man has a breaking point. Perhaps the soldiers of *La Grande Armée* have reached theirs.'

Napoleon nodded.

'The army currently occupies a line extending from Neidenburg, down the valley of the Orezyc to here at Pultusk,' he muttered. 'There are bridgeheads at Okunin and others under way here and at Sierock on the Bug. We have the advantage strategically and territorially. The military aspect of the campaign is to our advantage. Now time must be taken to organise hospitals, magazines and transport,' he said. 'The commissariat at Warsaw, in particular, is in dire need of attention.'

'Then *take* that time, sire,' Rapp interjected. 'If *you* feel it is right. You said yourself that the pursuit of the Russians cannot be conducted with the speed and efficiency you would normally expect and require.'

The Corsican did not answer. He merely picked up another of the pieces of paper scattered across the desk and ran his gaze slowly across the words.

'My next set of orders will be issued from Warsaw,' he said finally.

Alain Lausard dug the toe of his boot into the reeking straw that blanketed the floor of the barn. Several dozen fleas stuck to the mud on the battered leather. Nearby, something larger moved quickly through the straw. Lausard saw the rat scurry into a hole at the base of one wooden beam. He wondered how many others were inside the building. Erebus ran around barking frenziedly at several pieces of gnawed timber until even the large black dog himself tired of the game and wandered across to Gaston. The trumpeter reached down with one heavily bandaged hand and stroked the dog. Lausard looked up and saw that there was a loft. Approachable by a rickety-looking ladder, it would accommodate ten or fifteen men, sleeping closely together. The ground floor of the building would take another ten once some horses had been sheltered.

'So, this is to be our home until the Emperor decides otherwise?' said Rocheteau, gazing around. He scratched irritably at the back of his neck, finally pulling a flea away and cracking it between his thumb and forefinger.

'At least we have shelter,' Lausard murmured. 'And this straw will help to make a fire. It's fit for nothing else.' He wiped his nose on the back of one hand and shivered involuntarily. 'What are the other buildings like?'

'The same,' Rocheteau informed him. 'Rat- and flea-infested hovels. What we have come to expect of this country, Alain.' The corporal smiled.

Lausard merely nodded.

'How long are we to remain here?' Rocheteau wanted to know.

'As you said, my friend, until Bonaparte decides otherwise. A week? A month? I have no window to look into *his* mind.'

'What is the name of this place anyway?' Gaston asked.

'I believe Bonet called it Dabronsko,' Lausard answered. 'If you ask him, I'm sure he will point it out to you on his map.'

Erebus began barking once again and the three dragoons looked around to see a particularly large rat making its way across the floor of the barn. It stopped for a moment, quite unconcerned by the presence of either the men or the dog, scratched at its snout then continued towards another hole in the barn wall.

'Even rats can taste good when a man is hungry enough,' Rocheteau muttered.

'He is probably thinking the same about us,' added Lausard. 'No creature around here has an abundance of food. We all have to eat what we can. Even the rats.' He turned and walked out into the steadily falling snow. The earth was already covered by a thin layer of the white, powdery crystals but how long it would continue to fall the men could only guess. Judging by the conditions they had been forced to endure so far during the campaign, the snow could just as easily turn to rain or hail within the hour. Roads that were somewhat firmer due to a heavy frost would be quagmires again by evening. With the darkness would come rapidly dropping temperatures. The following morning could just as easily present them with an unwanted thaw. For the past two days that had been the pattern. Iron-hard frost followed by rapid thaw. Clinging mud, frozen slush and snow all combined to ensure the men were rarely dry, never comfortable and constantly exhausted. Their horses, if anything, were faring even more unfavourably. In the last two days, Lausard knew that more than fifty animals had died or been destroyed. Hunger and the intolerable conditions were proving to be enemies as lethal as those of Mother Russia.

The NCO looked in the direction of the thick woods that surrounded Dabronsko. They bent and swayed in the strong wind. It was from these woods that Kruger and Baumar emerged, guiding their horses over the slippery ground. They both reined in close to the other dragoons.

'There are wolves in the woods,' said Baumar flatly. 'I found droppings. Hunger must have forced them close to the village.'

'They won't have found much to satisfy them here,' Rocheteau offered.

Lausard turned and looked at Gaston and Kruger.

'Ride back and tell Lieutenant Royere to bring the rest of the squadron forward,' he said. Even as he spoke, Erebus began barking madly in the direction of the woods. Lausard shot out a hand and grabbed the huge black dog by the collar.

'Shut up, you black devil,' hissed Rocheteau, glancing first at the dog then in the direction that he was facing.

The animal's fury seemed to be focused on a small incline that sloped upwards away from a partially frozen stream about two hundred yards away. Lausard held on to him and narrowed his eyes in the thickly falling snow. It was impossible to make out what had so agitated the dog but, nonetheless, the animal continued barking loudly.

'Let him go, Alain,' Rocheteau suggested. 'Let him sniff out the problem. There may be Cossacks hiding in there.' The corporal smiled.

Lausard kept a firm grip on the dog and shook his head almost imperceptibly.

'We will see,' he murmured. Never once did his eyes leave the woods.

During his life as a soldier, Lausard had found that time had a habit of losing its meaning. That, in certain situations and circumstances, a man actually lost track of hours, sometimes days. The monotony of marches, drill, bivouac and forage blurred into one. In war time this routine was only occasionally punctuated by skirmishes or the savagery of battle itself. During times of peace there was precious little for a soldier to do except clean the equipment he relied so heavily upon or, in the case of cavalrymen like Lausard, ensure that the health of his mount was not neglected. The same had to be done during a campaign naturally, but, and he had found this to be particularly true in recent weeks, care of the horses seemed almost secondary. No matter how dedicated and devoted a man might be to his mount, in conditions such as those the French cavalry had endured in Poland, that care seemed wasted. Animals, Lausard had come to think, were perfectly capable of understanding the futility of life as much as men. Just as able to fathom when it made more sense merely to give up and die quietly in some waterlogged ditch than cling to such a miserable existence. In the icy, freezing, mud-clogged swamps of Poland, life was something to be endured, not embraced. For Lausard, only the promise of conflict forced him on. The NCO preferred the frantic, confused and potentially lethal tableau that was battle. The business of war held its own attractions for him. He knew it was a view he shared with few of his companions but then he was different from them in many ways. Most notably in that he cared little if he lived or died. When faced with the possibility of death, most men felt a twinge of dread. Not Lausard. For him, the thought of death on the battlefield offered the catharsis he had sought for so long. Death for him was not the end of a meaningful life but the exorcism of one made worthless by acts that still tortured him. When he closed his eyes, and concentrated, he could still see his family walking to their deaths beneath the blade of the guillotine in the Place de la Révolution. How many years ago? Twelve? Fifteen? Time, as he had reasoned, sometimes lost its meaning.

As he wandered around the village of Dabronsko, that feeling of lost time now weighed on him as heavily as the extra clothing he wore to keep out the biting cold. He sank up to his calves in the mud, pausing occasionally physically to pull his own feet free of the sucking ooze. Inside his boots he wore two pairs of socks and some gaiters he had stripped from a dead infantryman. It made the boots difficult to get on and off but it was a process Lausard insisted on every night. There were many in the squadron, he knew, who never removed their boots. Some were only too eager to do so. Desperate to warm their feet at meagre fires which they invariably slept too close to, their flesh swelled and they were unable to replace their boots. At least five of those men had been taken to the nearest field hospital where they were being treated for gangrene. If they were lucky they would lose some toes. Perhaps a foot. It might be enough to get them sent back to France but Lausard doubted it. *La Grande Armée* was so desperate for extra men that many of those suffering from ailments caused by the weather were simply given extra rations of brandy. Lausard pulled his thick green cloak around him, ignoring the fact that the frayed hem was dangling in the mud. He still wore a torn hussar's pelisse beneath the cloak, open over his own surtout. He had torn the fur from the pelisse and wrapped the strips around his hands. There was a flea-ridden scarf wrapped around his neck and lower face. His brass helmet offered some protection for his head but did little to deflect the cold. Lausard, like many other troopers, had long ago taken to wrapping bandages around his scalp to add warmth. His gauntlets were caked in mud, the leather worn and cracked. Beneath them he wore a pair of woollen gloves taken from the portmanteau of a dead cuirassier. He had also found some tobacco, two or three gold coins and some mouldy biscuits on the same corpse. He had taken them all. The tobacco he had sold to Charnier in the third squadron, the gold he would use to buy food or drink if they ever reached anything approaching civilisation and the biscuits he had eaten to temporarily satiate his ever present hunger.

A number of camp fires had been lit and men sat around them, silent for the most part, seemingly oblivious to the snow that fell. It settled on their clothes but few bothered to wipe it away. Lausard headed for the partially frozen stream, deciding it was simpler to wade through the water than to chance overbalancing on one of the icy stepping stones. He splashed his way to the far bank and struggled up towards the dense woods that surrounded Dabronsko like circled fingers. He nodded at several of the sentries who stood freezing in the chill night. Some managed to raise a hand in greeting but the most that the majority could muster was a nod of recognition. In such horrendous conditions, sentries were relieved every thirty minutes, not every two hours as was usual. Two hours away from a fire in such weather could kill a man as surely as a musket ball.

Lausard moved further into the woods and found the men he sought. Baumar was holding his carbine across his chest, walking slowly backwards and forwards. Two or three yards from him, Bonet was doing the same, occasionally stopping to peer into the stygian darkness of the wood. As Lausard drew nearer, the former schoolmaster turned and looked at him.

'There's something moving out there,' he said quietly.

'Russians?' Lausard wanted to know.

'No,' Baumar offered. 'Wolves.'

'How can you be sure?' the NCO wanted to know.

'I can smell them. I know their scent,' Baumar said. 'The heat and the light are attracting them.'

'And the horses?' Bonet wondered.

'They want food,' Lausard murmured. 'Like every other creature in this country.' He squinted into the gloom but could see nothing.

Bonet turned and looked longingly back in the direction of the camp fires burning in and around Dabronsko.

'Another ten minutes and I will send Moreau and Delbene to relieve you,' Lausard said. 'There is some food for you when you get back.'

'And brandy?' Baumar asked hopefully.

Lausard smiled then turned and headed back in the direction of the village. He passed more sentries and nodded greetings to them. Some of the men looked at him as if trying to understand why he would have forsaken the warmth of a fire to walk in the woods on such a bitter night but those who knew him had become accustomed to his nocturnal wanderings. Lausard made his way back through the stream and towards the barn in which he was billeted. As he approached the huge fire they had built, Rocheteau handed him a cup of dark-looking fluid.

'Drink it,' the corporal said.

Lausard did so without question, wincing slightly as the drink burned its way to his stomach.

'What is that?' he asked, massaging his throat with one hand and coughing.

Rocheteau laughed.

'I found a flagon of it hidden beneath the floor of one of the buildings,' he said. 'It's some kind of liquor distilled from potatoes. It warms the stomach.'

'It probably rots the stomach,' Lausard added, sucking in a cold breath.

Some of the other men laughed.

'How are the horses?' the sergeant wanted to know. 'Baumar says there are wolves in the forest.'

'Some have sensed that,' Karim informed him.

'They are well guarded, Sergeant,' Tigana added.

'Can you eat wolf?' Tabor wanted to know.

'You can eat *anything* if it's cooked properly, you half-wit,' snapped Delacor. 'Even human flesh.'

'Perhaps we should cook Joubert,' Giresse offered. 'We could feed half the army with *his* carcass.'

Some of the other men laughed. Joubert merely pulled the collar of his cloak up more tightly around his neck and shuffled closer to the fire.

'Rider coming in.'

The shout echoed through the snowy night and, at first, Lausard was not sure from which direction it had come. Then he heard the sounds of a horse's hooves drawing closer and glanced towards the solitary horseman who was guiding his mount over the freezing mud towards the camp fire. Sonnier reached for his carbine. Karim rested one hand on the hilt of his scimitar. The newcomer was wearing the long green cloak of a dragoon and the red plume that adorned one side of his helmet was not encased in oilskin as was that of Lausard and his companions, but on view for all to see. In the firelight, his brass stirrups gleamed. Lausard was joined by Lieutenant Royere who was also gazing intently at the man.

The rider reined in his mount, patted the animal on the neck and swung himself out of the saddle, his scabbard scraping the ground as he walked. He wore a patch over his right eye and there was heavy scarring around the eye and the temple on that side of his face. He stood still for a moment then pulled the scarf away to reveal his face.

A slight smile creased the corners of Lausard's mouth.

The newcomer also smiled.

'Captain Milliere,' said Lausard, stretching out a hand in greeting. 'We thought you were dead.'

The officer shook Lausard's hand warmly then did the same with Royere.

'There were times when *I* thought I was dead,' Milliere confessed, smiling again.

He moved among the other dragoons, all of whom were anxious to offer their hands in welcome. Even Erebus wandered over and licked at the officer's hand.

'I see this black devil is still thriving,' Milliere grinned, stroking the huge dog's head.

'He will outlive all of us,' Lausard said.

'It is good to have you with us again, Captain,' Royere said.

'The lieutenant is relieved to see you, Captain, because that means that *he* does not have to take command of the squadron,' smiled Lausard. 'Promotion would distance him from his ideals, would it not, Lieutenant?'

Royere chuckled and nodded. The other dragoons laughed.

'How was hospital?' Lausard wanted to know. 'Were the surgeons good to you?'

'They are butchers, the lot of them,' Milliere told him. 'But they saved my life. Even if they took my eye.' He tapped the black eyepatch gently with one index finger.

Lausard ushered the officer towards the camp fire where he sat on some damp straw, warming his hands at the dancing flames. Charvet pushed a metal plate in his direction and Milliere accepted it gratefully. He was not sure what was in the watery concoction but there were pieces of meat and vegetables, the offering was hot and, for that alone, he was thankful. He ate hungrily.

'Unfortunately, we have no more to share, Captain,' Lausard told him. 'This country, as you will be aware, is reluctant to offer us anything other than cold and discomfort.'

Milliere nodded and continued eating.

'Have you any idea how long we are to remain in winter quarters, captain?' Rocheteau asked.

The other dragoons drew nearer, as if eager to hear what the officer had to say.

'I wish I could enlighten you, Corporal,' Milliere said apologetically. 'From what I heard, the weather has certainly forced the Emperor into this temporary halt in his pursuit of the Russians. Without this freakish weather we would still be following the Muscovites now. I can only assume that once the roads become more easily traversible we will be ordered forward once again.' The officer tipped up the plate and swallowed the last of the watery gravy. 'In the meantime, you may or may not be glad to hear that we ourselves will not be confined to winter quarters indefinitely. I return to you not just to resume command of the squadron but also with orders.'

Lausard and Rocheteau glanced first at one another then back at the officer.

'It has been difficult to gather intelligence as to the exact whereabouts and strengths of the enemy in the last week or so,' Milliere said, rubbing his hands together. 'Light cavalry patrols have come under increasing attack from Cossacks. Also, the Emperor's attempts to improve the quality of the roads has been hampered by the harassing actions of these savages. Disciplinary units charged with working on the roads have been attacked and prevented from completing their task due to Cossack intervention. I have orders to offer protection both to our own light cavalry patrols and also to the disciplinary units working in this area. This squadron has been singled out for that assignment.'

'Criminals guarding criminals,' Lausard said flatly.

'The nature of your backgrounds is immaterial, Sergeant,' Milliere said.

'I beg to differ, Captain,' Lausard continued, holding the officer's gaze.

'You know as well as I do that the reason this squadron has been chosen is because many of you are still viewed as expendable. A view I do not share myself but my observations are unwanted. I know that there is no better cavalry unit in the French army. What others think is of no importance.'

'Have we not proved ourselves enough these past ten years?' Roussard protested. 'Are we always to be treated with such contempt? To be given tasks others would never even be considered for?'

'Perhaps they also see in you those qualities lacking in many of the other men in the army,' Milliere offered. 'Qualities I have come to know well. Whatever the case, the orders I was given will be carried out.'

'So we are to act as nursemaids to the light cavalry?' sneered Delacor.

'There is something else,' Milliere said quietly. 'The Cossacks pose the main threat on this sector of the line but there have also been attacks on supply lines by renegade French soldiers. Our own supplies are being taken by our fellow countrymen. Discipline is breaking down more quickly than anyone in the high command dare imagine. They know what is happening but I doubt if they realise its scale.'

'Are you telling us we are to fight our own countrymen, Captain?' Lausard asked.

'If the situation should arise, yes. Men who have left their units and now operate in loosely organised bands are preying on those they once fought side by side with. Deserters roam this land like wolves. The supply columns are their easiest target. They must be stopped.'

'We have no food,' snapped Delacor. 'Why can't we simply take what there is from the villages we come across?'

'The Emperor is anxious not to alienate a people he seeks to rule. If the Poles are treated badly they will begin to resent the presence of French troops in their country. They may even transfer their allegiance to the Russians.'

'They have done little or nothing to help us ever since we arrived here,' Roussard protested. 'Why should we care about their feelings when they do not want us here anyway?'

'I agree,' Delacor echoed. 'We are hungry. Let us take from the Poles rather than kill other Frenchmen.'

'Delacor is right,' Rostov added. 'To hell with the Poles. Let them starve. What difference does it make if they support the Russians against us?'

'That is not what the Emperor wants,' Milliere told them.

'Bonaparte is not here in some stinking, flea-ridden village eating slops, Captain,' Delacor hissed. 'He sits in splendour in Warsaw with a full belly.'

Some of the other dragoons murmured their agreement.

'That may be,' Milliere said, glaring at Delacor. 'But he is still our commander, our Emperor. As long as that is the case, any orders he issues will be carried out.'

'Despite their nature?' Roussard rasped.

'What would you do, Roussard?' Lausard snapped. 'Do you want to leave? Do you, Delacor? You, Rostov?' He raised his voice and turned slowly to look at each of the dragoons nearby. 'Do any of you wish to walk away? To desert? To join those who steal from their own countrymen? If you do, then proclaim it now.'

There was a long silence, broken only by the crackling of the fire.

Then, from somewhere in the woods, came the sound of a gunshot.

FOURTEEN

Lausard spun round, one hand falling to the hilt of his sword. Many of the other dragoons also turned in the direction of the sound that still reverberated through the stillness of the night. Then a second shot shattered the tranquillity. It was followed rapidly by a third. Shouts began to rise from the woods and Lausard wasted no more time; he set off at a run towards the source of the disturbance. Sonnier, his carbine already held across his chest, joined him. Rocheteau pulled his pistols from their holsters and the men hurried after their sergeant. Lieutenant Royere and Captain Milliere were also on their feet, anxious to discover what was happening. Erebus bounded along, barking frenziedly, his great jaws snapping.

Two more shots ripped through the night and then, as Lausard and the others drew nearer, they heard the first of several piercing screams. But the sergeant heard another sound, even louder than the shrieks. They were the unmistakable sounds of growls. Far louder than anything even Erebus could manage. The dragoons splashed through the partially frozen stream and up the slope, some slipping on the frozen mud. It was as Lausard reached the edge of the forest that he saw something staggering from the trees. For fleeting seconds it did not register that what was approaching him was a man. The sentry was covered in blood from head to foot. He was dragging one leg uselessly behind him, leaving a trail of crimson on the rancid earth. His cloak had been torn to shreds, his surtout ripped open and, through the rents, Lausard could see flesh and muscle. Blood was smeared over the sentry's face and most of his nose was missing. All that remained was a bloody hole in the centre of his face. His helmet had been knocked off and Lausard saw that his left ear was also missing. The man took another couple of steps then dropped to his knees, his eyes rolling upwards in their sockets. Lausard looked down at him and saw that there was a gaping wound in his throat, large enough to get a fist into. Blood pumped fiercely from it, condensation swirling around the hot fluid as it spurted into the air. The man tried to speak but his lips merely fluttered soundlessly.

Lausard ran past him into the trees, pulling his sword from its scabbard.

He saw the wolves immediately.

There were six that he could make out in the gloom. Huge, powerful creatures that stood as tall as his waist. Two of them had hold of another sentry. One had fastened its jaws on the man's face while another was tugging at his unprotected genitals. The high-pitched shrieks of the dragoon rang through the night like something from a fevered nightmare. Lausard rushed forward and swung his sword at the nearest animal, catching it across the rump and laying open its flesh. It yelped and let go of the sentry but only backed up enough to bare its bloodied teeth at Lausard. It fixed him in its cold stare and stood its ground. Rocheteau shot it twice, each lead ball slamming into its body, knocking the wind from it. Sonnier swung his carbine up to his shoulder and fired too. The .50 calibre round hit the wolf squarely between the eyes, caving in its skull. It dropped like a stone and Sonnier reloaded with lightning speed, glancing around him at the tableau that resembled some scene from the nether reaches of hell.

On all sides, wolves were swarming out of the forest, intent on attacking anything that moved. Sonnier saw ten, twelve, more of the ravenous creatures. The other sentries were battling them as best they could; most, having fired their single shot, were now attempting to keep the creatures at bay with their bayonets. Two or three of the men were already on the ground. It was obvious, even in the darkness, that at least one of them was dead.

'Bring fire,' roared Milliere, drawing his own sword, his eyes never leaving the wolf closest to him.

Behind him, several of the dragoons hurried to their camp fires and hurried to make torches. Kruger wrapped several lengths of cloth around a long branch and stuck it into the flames, waiting for the damp material to ignite. When it finally did it only burned with a dull blue flame. He hissed irritably and looked around for anything else to wrap around the staff to increase the ferocity of the blaze.

In the woods, Lausard held his sword steady and stood his ground as the wolves circled, teeth bared.

'Their hunger makes them brave,' said Baumar, his breath coming in gasps. He was clutching his carbine in both hands, the bayonet point lowered at the same wolf facing Lausard. It was a large grey animal, its teeth already stained with blood. Lausard took a step towards it, as if trying to provoke it. The wolf merely moved back slightly, its haunches lowered as it prepared to spring. Lausard kept his eyes locked on the beast, readying himself for the onslaught he knew would come.

All around him, dragoons and wolves faced each other in an eerie silence broken only by the occasional snarls of the animals or the continued shrieks of pain of men already mauled by the predators. The breath of both men and beasts clouded in the air as they exhaled. Erebus bared his teeth and faced another of the smaller pack members. Then, as if on a signal, the wolves attacked. The comparative silence of the night gave way to a cacophony of shouts, screams and maniacal roars. Lausard drove his sword forward as the first of the beasts launched itself at him. He gripped the hilt with both hands and lunged upwards, the powerful thrust piercing the wolf's body, bursting one of its lungs and erupting from its back. The weight of the carcass pulled the weapon from Lausard's grip and he raised an arm to protect himself from the next animal. It succeeded in clamping its jaws on his right forearm and the sergeant grabbed it by one ear, gouging at its exposed eye as it tried to rip through his clothes. He heard a swish of steel and the pressure on his arm was suddenly released. The wolf's body fell before him, now headless. He glanced across and saw that Karim had struck the animal's head from its body with one blow of his scimitar. Lausard tore his own sword free of the first wolf and spun round, preparing to meet another attack. To his left he saw Erebus shaking one of the smaller wolves by the throat, as a fox would shake a chicken.

Another of the pack ducked beneath the swing of a sword and buried its long canine teeth into the flesh of Collard's left thigh. He shouted in pain and slashed at the wolf but it tore away a sizable chunk of both his breeches and his leg as it shook loose. It lunged again but this time its teeth clamped around the cuff of his boot. Collard kicked it hard in the side and tried to struggle to his feet, perturbed at how deep the wound in his thigh was. It was bleeding badly and he struck furiously at the wolf, angered as much as injured by the attack. He could see his own blood glistening on the animal's teeth as it snarled at him. He hissed something under his breath and swung at the wolf once more but missed; the predator launched itself again, slamming into his chest and knocking him to the ground. Collard brought the sword up sharply, driving it into the belly of the wolf, pushing upwards until the sword point burst from its back and he felt warm blood pouring on to him. He rolled to one side, pushing the carcass off while, all around him, his companions were engaged in similar combat with the starving pack. He saw Delacor hack off one wolf's right foreleg with his axe while Karim gutted another with a flick of his razor-sharp scimitar. Sonnier, his face scratched and bleeding, shot another animal from close range.

Rocheteau found himself with two of the creatures coming at him. He met the leap of one, while the second was intercepted by the giant frame of Tabor. The big man gripped the wolf by the muzzle and twisted hard. The snapping of vertebrae was clearly audible. Tabor dropped the dead animal and turned in time to see a huge she-wolf hurtling towards him. He raised his arms again but the force of the impact staggered him and he went down, the wolf snapping at his face. He smelled its rancid breath as it tried to bite him. The big man struck out at it with one hand, kicking wildly in order to get the beast off him. Rocheteau, who had succeeded in hurling one of the beasts away, hauled himself upright and snatched up Tabor's carbine. Using the butt as a club, the corporal brought it down with incredible force on the she-wolf's back. The animal yelped in pain and drew back. But Rocheteau advanced on it with lightning speed, swung the butt again and smacked the wolf on the side of the muzzle. Several teeth were shattered by the impact but that only seemed to provoke a more frenzied response from the ravenous animal. It looked from Tabor to Rocheteau, both men moving slowly towards it.

Lieutenant Royere suddenly appeared between them and drove his sword towards the she-wolf, the tip of the blade catching it in one shoulder. It snarled and bit at the sword but the officer struck again quickly, wounding it again in the side. Rocheteau took his chance and rammed the carbine's fifteen-inch bayonet into the she-wolf's flank, using his weight to push it over, skewering it to the frozen earth. Royere struck it across the head with a powerful backhand blow that split its skull.

Lausard was suddenly aware of heat beside him. Of bright, yellowish flares of light in the gloom. He saw Kruger and Varcon carrying torches, waving them in the direction of the wolves. The animals barked and snarled at this new menace and some backed away, driven off despite their gnawing hunger. Behind them, other dragoons waved the blazing beacons. Pieces of lighted rag wound around branches or, in some cases, around the ends of swords or bayonets. One of the wolves dashed at Giresse but he jabbed the torch into its face. The creature yelped, spun around and ran off. A broken line of men advanced, driving the wolves back into the forest. One or two of the larger and more desperate members of the pack tried to hold their ground but it was useless. Lausard took one of the torches from Carbonne and continued to advance, his sword in his other hand. As he swept the flame back and forth it reflected in the eyes of the wolves. To his right and left, other men were forcing the animals back into the forest with the torches. One or two shots rang out. Lausard saw another wolf fall. When the first turned and sped into the enveloping blackness, it was only seconds before others joined it. The creatures were swallowed up like shadows by the umbra.

Captain Milliere, also carrying a torch, held up his hand to halt the men.

The officer was breathing heavily and there was blood on his cheek which he wiped away with the back of his gloved hand. He looked down at the body of a dead wolf then glanced at Lausard.

Rocheteau, Gaston and Baumar were already hard at work skinning the other carcasses. The fur would make a welcome addition to the reeking garments already worn by the dragoons. It would offer added warmth.

'I suspect that this was not the enemy you expected to face when you returned, Captain,' said Lausard quietly, his breath clouding in the air. He prodded the dead wolf with the toe of his boot.

Milliere merely shook his head.

Somewhere deep in the forest, several wolves howled mournfully.

FIFTEEN

Laughter echoed along the corridor of the palace, reverberating around the high vaulted ceilings and from the marbled walls and pillars. The sound mingled with the more strident clacking of boot heels on polished floors. Half a dozen voices, all speaking simultaneously, melded together to add to the sounds of gaiety. Napoleon Bonaparte, his face lightened by a smile, walked briskly along the corridor with several members of his staff. The Emperor of the French rubbed his hands together in an effort to restore the circulation but he knew that fires would have been lit and maintained in the state rooms he used. The biting chill of the Warsaw night air would soon be a distant memory. His servants would have mulled wine waiting for him. His bed would have been warmed for whenever he chose to retire. The men of his staff could expect similar luxury when they eventually retreated to the privacy of their own quarters.

At every door he passed, Napoleon nodded greetings to the huge Imperial Guard grenadiers that stood sentinel there. Each man raised his musket in acknowledgement of the Corsican's gesture. The two men guarding the room at the end of the corridor snapped their heels together smartly as Napoleon pushed open the door and walked past them. He was immediately enveloped by the warmth of the fire. Behind him, Marshal Berthier followed, slipping his blue cloak from his shoulders as he moved nearer the fire. Duroc, the Grand Marshal of the palace, took up position beside the Chief of Staff. Both men accepted wine from servants, as did Jean Baptiste Antoine

Marcellin Marbot, one of the Emperor's most senior aides-de-camp. Marbot ran a hand through his dark hair and watched as the other men in the room were also presented with their wine. General Rapp inhaled the bouquet and nodded approvingly. General Anne Jean Marie Rene Savary waited until all the men in the room were holding glasses then raised his in salute.

'With your permission, sire,' he began. 'I would like to propose a toast to the city of Warsaw. Although we would all, I am sure, prefer to be in Paris, I feel this city presents all the gaieties of our own capital.' He prepared to drink then smiled and added, 'with the exception of theatres, of course'.

The other men laughed and accepted the toast.

'Warsaw has, indeed, many delights to offer,' Napoleon echoed. 'Would that we were celebrating our victory over the Russians rather than merely a respite from the foul weather visited upon us by this country. For all the charms this city holds, I would sooner be pursuing our enemies back to their own borders.'

'That must only be a matter of time, sire,' Duroc offered. 'The weather that has forced us to seek winter quarters cannot continue for ever. Once the ground is firmer and supply lines have been more adequately opened, then it will just be a matter of time before the final reckoning is reached for the Tsar's armies.'

'And, until then, we must endure the delights of Warsaw and all it has to offer,' Savary mused.

The other men laughed.

'Your brother-in-law certainly seems to be enamoured with the city, sire,' Duroc offered. 'I heard that he had sent to Paris for twenty-six thousand francs' worth of ostrich feathers with which to adorn his uniforms and those of his aides.'

'Marshal Murat has a flair for flamboyance,' Napoleon smiled. 'He feels that the Poles will be impressed by his costumes. He is on a spiritual mission to bring some light into their drab existence. He feels he is the sun around which they orbit.'

More laughter filled the room.

'I can only hope that the radiance he seeks to emit will blind our enemies on the battlefield when that day finally comes,' the

Corsican continued. 'In the meantime, the Cossacks seem to be singularly unimpressed with my brother-in-law's demeanour or his attempts to keep them at bay along our perimeters. They attack at all hours of the day and night. Murat has increased the size of cavalry patrols from fifteen to thirty.'

'He has had little choice, sire,' Rapp interjected. 'As you yourself said, the Cossacks are everywhere. Marshal Murat has been forced to employ larger reconnaissance units.'

'Their size makes them more vulnerable,' the Emperor observed. 'They are more likely to be noticed. More likely to be attacked. That is why we have so little intelligence. Why the movements of the Russian armies are largely unknown to us.'

'They will sit and wait for us, sire,' Duroc said. 'As is their way.'

'We cannot be sure of that, Duroc,' insisted Rapp. 'Even now, they may be preparing to attack. Perhaps the constant Cossack harassments are merely to screen something larger being planned by the Muscovites.' He looked to Napoleon as if for confirmation. The Corsican merely shrugged.

'If that should happen then each commander already knows the places at which he should concentrate his corps,' said Napoleon, sipping his wine. 'Ney at Mlawa. Soult at Golymin. Davout at Pultusk. Lannes at Sierock and Augereau at Plonsk. All cover an area of country they are perfectly equipped to defend should that eventuality arise.'

'As you instructed, sire, orders have been issued for the collection of supplies and the establishment of hospitals at Marienwerder, Thorn, Plock, Wyszogrod, Lowicz, Pultusk and here on the outskirts of Warsaw itself,' Berthier added.

'We lose more men to this damned weather and to hunger than we do to Russian bullets and cannonballs,' snapped Duroc.

'I respect your orders to collect supplies, sire,' Savary began. 'But we have already seen how unyielding this land is. Where are such supplies to be found? The troops have already scraped the land clean and yet still they are starving.'

'Bread and biscuits are being baked, at Pultusk, ready for distribution among the army, even as we speak,' Berthier offered.

'Baked with what?' Rapp wanted to know. 'These Polish

peasants have no flour or corn to give us and, even if they have, they are far from forthcoming with it. They treat their liberators with the kind of caution one usually reserves for invaders.'

'Enough of this,' Napoleon said, raising his hand dismissively. 'We must not become too preoccupied with our own problems. Instead we must consider how best to cause inconvenience to our enemy. At the moment that can best be achieved by diplomatic rather than military means. Russia has many enemies other than ourselves. Steps have been taken to intrigue those foes against the Tsar and his men. To antagonise and galvanise Russian adversaries and create disorder against them on other fronts. I myself wrote to Sultan Selim of Turkey entreating him to declare war on Russia. I enjoined him to drive out the rebel Hospodars.* War in the Balkans will engage Russian reserves. Weaken them in their struggle against us *here*. They will not allow their southern border to be threatened.'

'And in the meantime, we are at the mercy of the elements,' Duroc intoned. 'Trapped in cantonments when we should be fighting.'

'Patience in war is sometimes as much a virtue as swiftness,' the Corsican remarked. 'What would you have me do, Duroc? Continue a futile pursuit of a foe intent only on retreating? Lose more men to weather and indiscipline? Men who will be needed for the remainder of the campaign?' The Emperor looked reproachfully at his ADC and Duroc nodded as if in supplication. 'All too soon the fighting will begin again, gentlemen, and, when that happens, I fancy that you will all gladly give up your tents in some freezing wood or mud flat for the warmth of the beds you now possess.'

The other men laughed and finished their drinks. One by one they bade goodnight to their Emperor and filed out of the room. Berthier was the last to leave. The Chief of Staff pulled his cloak around his shoulders and saluted his commander.

'I understand you have other matters to attend to, sire,' he said, a slight smile playing on his lips. 'I will not detain you further.'

* Russian settlers in Wallachia

'I fear you missed your calling, Berthier,' Napoleon answered as he watched the marshal striding towards the door. 'Your gift for diplomacy would have made you the equal of Talleyrand. You should have been a statesman, not a soldier.'

Napoleon stood for a moment in the room then finished his Chambertin and walked briskly to the double doors at the other side of the room. He opened them and stepped through into his bedroom. There was another fire burning in the marble hearth and the room smelled fragrant. It was lit with candles that cast long shadows and left the corners of the room in blackness. The Corsican closed the doors behind him and lingered there for a moment, his eyes fixed on the bed. Beside it stood the figure of Countess Marie Walewska. Aged just eighteen, she had the bearing of a woman twenty years older. She was clad only in a chiffon nightdress, the candles in the room making the material look diaphanous. Her long dark hair cascaded over her shoulders and she fixed the Corsican with a telling look.

'I trust I have not kept you waiting too long,' he said quietly. 'I realise you understand that, as much as I want to be with you as often as possible, I am sometimes constrained by the demands of my position.'

'Do you come here tonight as Emperor of the French or as a lover?'

'With you I am but a humble lover.'

'Of what did you speak tonight?' she wanted to know. 'Of the destruction of the Russian armies or of freeing my country? A promise you have yet to fulfil.'

Napoleon unbuttoned his tunic as he crossed towards her.

'Neither subject is fitting for a bedroom,' he murmured softly. He reached out and gently touched her cheek. The skin felt like warm alabaster beneath his fingertips. 'Politics and war have no place here.'

SIXTEEN

Alain Lausard gritted his teeth and dug his spurs into his mount, trying to coax more speed from the already lathered animal. It ploughed through the slippery mud, great gouts of the reeking muck flying into the air around Lausard and his fellow cavalrymen as they hurtled across the sticky terrain. Ahead of them, half a dozen Cossacks guided their powerful ponies over the ground with apparent ease but more than one of them glanced over his shoulder to see how close the pursuing French cavalry were. The gap between them was closing. Up ahead there was a range of low hills thickly covered by trees. If the Cossacks reached those then there would be little point following them, thought Lausard. The Russian light cavalry moved with greater ease in such surroundings and there was always the possibility that the dragoons were merely being led into a trap. Once they entered the confines of the wood there was every possibility they would be enveloped by swarms of the irregular horsemen or shot from the saddle by others already concealed in the gloom of the forest. But, as long as the Russians remained in the open they were open to pursuit. Lausard pulled his second pistol from the holster on his saddle and pointed it in the direction of the fleeing Cossacks.

To his left and right, Collard and Rocheteau were in the process of doing the same. Three shots rang out close together. One of the Cossacks toppled from the saddle, his twelve-foot lance falling from his hand, the point burying itself in the sucking mud. As Karim swept past he grabbed the shaft and pulled the lance free, hefting it before him for a second then slipping it beneath his arm in the manner of some medieval jousting champion. For fleeting seconds he indeed looked like a man from another age. Charvet allowed his horse to trample the wounded Russian as he passed. He glanced quickly over his shoulder to see that the prone figure was no longer moving.

The dragoons drew nearer to the Cossacks. Less than ten yards separated them now. Lausard reached for his sword and pulled it free, the metallic hiss audible even above the snorting and panting of the galloping horses and the thunder of their hooves. He shouted something unintelligible and leaned forward in the saddle. His mount, seemingly infected with the same fury as its rider, drew extra strength and speed from somewhere and Lausard found himself alongside one of the Cossacks. He looked briefly into the man's face before striking out with a powerful backhand swipe. The blade caught the Russian across the bridge of the nose, shattered the bone there and shaved off a sizable chunk of one cheek. The man shrieked and fell from the saddle, his horse veering wildly across the path of Rocheteau's mount. The corporal tried to avoid the fleeing animal but it was no good. His own horse collided with the lighter pony and both crashed to the ground. Protecting his head as best he could from the flailing hooves of the animals trying to get up, Rocheteau lay still, allowing the horses to struggle to their feet. He caught the reins of his own mount, patting its muzzle to calm it before swinging himself back into the saddle. He was drenched with reeking, cold mud from head to foot. His horse shook its head to dislodge some clods of earth from its mane and, as it snorted, the air clouded around it. Rocheteau quickly ran his hands up and down his thighs, ensuring that no bones had been broken. In such weather, it was easy to overlook injuries sustained to flesh already numbed by such murderously low temperatures. Sonnier reined in his mount beside the corporal, lifted his Charleville to his shoulder and aimed. Rocheteau watched as his companion rose in the stirrups and fired at the fleeing Cossacks. He hit one in the back but the man merely slumped forward over his pony's neck momentarily, gripping his reins with one hand, trying to keep himself in the saddle. The .50 calibre lead ball had passed through the several layers of clothing he wore and punctured his lumbar region just below the kidneys. He barely had time to straighten up before Karim drew close to him and rammed the lance into him, driving it deep into his side. The Circassian dragged it free then struck again. The second thrust caught the Cossack beneath the armpit and knocked him from the saddle. He crashed to the ground, a geyser of mud and blood rising from where he landed.

Karim spun the lance, brandishing it like a javelin. With all his strength, he hurled it at another of the escaping Cossacks, watching as the shaft whistled through the air. It missed its target and buried itself in the soggy ground. Lausard saw that the remaining three Russians were now pulling clear of their pursuers again and held up his hand to halt his men.

'Let them go,' he shouted, watching as the Russian light horsemen were finally engulfed by the trees. Around him, his men sucked in deep breaths, exhausted by the chase. Horses too gulped down lungfuls of air as they were guided back more slowly across the sticky terrain.

Lausard walked his horse over to one of the fallen Cossacks and looked down at the body. Blood had spread out in a wide puddle around the corpse, mingling with the filthy water and stinking mud. Rocheteau had already dismounted and was searching through the clothes of the other fallen horsemen. Sonnier reloaded and kept his eyes on the woods. Collard led his horse over to where Lausard and Karim were sitting motionless looking down at the dead Cossack.

'Is this to be our part in the war?' Collard asked, pulling the scarf around his face up a little higher. The biting wind was already making his eyes water. 'Chasing Russian bandits?'

'They are more than bandits,' Karim said. 'They are the finest light cavalry in Europe.'

'What else would you have us do, Collard?' Lausard wanted to know. 'We are following orders. That is the duty of a soldier, is it not?'

'We chase bandits, guard criminals and escort supplies. Those are not the duties of soldiers but those of nursemaids.'

'Do you long for battle?' Lausard asked flatly. 'Do you yearn to face cannon and musket balls?'

'The sooner the battle is fought, the sooner this war will be over and we can all go home,' Collard grunted.

Lausard smiled.

'Home,' he mused. 'A pleasing thought. Hold on to it. For that is all it will remain. A thought. It will take more than one battle to finish *this* war. The Russians are made of sterner stuff. Actions have already been fought at Liebstadt, Mohrungen and Ionkovo and still the Russians continue to oppose us. To mass their troops for more combat. We have been in the saddle since September of last year. It is the beginning of February now. We have known four years of peace in eleven. I doubt we will see its like again. Bonaparte will not stop until he is master of Europe and if that means we all die in the process then he will not give it a second thought. While there is a man alive who will fight for him and who can march or ride, he will not stop. He sees it as his destiny. We are merely instruments of that desire. To be used and discarded as he feels necessary. When *this* war is over, Collard, you will have many others to look forward to.'

Lausard wheeled his horse and called the other men to him. They formed themselves alongside him and headed back the way they had come. The first snow of the day had already begun to fall.

The tree crashed to the ground with a loud thud that seemed to shake the soggy earth. The impact sent up several geysers of mud. Those near the fallen timber stepped back momentarily then set about it with axes and saws. Lausard watched as the men of the punishment company swarmed over the fallen tree like ants. They were clad only in rough brown uniforms that looked as if they had been fashioned from hessian. Denied even the benefit of buttons to fasten the ragged tunics and with only sabots to protect their feet, they laboured hard in an effort to generate some warmth to protect themselves against the rapidly dropping temperatures. The snow that had started to fall earlier that morning was now drifting steadily down from the bloated clouds, dusting white the already rutted and disfigured earth.

The men of the disciplinary unit worked on, seemingly oblivious to the conditions, struggling with their tools but also finding it hard to move, hampered as they were by the eight-pound cannonballs fastened to their right ankles by metal shackles. Each ball was attached to an eight-foot chain that made movement awkward at the best of times; but then again, Lausard reasoned, they were not intended to travel with any speed. The solid lead balls often sank into the mud or were stepped on by others. Denied even the luxury of being called by their names, they were identified only by the large white numbers on their black caps. They varied in age from their late teens to their early fifties. All sentenced, for various crimes, to labour in the cause of the army. Many, he knew, were guilty of the crime of self-mutilation. Some men, it had transpired, saw the prospect of blowing their own foot or hand off as preferable to a life in the army but their attempts to escape service in this way had been unsuccessful. As Lausard looked on, he saw that a number of the men were missing appendages. Others lacked fingers. Many bore scars and, once more, he suspected they were self-inflicted.

Their task was to try and make the roads more passable, a thankless one at the best of times in the appalling conditions. All they could do was to line the inadequate thoroughfares with lengths of timber to prevent the marshy terrain on either side from encroaching on what was supposed to pass for a road. The constant round of iron-hard frost and rapid thaw had caused most of the roads in that part of Poland to become quagmires and Lausard felt that the work of the punishment units was little more than token. Roads that were already barely passable flooded on an almost nightly basis. However, they went about their task with the mechanical and soulless air usually associated with men who have nothing to live for and even less to look forward to. He watched as the officer who commanded them coaxed his horse back and forth between them, occasionally shouting warnings to those he felt to be less than committed to their work. The man wore the uniform of a captain of Line infantry and Lausard knew him as Carras, a lean, pale individual who rode a bay and puffed constantly on a pipe. He watched as several of the men hacked the fallen tree into ten-foot lengths of timber and others hammered the staves into place at each side of the road. It was a thankless task as the mud engulfed everything.

'Cowards and criminals,' said Delacor dismissively.

'Eleven years ago, that would have been *us*,' Lausard reminded him. 'How long do you think a rapist would serve in a punishment unit?'

Delacor narrowed his eyes and looked at Lausard.

'Or a horse thief?' Rocheteau wondered, jabbing Giresse in the back with one finger.

'Or a thief?' Giresse chuckled, looking at the corporal.

'At least they are being allowed to contribute to the army's cause,' said Bonet. 'Rather than being locked in cells and threatened with the guillotine as we were.'

'It isn't much of a choice, schoolmaster,' Charvet offered. 'Rot in a dungeon or freeze to death in Poland.'

Lausard swung himself out of the saddle and walked across to the small camp fire that was burning nearby. The flames were struggling to take on the damp wood and thick smoke was billowing from the fire. It made the sergeant's eyes water but he remained as close as he could to the fire in an effort to garner some warmth from it. Seated on a fallen log on the other side of the smoky blaze Lieutenant Royere was holding a piece of paper. He handed it to Lausard.

'The latest bulletin of the army, my friend,' Royere commented. 'I thought you might be interested in the words of our Emperor.'

Lausard glanced at the paper, raising his eyebrows slightly as he read it. He reached out with one hand and ruffled Erebus's black coat with his free hand. The large dog growled approvingly.

'What does it say, Alain?' Rocheteau wanted to know.

'Bonaparte tells us how close to victory we are,' Lausard said, without looking up. 'How he missed the decisive victory he wanted at Ionkovo by a hair's-breadth. That the Russians are only concerned with retreating and that it is our duty to continue pursuing them until they are forced to turn and fight.' Lausard shook his head.

'Pursue them,' Delacor grunted. 'All we do is chase Cossacks and play nursemaid to cowards.'

Lausard ignored the remark and continued reading.

'". . . The greater part of the Russian army's lines of communication have been severed,"' he read aloud.

'Does that mean there will be a battle soon?' Tabor wanted to know.

'Of course not, you half-wit,' snapped Delacor. 'All it means is the Russians are still on the run.'

'Good,' said Roussard. 'The longer they run, the longer it delays a battle.'

Erebus loped back towards Gaston and the young trumpeter pulled his cloak more tightly around as he crouched by the fire, extending a hand to stroke the dog.

'"The depots of Guttstadt and Liebstadt and part of the magazines of the Alle have been captured by our light cavalry,"' Lausard continued.

'Those peacock bastards,' hissed Delacor. 'They ride around in their pretty uniforms collecting the Emperor's praise while we suffer.'

'They have a job to do, the same as we have,' Royere noted.

'They suffer too,' Lausard added. 'Everyone does.' He brushed some snow from his face. The flurries that had been falling all day were becoming more intense. Despite the condition of the ground, the snow was settling. If the weather continued this way, they could expect drifts by nightfall. It would harden the ground but make their passage no easier. Battling through snow two feet thick was no more preferable to negotiating mud a foot or more deep.

'This damned country,' said Rocheteau, looking around him.

The punishment unit worked on.

Lausard stood and watched them for a moment. If one paused or dropped a tool, Captain Carras would walk his horse towards them and bellow something. The men returned to their labours with renewed vigour.

'What can you threaten men like that with?' the sergeant mused. 'Death? Surely that would be a merciful release for them. A firing squad would be preferable to what they are forced to do.'

'For some men, life is all that matters,' Royere offered. 'No matter how vile or intolerable it may seem to us.'

'Many of us lived like animals in the gutters of Paris before Bonaparte gave us the chance to be soldiers,' Rocheteau added. 'But did *we* ever think of giving in to death?'

'Not until we were caught and sentenced,' chuckled Giresse.

Some of the other men also laughed. Lausard said nothing.

'When I worked at the asylum at Charenton I used to envy some of the inmates there,' Varcon interjected. 'Men whose minds had gone. They had no comprehension of where they were. They did not long for freedom because they did not understand what it meant. When it was taken from them, they had no knowledge of it. Their ignorance was their salvation.'

'Did none of them ever try to escape?' Bonet asked.

'Occasionally,' Varcon answered. 'But many had been there all their lives. They had no reason to leave, even if they had been able. Charenton was their prison, but it was also their home.'

'It sounds as if it served the same purpose for them as the army does for us,' Bonet mused. 'We were reluctant to join but it offered us an escape. Now it is the only home we have.'

'Or will ever have again,' Roussard said quietly.

'I will find a home in the Kingdom of Heaven when my time comes,' Moreau said, crossing himself.

'I would settle for one back in France,' Gormier offered.

'You are more likely to find one beneath six feet of Polish mud,' Roussard grunted.

Rocheteau scraped some snow together, balled it up and threw it at his companion. Roussard snapped something at the corporal while the other men laughed.

'Where is Captain Milliere, Lieutenant?' Lausard wanted to know.

'He took some men and travelled to the west of here,' the officer said. 'He suspects that there will be more Cossack attacks. Perhaps even tonight. What of those you chased off?'

'We killed three of them,' Lausard shrugged. 'The others disappeared like spirits.'

'They do have an uncanny ability to become as one with the

land in which they move,' Royere remarked. 'They are unlike any enemy we have come up against before.'

'They ride with the skill of the Mamelukes,' offered Moreau. 'How could any of us forget *them*? Damned heathen savages.'

Some of the other men laughed.

'If you insult those bastards, you insult Karim,' chuckled Rocheteau. 'And who among us would want to do that?'

'I am Circassian,' Karim said flatly. 'I never had any allegiance to the Mamelukes. It is more of an insult to liken me to one of those slave-masters.'

'How do you compare the merits of Cossacks against them, my friend?' Lausard wanted to know.

'Both are perfectly suited to the terrain in which they choose to fight,' Karim said. 'But I say we are a match for either of them.'

Lausard smiled and patted the Circassian on the shoulder, then he turned as he heard the rumbling of horses' hooves away to his left. More than a dozen dragoons, led by Captain Milliere, reined in their mounts less than a hundred yards from where Lausard and the other men huddled around the sputtering fire. Milliere looked up at the bloated grey clouds and strode across to join the waiting men.

'There are tracks everywhere,' the officer said. 'Cossack ponies. The woods and countryside around here must be swarming with them.' He watched as Delbene fed more kindling into the fire but it seemed to do little to aid the struggling flames. Milliere looked into the fire for a moment. 'We will bivouac here for the night,' he said finally. 'I want fires lit around the perimeter of the camp and double the sentries. There is no point trying to hide from the Cossacks, they already know where we are. At least, should they decide to attack, we will be in some small measure prepared for them.' He looked first at Royere then at Lausard. Both men nodded. The sounds of toil still came from the punishment unit. The snow continued to fall.

Napoleon Bonaparte read and reread the reports before him, his face belying little of what he was feeling. The Corsican ambled back and forth inside the abandoned inn, his boots beating out a tattoo on the wooden floor. Marshal Berthier watched him for a moment then returned to his work, his quill scratching across paper with incredible speed. The Chief of Staff stopped occasionally and examined the tip of the quill as if afraid that the ink might have frozen upon it, such was the ferocity of the cold that penetrated every crack in the building and drove icy teeth into everything it touched. The snow that had been falling for most of the day was still coming down in thick flurries, occasionally made worse by the increasingly strong wind. Every so often, a grenadier of the Imperial Guard, his blue overcoat dusted with snow, would enter the inn and push more wood on to the fire but, no matter how much the flames were fed, they seemed incapable of driving out the fearsome chill. General Rapp rubbed his hands together and waited for the Corsican to speak.

'And where is Bennigsen now?' he said finally.

'On the road from Landsberg to Königsberg, sire,' Rapp said. 'With all of his army apart from his artillery. Intelligence suggests that he has directed his guns to make for the village of Preussich Eylau some eight miles to the north of here.'

'Will he stand and fight there?' murmured Napoleon, crossing to a map laid out on one of the tables close by.

'Eylau itself is a strong position, sire,' Berthier remarked. 'The roads from Landsberg, Kreuzberg, Königsberg, Friedland, Bartenstein and Heilsberg all converge there.'

'What of the terrain itself?' the Corsican demanded.

'Forest and plain, just like most of Poland,' Berthier said wearily. 'The village itself appears to be large.'

'So it will offer much cover to defending troops,' Napoleon mused. 'The ground between these two lakes, Tenknitten and Waschkeiten, is also slightly elevated, is it not?' He ran an index finger over the map, studying the contours it showed. 'What is the distance between these lakes? A thousand yards?'

Berthier nodded.

'The lakes themselves should present little problem,' the Chief of Staff continued. 'They will be frozen solid. Both cavalry and artillery will be able to manoeuvre freely over them.'

'The village itself is in a shallow valley,' Rapp offered. 'Protected by woods on two sides.'

Napoleon stepped back.

'If you were to choose a defensive position, gentlemen, you could do worse than choose *this* one,' he remarked. 'Bennigsen will know this ground. It suits the way he fights.'

'He fights on the run,' said Rapp dismissively. 'The battle at Hoff was against his rearguard. He loses two thousand men, five cannon and two standards and then retreats once more. He seems to have no wish to consolidate his position.'

'Not until the ground is right for him to do so,' Napoleon said. 'But, for once, this cursed weather may well work to our advantage. As you both know, the Russians have a liking for building earthworks. It will be impossible for them to dig in ground as hard as steel.'

'If they cannot shelter behind ramparts of their own construction, sire, then surely they will use what is available to them,' Berthier commented. 'The buildings of Eylau itself.'

Napoleon nodded and peered once again at the map.

'The village lies before a small incline,' he said. 'According to this map, the church and cemetery are on a mound. Possibly a commanding position for defending troops, especially with the benefit of houses around them too.' He looked at Berthier. 'What are the current dispositions and strengths of our troops in this area?'

'The corps of Marshals Soult and Murat are closest, sire,' the Chief of Staff said. 'Accompanied by the Guard and the men under the command of Marshal Augereau. But even they will not be able to reach Eylau before Bennigsen and his army. Marshal Ney has close to fifteen thousand men under his command to the north but he is charged with the task of preventing Lestocq and his Prussians from uniting with Bennigsen. Marshal Davout's corps, numbering some fifteen thousand, is currently marching from Bartenstein.'

'How many men in total do I have at my disposal?' Napoleon snapped.

'If Davout and Ney can reach here by morning then around forty-five thousand, sire,' Berthier said flatly. 'We can call upon two hundred cannon to support them.'

'And Bennigsen?'

'Intelligence reports indicate between sixty-five and sixty-seven thousand Russian troops, sire, supported by four hundred and sixty cannon. There is always the possibility that Lestocq and his Prussians will reach Bennigsen, swelling his numbers to around seventy-five thousand.'

'It would, I feel, be a mistake to engage the enemy until the corps of Ney and Davout have arrived,' said Napoleon. 'It would also be remiss of me to continue planning troop movements without first *seeing* the terrain. First thing in the morning I intend to view Eylau and its surrounding hamlets. Perhaps, by then, I will have a clearer idea of what Bennigsen intends to do and what *I* can do to stop him.'

SEVENTEEN

Lausard looked at his pocket watch and noted that it was approaching 10.37. The snow that had been falling so heavily during the day had hardly abated with the coming of night and the hours of darkness had brought with them the added misery of frost. Even as the snow fell, it seemed to be hardening, adding to the already bone-hard white covering that stretched across the earth below and imparted that peculiar silence to the air that snowfalls bring.

As the sergeant walked, he glanced at the men huddled around the camp fires that formed the perimeter of the dragoons' bivouac. Without exception they looked chilled to the marrow, some ready merely to sink back into the snow and accept the deadly embrace of the elements. The looks on their faces seemed to say to him that they could not care less whether or not the snow covered them in the night. He had heard that men with frostbite were overcome with a gradual feeling, not of painful cold but of pleasing warmth. Lausard thought how easy it would be to give in to this silent assassin. To lie in the arms of death and feel comforted instead of tortured. For this reason, some men made no attempt to sleep. He saw a number of them continually walking back and forth, wearing ruts in the snow. Others did their best to busy themselves with the routine tasks they would normally undertake once ensconced around a camp fire. They tried to clean their carbines with oil that froze on the rags. They wiped down sword blades. Others tended to their horses. The animals were suffering as badly as the men and many had already succumbed to the savagely low temperatures. For every three horses that died, one carcass was kept, cut up and used for meat. The flesh was distributed evenly among the squadron. Melted snow was mixed with what few coffee grains the men could scrape together. Liquor, even more precious in the freezing conditions, was handed around almost grudgingly between companions. Lausard had never experienced conditions like these before and he hoped he never would again, although he decided not to dwell on the possibility for too long.

His stroll around the camp took him from fire to fire but also beyond the sputtering flames and into the woods that grew so thickly on either side of the road. He spoke to sentries, many of whom had the firing mechanisms of their muskets wrapped in oilskin to prevent the hammers and their internal parts from freezing. Only one man in every pair had done this, thereby enabling at least one of the two to get off a shot quickly should the need arise. Lausard came to Rostov and Laubardemont and found the Russian pacing back and forth rubbing his hands together.

'Any sign?' he asked.

'No Cossacks. No wolves,' Rostov said, the breath clouding around him as he spoke.

'It's so quiet,' Laubardemont commented, gazing into the black woods.

'Let us hope it remains like that,' Lausard muttered as he moved on.

He passed another bivouac fire that, he noticed, was burning low.

'Keep that fire burning there.'

He heard the voice and glanced around to see that the words had come from Captain Milliere. The officer was also wandering around the camp, checking the dragoons' defences. Lausard dragged himself through a particularly deep snowdrift to join the officer who stood by while two men pushed more pieces of wood into the fire, waiting for it to ignite. One rolled some of the embers with the tip of his bayonet and the fire grew slightly in strength. Its dull yellow glow illuminated the faces of those who crouched around it. Wrapped in their thick woollen cloaks they glanced up at Lausard and Milliere but little registered in their eyes. Lausard felt as if he were looking into the eyes of dead men. There was no emotion there, no feeling. Only emptiness. As if every last shred of hope, joy and humanity had been sucked from them. They looked like phantoms crowded around the flames in an untidy group that uttered barely a word.

Milliere walked with him as they struggled on, through the ever deepening snow, back towards the fire where most of Lausard's companions waited.

'The Church threatens sinners with the fires of hell,' Milliere mused. 'Perhaps they would be better served promising eternity in a climate such as this. I for one would find that infinitely more terrifying at the moment.'

Lausard smiled beneath the scarf wrapped around his face.

'I didn't know that you believed in God, Captain,' he said.

'I believe that God must have been insane when he made a country like this. There must be more ways for a man to die here in these woods than there is on a battlefield. Cold. Hunger. Wolves.'

'I am sure a battlefield offers a more varied selection of suffering, Captain. Perhaps you more than most should know that.'

Milliere nodded and touched his black eyepatch.

'At least a cannonball or a bullet are quicker,' he observed. 'Better to die like that than by inches. To have the life frozen from you the way it is taken from men now. That is no way to die.'

'Is there a *good* way to die, Captain?'

Milliere shook his head.

'Probably not, Sergeant,' he said. 'But you can be sure that we will all find a way sooner or later. Starvation or sword thrust. Cold or roundshot. It is surely only a matter of time for all of us. I speak, I hope you appreciate, as a realist and not a fatalist.'

'I appreciate *exactly* what you mean, Captain,' grinned Lausard. Both men laughed and it was a sound unusual enough to attract the attention of those close by.

One of the men who looked up was Captain Carras. He was seated on a tree stump close to the fire, his pipe jammed between his teeth. Lausard saluted him and the officer returned the gesture.

'Your men must find it hard in these conditions, Captain,' said Milliere. 'We ourselves suffer and we have the benefit of better equipment and uniforms than they.'

'Let them suffer,' Carras said, gazing into the flames. 'I do not concern myself with their wellbeing.'

'How is it that you are in command of such a unit, Captain?' Lausard asked.

Carras puffed on his pipe but did not look at the sergeant.

'A minor lapse,' he said quietly. 'A penance, if you will.'

'You wear the uniform of a Line infantry officer,' Milliere said. 'What kind of lapse could bring you to where you are now?'

'I stole from a church in Berlin,' Carras confessed. 'I and so many others like me. But our colonel is a religious man. He felt that my misdeed should be paid for. He transferred me to this punishment unit. I do not rejoin my own regiment for another month. Another four weeks of watching those fools,' he nodded in the direction of the men of the punishment unit. 'Twenty-eight more days before I can call myself a *real* soldier once more.'

'It could have been worse,' Royere offered. 'You could have lost your rank. Been court-martialled. Sentenced as were the men you now command.'

'I do not *command* them,' snapped Carras venomously. 'One commands soldiers, not criminals. I *herd* them as a shepherd does wayward sheep. That is my penance.' He puffed on his pipe.

There was a loud whoosh, similar to a swift exhalation of air. It was followed by a thud as the arrow that had sped through the air buried itself in Carras's chest. He remained seated, the long shaft protruding from his sternum, then his eyes rolled upwards in their sockets and he toppled backwards. Immediately, dozens more arrows came hurtling through the air. Some hit the ground and skidded away, others found human targets. Lausard saw two hit a dragoon close to him. Another caught Tabor in the left shoulder. The big man grunted and grabbed the shaft, tugging it free.

'Kalmucks,' hissed Karim, drawing his scimitar and looking towards the woods.

Several shots were fired and, for interminable seconds, Lausard could not be sure if they were coming from the trees or not.

Sonnier snatched up his carbine and pressed it to his shoulder, unsure of where to fire.

The rest of the dragoons were on their feet, some moving towards their tethered horses. There were more shots and, this time, Lausard saw smoke drifting lazily from some trees to his left. A bullet hit the ground close to his foot. Sonnier spun around and fired in the direction of the smoke, reloading with lightning speed.

'As long as the darkness hides them they will remain in the trees,' said Milliere, ducking down beside the body of Carras. He shook the officer gently but, on seeing the blood streaming from his mouth, he was sure the captain was dead.

'And as long as we have fires they will see us,' Lausard snapped, kicking snow on to the feeble blaze before him. The flames sputtered and died as Rocheteau joined him in extinguishing the precious source of light and warmth.

'Put out the fires,' roared Milliere.

Men hurried to complete the order as more salvos of arrows and bullets cut into the dragoons. Three more went down. A horse fell heavily, crushing its rider. As more and more of the bivouac fires were put out, the blackness of the night began to wrap itself around the men like a freezing glove. Visibility was reduced from twenty feet to ten then to five.

'We'll be killing each other in this,' hissed Rocheteau, drawing his sword, barely able to see two feet ahead of him.

The darkness was now almost total. The rattle of swords and carbines echoed through the umbra, mingling with shouts of men and the frightened whinnying of horses. Every so often the sound of a shot would split the snowy night. Erebus barked loudly in the gloom, able to see better than the soldiers. The huge black dog snarled in the direction of some trees less than thirty feet away.

'Find them,' Lausard hissed into his ear and the dog loped off, followed by the sergeant and half a dozen of his companions.

'This is madness, Alain,' Rocheteau said, stumbling over some fallen branches. 'How can we fight men we cannot see?'

'If *we* are blind then so are the Cossacks,' Lausard told him. 'We fight on equal terms now.'

Lausard followed Erebus into the woods. The dog was barking madly. The sergeant saw a shape move in the gloom, as if part of the umbra had detached itself and taken on tangible form. He struck out at it with his sword, satisfied to feel the blade connect and also to hear a scream of pain. Something heavy fell at his feet. He could just make out the shape of a man and drove his sword into that shape again. When he withdrew it, the blood on the blade was steaming.

From the far side of the camp there were more gunshots. Sporadic, uncoordinated fire that came from both sides. Lausard heard a bullet hiss past his ear but was not sure which direction it came from. He ducked instinctively, bumping into one of his own men as he did so. He felt his heart thudding hard against his ribs, his breath freezing in his lungs as he gulped it down. He squinted in the gloom, trying to pick out shapes but it was virtually impossible. There was no way of seeing a man in such stygian blackness unless he was virtually touching you. By the time you spotted your foe, he could run a sword into you, press a musket to your chest or ram a lance through you.

Lausard stumbled on into the woods, occasionally striking out to his right and left with his sword. The blade hacked into trees on more than one occasion. All around him he heard voices. Most of them were French, most jabbering incoherently, as much to let their companions know of their whereabouts as anything else. He heard whispered prayers, curses and grunts as men stumbled around blindly, reluctant to use their weapons but afraid not to. Close to him Erebus barked loudly. Lausard struck out again with his sword and, this time, the blade connected with something soft. He heard a scream and the sound of snapping twigs as someone just ahead of him fell over on the carpet of fallen branches that lay on the forest floor. Erebus snarled and gripped the fallen shape in his huge jaws. Lausard drew closer, guided by the dog's wild snarls and the shouts of the fallen Cossack. The sergeant drove his sword forward and felt it puncture flesh. He heard another scream. And now, from all directions, shouts, screams and gunshots began to fill the void.

Like blind men, the dragoons stumbled about in the woods hacking at foes they could not see, firing at shadows. While, from the cover of the trees, the Kalmucks, as helpless as their intended targets, tried to strike back.

It was insanity personified. Two sets of men trying to kill each other in a darkness so total they could barely see their own hands in front of their faces. Yet still they fired their muskets and carbines and swung swords and sabres, more often than not at the air. Occasionally against their own companions. Lausard had no idea who or what he was striking at; he merely blundered on deeper into the woods, his sword parting air, occasionally cutting into trees, sometimes connecting with human flesh. Flesh that he could only hope belonged to an enemy. And, all the time, the dreadful cacophony of sounds rose into the snow-filled sky. Despite the chill, Lausard felt perspiration beading on his face, such was the extent of his exertions. More than once he felt something warm splash on to his skin and he knew it was blood. He wished he could be certain that it came from a Russian. Less than a foot away from him there was a deafening bang and, in the muzzle flash from the carbine, Lausard and those around him saw, for fleeting seconds, everything before them.

Several Kalmucks were gathered less than a yard from them, some carrying bows, others armed with carbines, pistols or swords.

Lausard had dragoons to his left and right, also heavily armed. He realised that the same thing must be going on all through the woods, all over the camp. Impenetrable blackness suddenly broken by a second of yellowish-red brilliance. A light to kill by. Before the searing flash had even left his retina he struck out with his sword. As he did, he heard other movements. More weapons were discharged. An arrow thudded into a tree, missing him by inches. He heard a scream to his right. Another ahead of him. The sergeant felt something crash into him, the weight knocking him off his feet. He brought the pommel of his sword up and slammed it into the face of the figure that pinned him down, using his strength to roll over and straddle the shape. He managed to drive his sword into the chest, pushing the blade deep. He heard the soft hiss of air escaping from a punctured lung. The bubble of blood rising in a throat and the rattle he knew so well that signalled the end of life. Lausard ripped his blade free and stumbled to his feet, crashing into another figure running through the blackness. He seized the newcomer by the shoulder and spun him round, hurling him up against a tree. As he did he felt the cold touch of a knife blade against his own face.

'Alain.'

He recognised the voice.

It belonged to Rocheteau.

Lausard felt the blade being withdrawn and he himself pulled his sword away from the corporal's stomach. Both men were breathing heavily. A combination of fear and sheer physical effort. They remained locked together for a second longer then Lausard stumbled away. Rocheteau shot out a hand to stop him.

'Let them go,' he hissed.

Two more shots sounded nearby. The fire from the muzzles lit the forest again for a split second.

There were bodies all around them. Kalmucks and dragoons. Some dead, some dying.

'They're running,' Rocheteau said. 'Let them run.'

Lausard sucked in a deep breath and nodded.

From somewhere off to his right he heard another shout, a French voice.

'Cease fire.'

He recognised it as belonging to Captain Milliere.

'Stand where you are,' called Lieutenant Royere.

Erebus barked loudly as if reluctant to give up the battle.

Gaston, the sleeve of his jacket ripped open by an arrowhead, grabbed the huge black dog by the back of the neck and held him firmly.

Time seemed to stand still. For what seemed like an eternity, no one moved. Lausard remained motionless, his breath clouding before him, his sword still gripped in his fist. It was as if none of the dragoons dared take a step forward or back for fear of being shot or hacked at by their own comrades.

'Call out your names,' Lausard said, raising his voice slightly.

'Rocheteau.'

'Baumar.'

'Carbonne.'

'Sonnier.'

The sounds came from all around him. Some slightly ahead.

'Tigana.'

'Karim.'

'Gaston.'

Lausard nodded in the gloom and swallowed hard, his heart beginning to slow somewhat.

'The Kalmucks have fled,' he called. 'Those around you in the darkness are your own companions. Do not open fire or strike out.'

He heard heavy breathing from nearby.

'I said it was madness,' Rocheteau gasped.

Lausard did not reply. Only as he strode back towards the camp site did he think to wipe the blood from his face.

'Will they attack again?'

Roussard moved closer to the fire and looked around him in the direction of the woods.

'Hard to say,' Milliere answered. He looked at his own pocket watch.

It was 2.35 a.m.

'Have all the dead been buried?' the officer continued.

'As far as it was possible, Captain,' Lausard said. 'The ground is like iron. The punishment unit could hardly turn the earth.'

'How many did we lose?' Milliere wanted to know.

'Nine dead, twice that number wounded,' said Lieutenant Royere.

'Killed by which side?' Delacor mused.

'We all know who killed Captain Carras,' Tabor offered. 'We all saw him die.'

'We know that, you half-wit,' snapped Delacor. He looked scornfully at the big man. His shoulder was bandaged but the arrow had not penetrated too deeply mainly due to the thickness of the clothing he wore. Bonet patted him on the arm reassuringly.

'Captain.'

All eyes turned in the direction of the shout.

The dragoons huddled around the fire got to their feet, some reaching for their weapons.

Lausard heard a low rumble coming from the south. Erebus began barking loudly.

'It's a light cavalry patrol,' Varcon shouted.

'Ours or theirs?' Laubardemont muttered warily.

Lausard squinted through the gloom and saw the leading horsemen canter into view. He saw the red pelisses they wore, their shakos protected by oilskin. Their horses looked lathered despite the cold and the men themselves were as white as ghosts. They looked as if they had been in the saddle for hours. The leading rider, a lieutenant in his early thirties with a huge bushy moustache, ran appraising eyes over the dragoons and reined in his horse.

'Who is in command here?' he asked.

Captain Milliere stepped forward. The lieutenant of hussars saluted and handed Milliere a rolled-up piece of paper which he scanned quickly then tossed into the fire. It caught and flared brightly for a second.

'We are to rejoin the rest of the army,' he said.

'As quickly as possible,' the hussar officer urged.

'I read the order, Lieutenant,' Milliere said dismissively.

'A battle?' Lausard wondered aloud.

'The Russians are massing before us at Eylau,' said the hussar.

'Ten miles north-east of here,' Bonet mused, glancing at the map he had pulled from inside his tunic.

'The Emperor needs all his men at that place,' said the hussar.

'We will be there,' Milliere assured the light cavalryman.

The patrol rode on, along the snow-covered road, gradually disappearing into the enveloping woods.

'What of those men?' said Bonet, indicating the punishment unit.

'They are no longer our responsibility,' Milliere said, walking towards his horse. 'I want the entire squadron saddled, mounted and ready to leave within the hour. The conditions will slow us down. It will take us until daybreak to reach Eylau even if we ride all night.'

'And are not ambushed by Cossacks on the way,' Royere offered.

Many of the dragoons scurried off to prepare their mounts. Only Lausard hesitated.

'The chasing is over, Sergeant,' said Milliere. 'Are you not grateful for that? You always seem more eager than most to enter a battle. It seems you have your wish.'

'A soldier's business is fighting, Captain. You know that.'

Milliere nodded.

'Forgive me for not welcoming yet another confrontation with quite the relish *you* reserve for it, Sergeant,' said the officer.

'I always thought I would find my destiny on a battlefield, Captain,' Lausard said quietly. 'If I am to find my death upon one too, then so be it.' He turned and walked towards his horse. All around him, the woods were filled with the sounds of hundreds of men preparing themselves and their horses for yet another conflict. And more than one of them wondered if this night would be their last on earth. As the snow continued to fall, the squadron formed itself into a well-drilled column and moved off into the blackness.

EIGHTEEN

Napoleon Bonaparte pulled gently on the reins of his magnificent white Arab stallion, causing the animal to slow its pace slightly. Due to the rutted, snow- and frost-encrusted ground, the Emperor's progress had been unbearably slow and he was becoming impatient. It showed in his expression. He pulled up the fur collar of his greatcoat and shivered in the saddle, patting his horse's neck. The animal snorted, two thick jets of condensation blasting from its nostrils, forming a dense cloud as it combined with the breath of the other animals around the Emperor. Ahead of the Corsican rode twenty mounted chausseurs, their fur kolpacks and their red-tipped green plumes covered with oilskin to protect them from the elements. Another fifty formed the rear of the small column. All of the men of his escort were wrapped in cloaks or encased in extra jackets in an attempt to keep out the searing cold. Beside him, Marshal Berthier rode with his head slightly bowed to protect his eyes against the biting wind. The feathers on his bicorn danced madly in the wind as it blew. More than once he had to keep a grip on the headgear to prevent it being torn from his head by the growing strength of the gusts. His blue cloak was flecked with snow, the worst of which had stopped during the night. For that, at least, the French were grateful. However, the passing of the snow had given way to a drop in temperature and Napoleon glanced at his Chief of Staff as if for a confirmation of this. Berthier pulled a thermometer from his pocket and held it up in one gloved hand, watching the mercury fall steadily. It finally settled at minus eighteen degrees. The Corsican nodded ruefully, his eyes fixed once more upon the sight that had made not just him but his entire escort slow its advance.

A single rider was spurring his bay mount through the powdery snow at incredible speed. He had one gloved hand raised above his head and Napoleon could see that he held something in it. Berthier pulled his telescope from his portmanteau and trained it on the rider. Other men around the Emperor began doing the same. Finally the Corsican himself trained his glass on the rider, watching as he sped onwards. The entire escort had slowed to a walk and the officer commanding the chausseurs glanced back at his men, preparing to give the order to draw swords should it be necessary.

General Rapp squinted through his own telescope, picking out details of the man's uniform. The rider was clad in a uniform like that of a hussar but weeks of campaigning in such hostile conditions had robbed the light cavalryman of the usual vibrant demeanour associated with those of his kind. His uniform looked washed out and filthy. His shako was wrapped in oilskin and he wore a grey cloak over his pelisse. Colours like white, fawn and amaranth were hidden beneath layers of dirt.

'Aide-de-camp,' murmured Duroc, able, by now, to make out the man's features. He could see the huge bushy moustache the rider sported and the long plaits that hung from each side of his head and lashed around like serpents' tails as he rode.

'But from who?' Napoleon mused. 'Murat? Soult?'

'He seems to be attired in the manner of your brother-in-law, sire,' Rapp mused. 'Those who carry messages for Marshal Soult wear yellow and sky blue and have a tendency to be less flamboyant. As befits the character of their commander.'

Napoleon managed a smile and some of the other staff officers chuckled quietly.

The aide was now less than a hundred yards away and the escort of chausseurs parted to allow him passage to the Emperor. He rode towards the Corsican, reining his horse in and saluting. Berthier took the communication from the ADC then handed it to the Corsican who scanned it quickly before passing it back to his Chief of Staff.

'The Russians are in considerable strength before, within and around Eylau itself, sire,' said the aide breathlessly. 'Marshal Murat requests reinforcements immediately if he is to take the village and hold it.'

'I gave no orders for such an action,' snapped Napoleon. 'What of the corps of Marshal Soult? Are they similarly engaged?'

'Most of the infantry have been committed, sire,' the ADC remarked. 'The 18th and 46th Line regiments in particular have already suffered considerable casualties both from cannon fire and the attacks of Russian cavalry.'

'If Bennigsen thinks this is the beginning of an attack he may well retire once more,' Napoleon hissed. 'He will continue to run. Deprive me of the battle I desire.'

'You said yourself, sire, that Bennigsen would not forgo the chance to use Eylau and its surrounding countryside as a defensive position,' Berthier reminded the Emperor. 'It is of outstanding merit for the Russians if they are to stand and fight.'

'*If* they do?'

'They show every sign of holding their position presently, sire,' the aide remarked, sucking in a deep breath. 'What am I to tell Marshal Murat?'

Napoleon looked once more at the communication sent from his brother-in-law, his eyes narrowing slightly.

'He and Soult have committed men too early,' the Corsican said angrily. 'They have compromised me. Why did they show such a lack of discipline? Such a disregard for my wishes?'

'The fault was not all theirs, sire, if you will forgive my impertinence,' the aide said, holding his Emperor's stare. 'They were placed in a position that gave them little choice but to commit men forward.'

'What set of circumstances can have forced them into such rash and impetuous action?' the Corsican demanded.

'Apparently, your own personal attendants, complete with your baggage and field kitchen, arrived in Eylau, unaware that the Russian outpost lines were only yards beyond the village itself at that time.'

Napoleon listened intently as the aide continued.

'They were attacked by an enemy patrol, sire,' the ADC went on. 'One that possibly sought or hoped to find you yourself within their reach. A detachment of the Imperial Guard prevented their destruction. Marshal Soult's men, who had been positioned at the gates of the village, entered Eylau to support the guard. The Russians then assumed our men were in the process of claiming the village for themselves and ordered up reinforcements to seize it. That was three hours ago, sire.'

'So, what began as a skirmish has escalated into a full-scale battle,' Napoleon said flatly. 'A battle that still rages even with the coming of darkness.' He looked up at the sky. It was already darkening alarmingly with the onset of dusk. Another two hours and night would have fallen across the land like an impenetrable black blanket.

'If you do not send them support, sire, they will be destroyed,' the aide offered.

'If they *can* take Eylau and hold it, sire, then surely it is *we* who will be in the strongest position,' Duroc interjected.

Berthier had already unfurled a map and was jabbing a finger at part of it.

'A plateau overlooks the valley and the village within it, sire,' he offered. 'It would, indeed, be advantageous to us to be in possession of such high ground.'

Napoleon gazed straight ahead for an instant, apparently lost in his own deliberations. Those around him fixed their stares upon him, waiting for some kind of decision. The bay ridden by the ADC tossed its head wildly as if also impatient for an answer. The Corsican finally turned to Berthier who had produced a quill and some ink and was struggling to balance them while still in the saddle.

'Tell Murat and Soult to hold the village,' Napoleon said sharply. 'They may draw upon support from the corps of Marshal Augereau if necessary. But Augereau is to commit his troops at his own discretion. Tell him I will be with him just after nightfall.'

Berthier scribbled frantically and handed the order to the ADC who saluted and took the piece of paper. He turned his horse in one fluid movement and galloped away. Napoleon and his companions watched as the aide drove his horse back across the snow-covered ground, finally disappearing over the low rise he had originally crested.

'It seems the battle I sought has begun without me,' Napoleon murmured.

Lausard heard the sound of cannon fire and felt his heart begin to thump that little bit harder. Across a land covered by snow, the sound seemed to carry further. Every bang and explosion was amplified. He urged his horse on slightly, aware that the fighting was close now. The sky, already heavy with cloud and darkening with the approach of late afternoon, was also filled with thick smoke rising from what the sergeant guessed must have been a considerable number of cannon and muskets. The dragoons were approaching the engagement via an icy road that rose at a gentle angle towards the crest of a slope. Another hundred or so yards and they would emerge on the ridge. Lausard kept his eyes firmly fixed on the slope, eager to see beyond. Just ahead of him, Captain Milliere and Lieutenant Royere also seemed to be exhorting greater efforts from their tired mounts and, all around him, Lausard knew the usual mixture of expressions would be colouring the faces of his companions. Expectation. Fear. Doubt. All those emotions ran through the mind of a soldier before a battle and many more too.

The dragoons crested the ridge and Milliere held up his arm to slow the column slightly.

'My God,' whispered Varcon looking upon the scene that lay before him.

Lausard said nothing. He merely allowed his gaze to travel over the terrain before him and, more importantly, the action that was unfolding upon it. The ridge on which they now waited sloped away before them into a shallow valley. Lausard saw thick woods to the left and right and also beyond, on the far slopes. These more distant ridges were a sea of green-uniformed Russian troops, drawn up in two or three impenetrable lines that seemed to stretch the full length of the valley. Before them, artillery batteries were firing sporadically into advancing French infantry and cavalry. But, Lausard noticed, most of their fire was directed at the large village in the valley. Smoke was already billowing from several of the buildings and he could see troops of both sides advancing towards the conglomeration of buildings. A church spire thrust upwards towards the heaving sky like an accusatory finger.

'Eylau,' Bonet murmured, nodding in the direction of the village.

Lausard could see bodies scattered over the snowy ground. Dead horses also lay around, as if dropped from the sky like bloodied confetti. Some had their riders with them. Some slumped across their mounts, others sprawled out beside them. The snow that had not already been trampled to mud by marching feet was stained crimson in many places around the approaches to Eylau itself.

Milliere pulled his telescope from his jacket and trained it on the village. Lausard did likewise but he swept his back and forth across the lines of enemy troops standing motionless on the far side of the valley. Some were partially hidden by the woods, others momentarily obscured by rolling banks of smoke that drifted across the terrain as artillery continued to blast away at Eylau and the French troops assaulting it. A number of aerial explosions sent jagged lumps of metal raining down on the attacking French and Lausard saw many fall. He searched the Russian lines for the batteries of howitzers that were lobbing explosive rounds so effectively into the air but he could not see them. He guessed it was incendiary rounds that had started the fires in Eylau itself.

'Little wonder the Emperor wanted all his troops here,' Milliere murmured, watching as a detachment of French hussars charged towards a battery of Russian six-pounders a little to the south of Eylau. The guns roared and simply swept away most of the hussars. By the time the smoke from their gaping barrels had cleared, only a few horses and men were still standing. They turned and retreated with the sweating Russian gunners pouring grapeshot into them as they fled.

A battery of French horse artillery situated at the bottom of the ridge, less than one hundred yards from where the dragoons sat, fired back and Lausard noticed that, despite the cold, many had discarded their tunics and were working furiously in just their shirts and breeches. He watched as one man swabbed out the barrel and another immediately pushed a four-pound lead ball into the yawning maw. Along with its charge, the ball was pushed down the barrel and, as the troopers stood clear, another of their companions applied the portfire to the touchhole at the end of the barrel. There was a loud blast and the gun shot back six or seven feet. The gunners, wreathed in smoke, immediately set about manoeuvring the weapon back into position and, as soon as that was done, they repeated the process again. This continued with robotic regularity as all four guns in the battery kept up a constant fire. Blind in the sulphurous clouds spewing from the muzzles of their guns, the artillerymen continued with their task, returning fire as best they could in the direction of a much larger Russian battery located on a slight rise between the intersection of two roads. Lausard could see two columns of French infantry swinging round from the direction of Eylau itself to meet the threat of this battery. An officer mounted on a grey led them, his sword gripped in one bloodied hand. Through his telescope, Lausard could see that the officer had also been wounded in the shoulder and knee. He was gripping the pommel of his saddle with his free hand, trying to prevent himself toppling to the ground. The eagle bearer of the unit lifted the flag high into the air and the infantry advanced towards the Russian battery. The three-coloured oiled silk standard itself was holed in many places and one corner was burned black.

The infantry had gone barely twenty yards when the double ranks of green-clad Russian infantry protecting the battery opened fire. The musket balls cut into the column, downing many of the French and they hesitated. Two of the Russian cannon were being turned to face them and, seconds later, while the French were trying to reform, Lausard saw them blasted by two massive volleys of canister fire. Thirty-six three-ounce lead balls in each discharge tore through the French infantry like a scythe through wheat. The officer on the grey was hit several times and blown from his saddle. He crashed to the ground close to his horse, the animal also being killed in the monstrous blasts. Dozens of men went down in heaps, sprawling on ground already saturated with blood and littered with corpses.

'What do we do, Captain?' Lausard wanted to know.

'We cannot stand by idly while our countrymen are slaughtered,' Royere offered.

Milliere nodded almost imperceptibly and glanced at Gaston. The bugler understood and pulled the brass instrument from his portmanteau. He wiped the mouthpiece then blasted out the first few notes that told the dragoons they were to form up in lines. The manoeuvre was completed with consummate skill and speed, such as can only be done by men hardened and drilled for so many years in the ways of war.

'I will lead the first squadron,' Milliere said to Royere. 'Bring the second yourself.'

The lieutenant nodded and put spurs to his mount, gathering the second squadron behind him in two long lines. Horses pawed the icy ground impatiently. Riders took advantage of the brief moment of calm to prepare themselves. Weapons were checked. Prayers were whispered or oaths murmured. Moreau, close to Lausard in the front line, crossed himself. Rocheteau merely sat motionless, gazing first at the smoke rising from Eylau and then at the Russian battery on the far side of the valley that he knew was the dragoons' target.

'Prepare to advance,' roared Milliere. 'Draw swords.'

There was a deafening metallic hiss as hundreds of three-foot blades were pulled simultaneously from their scabbards. Lausard saw some of the horse artillery at the bottom of the slope look around at the lines of dragoons arrayed behind them. An aerial shell-burst tore across the sky. More choking smoke, blown by the wind, gusted across the valley bringing with it the smell of gunpowder and death. It was a smell Lausard had come to know well. He swallowed hard, his pulse now racing. The adrenalin sped through his veins and he tried to control his breathing, anxious to be moving. To be hurtling towards the Russian battery, seemingly oblivious to the fact that the six-pound cannons were spewing death with every blast. Lausard had no fear of death. If death was to come, he hoped it would be relatively quick and the pain should be over quickly, if he was lucky. Only a life without purpose caused pain every day. He gripped the hilt of his sword more tightly and waited for the signal to advance. Ahead of him, the guidon of his regiment fluttered in the breeze. Lausard felt a swell of pride as he looked at it, his heart now thudding hard against his ribs.

The thundering of hooves to his left caused him to turn and he saw several men heading towards the dragoons. All were dressed in the dark blue jackets and breeches of staff officers and aides. All wore bicorns, some adorned with the white plumes of colonels. Others sported red, or a combination of the two colours. They were accompanied by a small detachment of mounted Line chausseurs. Lausard saw that the man they flanked was mounted on a powerful-looking black horse and the elaborate lace and embroidery on his red shabraque and pistol covers immediately marked him out as being of very senior rank. As he came closer, Lausard saw the wisps of dark hair protruding from beneath the man's gold-trimmed bicorn and he recognised the newcomer as Marshal Nicolas Jean de Dieu Soult.

'Where are you sending your men, Captain?' Soult called, reining in his mount. His entourage came to a halt around him.

'That Russian battery is doing murder, sir,' said Milliere, pointing to the six-pounders across the valley. 'I sought to relieve the pressure on our infantry in that area.'

'A noble idea but there is pressure on our troops everywhere on this field,' Soult said. 'I have more use for your men there.' He jabbed a finger behind him in the direction of Eylau.

More than one of the dragoons within earshot shuddered as they looked towards the smoke-shrouded village.

'And the Russian artillery, sir?' Milliere persisted.

'One cavalry charge will not stop them, Captain,' Soult announced. 'If it could I am sure Marshal Murat would have launched his men at them before now.' There was a note of scorn in Soult's voice and he glanced around at some of the staff officers close to him, as if to support his statement. A number of them nodded sagely but said nothing.

'Are we to fight on foot or horseback, sir?' Milliere wanted to know.

'You will fight however I deem it necessary for you to fight, Captain,' Soult said, his voice low. He made no attempt to raise it despite the constant thudding of cannon fire rolling across the battlefield. 'Now take your men down into the valley. Support the infantry already within Eylau and cover those on its outskirts.'

Milliere saluted.

As Lausard and the others watched, Soult turned his mount and, with his staff following, he rode quickly across the top of the ridge towards the southern end where many of them saw him pull out his telescope and survey the battle.

'Darkness is less than an hour away,' Lausard said, glancing up first at the sky then at the masses of men on both sides arrayed around and within Eylau. As the dragoons moved slowly down the slope towards the village, the rattle of musket fire became more audible, mingling with the ever present roar of cannon. Orders were shouted and Lausard saw dozens of wounded being removed to the rear, some on flat wagons that bumped over the icy ground and only served to increase the suffering of those they carried.

The dragoons continued in the direction of Eylau, the land flattening out beneath them.

'I looked at the map shortly before we arrived here,' said Bonet. 'The land we are on now is usually marshland and streams. We are on nothing more than frozen water.'

'I hope it can take our weight,' said Roussard.

'If it can take Joubert's weight it will accommodate *us*,' Rocheteau said, grinning. He slapped the big man playfully on the shoulder.

Delbene looked grimly towards the seething mass of men around Eylau. Moreau crossed himself. Delacor felt for the axe in his portmanteau. Karim tapped the hilt of his scimitar.

'And you volunteered for *this*?' Giresse said, glancing at Gormier.

'I felt it was my duty,' Gormier told him. 'I would give my life for the Emperor. For France.'

'That is exactly what it looks as if you will be doing,' Lausard told him.

Some of the other men managed to laugh.

Laubardemont did not.

'And *you* should have stayed in the artillery,' Rocheteau said to the former gunner. 'Better to fire at an enemy from a thousand yards away than to have him as close as the length of a bayonet.'

Laubardemont did not answer. His face was pale and he was shivering slightly. He feared that it was not all merely due to the savage weather.

'Infantry, cavalry or artillery. What difference does it make which uniform you're wearing when you get your head blown off?' Delacor snapped.

'Shut up,' hissed Roussard. 'Do you think any of us *wants* to die?'

'I don't *care* if you want to die. It isn't up to me,' Delacor said. 'It's up to the Russian who shoots you or stabs you or clubs you to death with his musket.'

'It is in the hands of God who will die and who will not,' Moreau said, crossing himself.

'Our destinies lie in the hands of Bonaparte,' Lausard interjected. 'They always have and they always will. For as long as we wear these uniforms.'

Above them, a howitzer shell exploded with a loud bang.

'That might not be for too much longer,' Rocheteau said, ducking involuntarily as several pieces of shrapnel struck the ground a little ahead of the dragoons.

Two columns of infantry were advancing towards Eylau. Lausard saw that the uniforms of most were filthy, most already stained with blood. Many had been wounded, their injuries rapidly and crudely bandaged in readiness for what was obviously another assault. They passed the waiting horsemen, some of whom glanced disdainfully at the dragoons.

'That's it,' said Delacor. 'Let the dog-faces have their day. Street fighting is for infantry. Not for us.'

There was more musket fire from the direction of Eylau. It was virtually non-stop now and, Lausard thought, even increasing in ferocity. The entire village was blanketed in reeking smoke and, from within that man-made fog came shouts, screams and curses. They mingled with the roar of cannon and the blasts of howitzer and mortar rounds that were exploding almost without interruption. The sky was definitely darkening but Lausard realised that the noxious fumes hanging over Eylau were reducing visibility even more. A battery of French eight-pounders were towed into the village by struggling teams of horses. Once unlimbered, they swept the streets with canister shot, sometimes killing friend and foe alike. The large lead balls cut holes in the walls of buildings, so great was their power and so short the range at which they were fired. Any men hit by the murderous blasts merely disintegrated. The dragoons moved closer to the village, supporting the infantry columns as they strode into the streets.

'First squadron, dismount, fight on foot,' shouted Milliere. 'Lieutenant Royere, you keep the second squad here. Guard our horses, but be prepared to move up if I send for you.' Royere saluted. The leading ranks of dragoons swung themselves out of the saddle. Lausard pulled his Charleville free and quickly inspected the firing mechanism, ensuring that it had not been frozen by the weather or damaged by any stray shrapnel. He pulled the oilskin cover from around it then slotted the fifteen-inch bayonet on to the end of the barrel and moved closer to Milliere. The dragoons moved forward in open order, ready to pick their way through streets already piled high with the dead of both sides. Lausard and his companions had no idea how long the fighting had been raging before their own arrival upon the battlefield but, from the large numbers of dead clad in both French and Russian uniforms, it appeared to the sergeant as if the village could already have changed hands more than once. He saw several dead Imperial Guard troops, one propped up against the wall of a house, his body untouched apart from a single bullet hole in the middle of his forehead. His eyes were still open and he seemed to be watching the advancing dragoons. The man lying next to him had been cut in two by a roundshot. The six-pound ball still lay close to the body. The street was awash with blood.

Lausard looked ahead, squinting through the smoke, and saw

that the worst of the fighting seemed to be taking place around the church. French infantry and artillery were positioned behind the low walls, keeping up a murderous fire, despite the hail of mortar shells and roundshot that the Russians were pouring into the area. Lausard saw even more bodies heaped around the entrance to the cemetery and he and Karim were forced to clamber over several corpses as they made their way into the graveyard. Some bodies had even been dragged across holes in the wall to create grotesque ramparts behind which the French infantry sheltered. Every now and then a cannonball would hit one of these fleshy fortifications, further pulverising the corpses there. Body parts lay everywhere. Lausard stepped over a severed arm as he took up position behind a shattered gravestone and sighted his musket.

All around him, his companions found their own positions, some mingling with the exhausted and bloodied French infantry, others using the carriages of eight-pounders as cover. There were two guns in the cemetery, both spewing canister in the direction of the oncoming Russians. Within minutes, Lausard was finding it difficult to breathe, the noxious stench of gunpowder, burning cartridge paper, scorched flesh, sweat, excrement and blood all mingled together to form a smell he knew only too well from previous battles. Millions of tiny cinders filled the air and he had to blink constantly to ensure his vision did not become too clouded by the black embers. He tore the top from a cartridge with his teeth and loaded his carbine, firing quickly and expertly into the mass of Russian infantry before him.

To his right, Sonnier shot a Russian officer down then ducked as a roundshot thudded into the earth close to him. It sent up a small fountain of iron-hard mud, a piece of which struck him in the side of the head. The man next to him was not as fortunate. The six-pound shot spun across the ground and took off his leg at the knee. Seconds later another mortar exploded close to the church. Lumps of hot lead cut down anyone close. One piece punched another hole in the door of the building. Smoke was already rising from the church and Sonnier glanced up to see that there were French troops in the bell tower, sniping at the attacking Russians from their lofty perch.

Gormier screamed in pain as a sliver of lead cut through his cheek. It carved effortlessly through the flesh and tore out two teeth before exiting through his other cheek. Blood filled his mouth and he slumped forward momentarily. Joubert reached across to him, pulling him away from the wall behind which they sheltered. Gormier could see the big man mouthing words but he could barely hear them. The constant roar of cannon and musket fire was deafening. Joubert himself ducked low as a roundshot struck the earth less than a foot from him. It bounced twice, smashed one of the crosses in the cemetery then hurtled on, bringing down part of the outer wall before rolling to a halt against a pile of corpses in the street beyond.

Lausard could see that the Russian infantry, moving in three ponderous columns, were almost upon Eylau now. He and his companions reloaded with even more immediacy, their mouths filled with grains of powder, their throats already parched. Eyes bleary with tears and pricked by the cinders filling the air. Few could see more than a few yards around them because of the choking smoke. Seven or eight of the dragoons were gathered together by Milliere and waited for his order before sending one concentrated volley into the head of the nearest column. Then a howitzer shell exploded in the air above the cemetery and Lausard saw three of them hit the ground as the hot shrapnel cut through them. Charvet was hit in the left calf. The metal ripped easily through his boot and tore into the fleshy part of his leg. As Tigana scrambled to help him he too was hit. A piece of metal caught him on the left temple, slamming into his brass helmet and knocking him off balance. He pitched sideways, barely conscious. Lausard ran forward, ducked low to avoid the concentrated volleys of musket fire now pouring from the leading ranks of the Russian troops. Two lead balls sang off his helmet, another struck his shoulder but he ran on and grabbed Tigana under both arms, dragging him towards the church.

Rocheteau and Delbene moved in on either side of him, carbines levelled as the first of the Russian infantry began scrambling over the low wall of the cemetery. They were met by bayonets, bullets and a final, devastating volley of canister from the two eight-pounders there. Screams of agony could be heard through the constant roar of gunfire as men of both sides fought hand to hand in the churchyard. High up in the bell tower, the French voltigeurs continued to fire down into the green-clad mass that was not only battering its way into the cemetery but sweeping around both sides of it.

'We'll be cut off,' shouted Lausard, glancing to his left and right.

'Fall back,' roared an infantry officer, waving his sword in the air. Seconds later, two Russian bayonets were rammed into his back, one driven so hard it erupted several inches from his chest.

The infantry needed no second order. They scrambled away as best they could and Lausard and his companions did likewise. The gunners abandoned their artillery to the Russians, although Lausard did see one gunner using his long barrel swab like a staff, flooring several Russians before he was shot down and bayoneted. However, when the French reached the gates of the cemetery, they re-formed into a ragged line and fired another volley into the Russians. Those up in the bell tower added their fire to the frantic last salvo, knowing now that they were cut off from their companions. Their options seemed limited, Lausard thought. Either attempt to fight their way out or wait for the Russians to overrun them inside the building. Either way they seemed doomed.

There was gunfire coming from the houses all around the cemetery and Lausard realised that the French infantry barricaded within the buildings had held their fire until they were sure they would not hit their own men. Now, as the French fell back, these hidden infantry opened up on the Russians as the leading troops spilled out of the cemetery into the streets. Dozens went down but by sheer weight of numbers the green-clad infantry poured out into the streets, cursing in their mother tongue. One of the leading troops carried a standard. Lausard saw him shot down and watched as the next man snatched up the valued flag. He too was hit but yet another infantryman rescued the standard and bellowed encouragement to his countrymen as they swarmed around him and towards the houses occupied by the French.

'Pull back,' bellowed Milliere, firing his own carbine at the oncoming hordes.

Dragging their wounded, the dragoons made their way back through the streets of Eylau. Lausard could barely breathe now, so thick was the smoke that filled the narrow thoroughfares. That, combined with the rapidly descending darkness, had already cut visibility to less than twenty yards. In places, only the blinding flare of muzzle flashes revealed the presence of men. But their screams and shouts could be heard, rising into one deafening cacophony, reaching to the sky itself.

Delbene hit the ground hard, clutching at his right shoulder, but Kruger and Roussard dragged him to his feet, urging him on. French infantry, driven from the houses by the savage Russian attack, were also spilling on to the streets now and Lausard and his companions found themselves caught up in this flood of humanity. The French re-formed and retreated slowly, seemingly oblivious to the now more concentrated fire being directed at them. Two infantrymen, less than a yard from Lausard, were hit by the same roundshot. One was decapitated, the other cut in two at the waist. The dragoon sergeant felt something warm soaking through his already sodden clothes and he knew only too well what it was. Most of the men around him were also spattered with blood, some of it their own. Lausard hawked and spat, trying to clear his mouth of the taste of gunpowder and smoke. Men around coughed and rubbed their eyes. Most were blacked by smoke and dirt, grimed further by blood. The dragoons staggered from the village watched by their companions in the second squadron, a number of whom dismounted to help the dazed and battered survivors. Lausard saw more French infantry formed up in column, ready to march back into the living hell that was Eylau. He sucked in a deep breath and gripped his carbine more tightly. The barrel was hot in his hand.

'Let them have the stinking village,' Delacor hissed, wiping blood from his nose.

'It will be dark in fifteen minutes,' Lausard said, looking up at the lowering heavens. 'With the night will come frost. Where would you rather spend the night, Delacor? In the open on these ridges or inside one of the houses in there?' He nodded towards the village.

'Do you think they will make us retake it, Alain?' Rocheteau asked breathlessly.

Lausard did not answer, but merely looked around at the drained faces of his companions.

'We will see,' he said, finally.

Within the village, the sound of gunfire continued.

NINETEEN

Within the square formed by the grenadiers of the Imperial Guard, Napoleon Bonaparte sat on a bundle of straw and gazed into the roaring flames of the fire. More than a dozen potatoes were baking in the embers and the Corsican used a long stick to turn them over, careful not to cook them for so long that the skins split. He could smell the aroma of the cooking vegetables as he sat quietly amidst the men who formed his personal bodyguard. Every now and then, the blue-clad men, all over six feet tall, would approach the fire and place more kindling on it, stoking it to even greater heights. Napoleon was not sure where they found the wood but he did not care. These men he called his children would sooner starve or freeze themselves than see *him* suffer any form of deprivation. He looked around at them and felt a great swell of pride. The Corsican turned another of the potatoes and then glanced at his pocket watch. It was almost nine thirty. The blackness of the night was total apart from the sputtering camp fires that marked both the French and the Russian lines on either side of the valley. Within the depression itself, the village of Eylau was surrounded by camp fires, French troops gathered around them in a desperate attempt to keep warm. The Emperor had a clear view of the entire valley and its surrounding ridges from his precipitous position on the plateau of Ziegelhof. The only problem was that the height of the plateau meant it was even more exposed to the icy wind that was gusting across the landscape. Napoleon moved a little closer to the fire, unable to drive the chill from his bones. He had known cold before but never anything to compare with these intolerable conditions.

'It is already minus twenty-five, sire,' said Berthier, consulting his thermometer, 'and the temperature is dropping constantly. By midnight it will be forty below freezing. One of the engineers says we are to expect thirty degrees of frost before morning.'

'No heat, no shelter and no food,' said Napoleon quietly. 'Do I ask too much of my army, Berthier?'

'Every man in *La Grande Armée* would follow you to the very ends of life, sire, you know that,' the Chief of Staff remarked, himself moving nearer the roaring flames.

'Many already have, this very day,' Napoleon remarked. 'What are our losses so far?'

'Close to four thousand, sire, but we *are* in possession of Eylau once again. At least the men there will pass the night in some measure of comfort, although perhaps that is a somewhat inadequate word to describe their position.'

'Why did Bennigsen withdraw?' the Corsican mused, looking into the fire as if expecting to find an answer in the flames. 'Why give up such a strong defensive position? Does he mean to run again during the night? Will he once more deny me the battle I seek?'

'It does not appear so, sire,' Marshal Soult offered, pulling up the collar of his cloak. 'I feel that the Russian intention is to give battle come the morning.'

'What are their current dispositions?' Napoleon wanted to know.

'After Bennigsen withdrew his men from Eylau he repositioned his fourth division on the eastern heights,' said Berthier, gesturing in the direction of the Russian lines away in the darkness. 'General Barclay has withdrawn to the left of Bagavout and his men around the village of Serpallan. Bennigsen's first line extends from Serpallan along the heights to Schloditten, passing across the Friedland road less than one thousand paces from Eylau itself. The slope leading up to his positions seems relatively easy to traverse, as is the one leading down from our own positions here.'

Napoleon took a potato from the fire and split it with a knife.

He then began to eat, cradling the hot vegetable in his gloved hands. He passed one to Berthier, another to Soult and another to those aides who stood close by. The men ate hungrily.

'Intelligence reports that, commencing from the extreme right at Schloditten, there are twelve cavalry regiments with possibly six more slightly in advance of this line,' the Chief of Staff continued. 'Beyond those are Cossacks, hoping to make contact with Lestocq and his Prussians who are reportedly marching to this location.'

'Let us hope that Marshal Ney can prevent their arrival,' Soult offered. 'We are already outnumbered here without any more hostile troops joining the enemy.'

Napoleon looked briefly at Soult then back at Berthier who continued.

'Eleven infantry regiments connect Markov's cavalry with the rest of the line,' said the Chief of Staff. 'There is a second line comprised of ten more infantry regiments. A third line of five more is to be used as the Russian reserve. They are positioned around the village of Anklappen, Bennigsen's headquarters. Tutchkov commands the right, Sacken the centre and Tolstoi the left. Doctorov has the reserve.'

'What of Bennigsen's remaining cavalry and artillery?' Napoleon wanted to know.

'It is behind the centre and the left flank, partly deployed and partly in column, commanded by Gallitzin.' Berthier said. 'Of the artillery, sixty horse artillery guns are at Anklappen. Four hundred guns and howitzers are ranged in front of the first line of Russian troops. Bennigsen has drawn up a battery of seventy heavy guns directly opposite Eylau. Another of sixty on the right and a third, numbering forty, between the central battery and the village of Klein Sausgarten slightly to his rear. It is a formidable array of firepower, sire.'

Napoleon nodded.

'I, better than most, know the value of artillery, Berthier,' the Corsican mused, a slight smile on his face. The smile vanished as a flurry of snow swept across the plateau. He shivered once more.

'The entire Russian army covers a frontage of less than two

miles, sire,' Soult added. 'Their formations are dense, tightly packed. They will be easy targets for our own artillery. Our own men are spread more thinly and are more extended than the Muscovites.'

'Because there are fewer of them,' the Corsican mused. 'Our forty-five thousand against their sixty-seven thousand. How are our own troops placed?'

'As you ordered, sire,' the Chief of Staff replied. 'Legrand's division is just beyond Eylau between the Königsberg and the Friedland roads. Schinner's brigade are in the houses near the church of Eylau. Ferey's hold the left of the village.'

'They at least have some degree of cover against the elements, then,' Napoleon mused.

'Unlike St Hilaire's division,' Berthier continued. 'They are bivouacked in the open ground towards Rothenen. Ahead of them are Milhaud's cavalry. Grouchy's and Klein's horsemen are behind Eylau to the left and right of the Landsberg road. To the left of the village are the cavalry brigades of Colbert, Guyot, Bruyere and d'Hautpol. Marshal Augereau's corps are camped within and to the front of Storchnest and Tenknitten. Marshal Murat has the cavalry reserve to the right, level with where we stand now.'

'I would move the guard back but I do not want the Russians to have any idea that they hold the upper hand in numbers,' said the Corsican. 'I am forced to place my most valued troops within range of the enemy before a shot has even been fired.'

'What choice do you have, sire?' Berthier insisted.

Napoleon did not answer.

All heads turned at the sound of approaching horses. Napoleon stood up when he saw the two horsemen. He recognised them immediately as Marshal Pierre François Charles Augereau and his aide-de-camp, Captain Marbot. Augereau swung himself off his horse with some difficulty, then paused a moment before making his way stiffly over towards the huge camp fire around which the other marshals and staff officers were gathered. Augereau, a lean, tall man with greying hair, refused the baked potato offered to him and warmed himself at the fire. Napoleon crossed to the older man and took his arm.

They wandered several yards from the fire, aware even more of the biting chill.

'Some of them want me to storm Eylau this evening,' said the Corsican quietly. 'But I do not like night fighting and, besides, I do not wish to push my centre too far forward before Davout has come up with the right wing and Ney with the left; consequently, I shall await them until tomorrow on this high ground which can be defended by artillery and offers an excellent position for our infantry. When Ney and Davout are in line, we can march simultaneously on the enemy.'

'A wise decision, sire,' Augereau answered. 'It seems unfortunate then that the impetuosity of your own brother-in-law saw the needless deaths of so many of our men earlier today.'

'What do you mean?' snapped Napoleon.

'He blundered into Eylau like some raw officer looking for glory on his first day in the saddle,' Augereau said haughtily.

'The village had to be held,' Napoleon said irritably. 'And now it is back in our hands.'

'Even at so great a cost? Then why do you speak of storming the village when we already control it?'

'Have you come to me this night to criticise what has gone before or to bring me news? If it is the former then feel free to return to your corps now.' There was anger in the Corsican's voice.

'I have come to ask that you excuse me from my command, sire. I have a fever. I can barely stay in the saddle.'

'I urge you not to give up your command. Come the morning, I will need all my marshals to be as committed to this struggle as the humblest infantry private and the lowliest battery gunner. I cannot spare your expertise and your bravery. There is no man in this army I could name who would be an adequate replacement for you. Do not desert me now.'

Augereau nodded almost imperceptibly.

'I will do what you ask of me, sire,' he said quietly. 'Even if I have to be strapped to my horse. You may rely upon me.'

Napoleon patted the marshal's shoulder and led him back towards the fire where the others waited, warming themselves and eating their meagre meal.

'What is your plan, sire?' Berthier asked, rubbing his hands together in a desperate attempt to restore the fast fading circulation.

Napoleon looked at each of the marshals and officers around the fire, his own face appearing to glow orange in the light of the dancing flames.

'Soult, your division will undertake to engage the Russians first and to hold them,' the Corsican said. 'Inflict maximum casualties on the Russians but, above all, delay them in *their* attempts to launch an assault at least until Davout and the Third Corps have arrived on our right. Davout himself will turn the Russian left. Augereau, you and Murat will deliver the crippling blow against the Russian left when the time is right. If Ney arrives to cut off their retreat towards Königsberg then this war will be over by tomorrow night.' The Emperor moved nearer to the fire then looked up into the sky. Snow was beginning to fall more heavily.

Lausard could barely move. He wondered, for fleeting seconds, if his joints were frozen stiff. If somehow the savagely low temperatures had solidified the blood in his body and turned him into some kind of living, snow-flecked statue. He managed to get to his feet, stamping on rock-hard earth already covered by six inches of snow. The camp fire that he and his companions had built was now little more than a spluttering, smoking pile of embers. It gave off very little heat and even less light. There was simply nothing else to put on it to make it burn. Every soldier in *La Grande Armée* had been scouring the slopes and valleys around Eylau for wood, straw and hay. Anything that would burn. This was made even more difficult for Lausard and his fellow cavalrymen because at least half of the meagre supply of straw they acquired had to be fed to their starving horses. The animals, for the most part, were quiet. Too cold and weary even to protest at their plight. Much the same could be said of the troops. Lausard had known his colleagues to complain about lack of food, drink and shelter, to vent their anger about the elements; but the men barely spoke. Gormier's face had been bound so thickly with bandages he resembled an Egyptian mummy but,

Lausard reasoned, at least he had extra protection against the snow and frost. The other men of the squadron who had been wounded had been attended to as adequately as possible. For the majority of the French wounded, a field hospital had been set up inside the church within Eylau itself. When casualties had filled the place to bursting, a series of field hospitals had been established in barns along the Landsberg road. Charvet had returned from one of these not long ago, telling how the attendants were unable even to *hold* the instruments required by their surgeons, so intense was the frost.

Sleep was virtually impossible. With no bed but the snowy ground and in temperatures that were dropping by the minute, even the weariest of men could find no escape in the oblivion of sleep. Joubert was pacing back and forth. Lausard noted that the big man was usually able to sleep no matter what the circumstances or conditions but this night was unlike anything they had ever experienced before. They had known cold. Marched in it. Fought in it. But not cold like this. Men dared not take off their helmets or the scarves wrapped around their heads for fear their ears would simply wither away in the numbing gales. The snow was whipped into their faces like slivers of frosted glass. It stung when it struck what little bare flesh they left uncovered. None dared expose even so much as a hand for more than seconds at a time. The frost dug searing barbs into every part of the body it touched.

Lausard himself saw two figures approaching the camp fire around which he and his companions huddled and he recognised them at once as Rocheteau and Gaston. Both men moved stiffly, as if the very effort of walking in the terrifyingly low temperatures was a gargantuan one. Every so often the blizzard that was now sweeping across the open ground would cause them to sway and stumble as it buffeted them mercilessly.

'Nothing,' Rocheteau mumbled through his scarf, getting as close to the fire as he could without setting fire to his cloak. 'No food in any of the villages. A handful of potatoes. Some water. Nothing else. If there are any vegetables in the ground then they cannot be dug up. The Guard have scraped everywhere clean. No fuel to burn either.'

Erebus trotted over to Gaston and the trumpeter pulled the

dog close to him as if to draw some warmth from its huge black body.

'Whatever the morning may bring will be preferable to this,' Rocheteau said, his eyes half-closed, his teeth chattering.

Lausard looked out across the dark valley separating the French from the Russians and saw the hundreds of camp fires of their adversaries. However, in the growing blizzard, it was becoming ever more difficult to pick out the enemy lines. They showed only as black outlines against the white landscape.

'The morning may bring death,' Roussard said quietly.

'So may this night,' Lausard murmured.

'Can blood freeze?' Tabor wanted to know.

'Not inside the body,' said Bonet, patting his huge companion on the shoulder.

'Are you sure of that, schoolmaster?' Lausard asked. 'The scholar who declared such a fact never endured a night like this, did he?'

Bonet merely shook his head feebly and continued gazing at what remained of the fire.

'How long until dawn?' Varcon wanted to know.

Lausard did not even look at his pocket watch.

'An eternity,' he said flatly and wandered off into the unceasing snow flurry. No one followed him.

The house smelled of blood, gunpowder and death. Even the smoke belching from the hastily built fire could not conceal that familiar odour. The pine logs burned with a low flame and the constant crackling was like the sound of distant musket fire. Napoleon Bonaparte sat on a chair before the hearth staring into the flames, occasionally dropping into a fitful sleep. He had been inside the small building for nearly two hours. The house was on the outskirts of Eylau, secured on the outside by twenty men of the Imperial Guard. It had been cleared of a number of corpses, both French and Russian, before the Corsican had taken up his temporary residence within it. Marshal Berthier moved as silently as he could across the room, anxious not to wake his Emperor. He shivered slightly and the building seemed in danger of being blown away by the powerful wind.

'I'm not asleep, Berthier.'

The words startled the Chief of Staff who paused and crossed to his commander.

'I apologise if I woke you, sire,' Berthier said.

'How can I sleep?'

'I know, sire, the cold is—'

'The weather has little to do with it. I was thinking about our situation here. About what could happen tomorrow. The consequences of defeat.'

'I have never heard you speak of defeat before, sire.'

'Once before, in my life, I came close to losing a battle. At Marengo. It seems like a thousand centuries ago. Time has become irrelevant to me these past seven years, Berthier. What I have achieved would make God himself pause.'

'Then why do you doubt yourself, sire? We have beaten the Russians before.'

'But this entire campaign has so far denied me the victory I need. The victory the army needs. The triumph the whole of France cries out for. The Russians have fought with unexpected resistance everywhere we have encountered them and, tomorrow, Bennigsen knows that defeat would force him to lose his army. But, should *I* suffer defeat then I would lose more than an army. I would lose everything I have built within France herself. I know that without the army I cannot rule. Bennigsen risks humiliation. I risk my destiny. There are those who would gladly see France restored to the keeping of those same lawyers who ruined her. If I lose tomorrow then they will rejoice. Try to take from me that which *I* have created.'

'The people will not follow anyone other than you, sire.'

'I am hundreds of miles from my people, Berthier. The population of any country is fickle. They would have followed me to the stars after Austerlitz. But now, two years and two campaigns later, with so many sons of France dead in foreign fields, the mood of the people is different. They want peace, Berthier. An end to these wars I fight for *their* betterment.'

'You cannot expect the common man to understand your motives, sire. When France is the most powerful nation in Europe *then* they will thank you.'

Napoleon continued to gaze into the flames.

Outside, the blizzard grew ever more fearsome.

Lausard patted the neck of his horse and watched as it picked at the straw scattered before it on the snowy ground. The animals on either side did likewise. Some were being attended to by their riders, others stood alone with just their blankets to protect them from the blizzard.

'They hate this weather as much as we do,' Tigana said, emerging from between two undernourished mounts.

'I cannot say I blame them,' Lausard added. He looked up towards the plateau to their rear and saw the dull glow of camp fires staining the swollen sky.

'The Guard seem to find wood,' said Delacor irritably. 'I bet they have food, too.'

'I doubt it,' Lausard muttered. 'I doubt if any man or beast on this field, on either side, has anything to eat tonight.'

'Some of these mounts will have trouble carrying riders tomorrow, Alain,' Tigana said, glancing at the lines of horses. A few whinnied in protest at the cold but most were as silent as the men camped around them. 'Some have been pushed to their limits.'

'As we all have,' Lausard noted.

Karim wandered over to join his companions, his scimitar in his hand. He was wiping the blade with an oily rag. He did this two or three times before sliding the wickedly sharp weapon back into its scabbard.

'The frost,' he explained. 'Sometimes it makes the blade stick. Best to keep it well oiled.'

Lausard nodded.

'Will we get close enough to the Russians to use our swords?' Tigana mused. 'I have heard that they have hundreds of cannon protecting them. We could all be blown to pieces before we have a chance to reach them.'

'We will see,' the sergeant replied, still stroking his horse's neck.

'The Emperor will not sacrifice us needlessly,' Tigana continued, trying to inject a note of optimism into his voice.

'Bonaparte will do whatever he has to do to gain victory,' Lausard answered. 'He cares nothing for us as men. We are merely the tools of his ambition. And when morning arrives, we will see to what extent he is willing to further that ambition.'

All around them, the wind continued to blow with unabated fury. Lausard glanced once more in the direction of the Russian lines before a particularly dense flurry of snow blurred his vision. The temperature continued to drop.

TWENTY

The bloated banks of low grey cloud, buffeted by the numbing north wind, seemed barely able to rise above the hills that surrounded Eylau. Like huge, monolithic slabs of floating stone, they lowered over the white-covered terrain, so weighed down with snow it seemed they would, at any time, plummet to earth and simply crush the lines of troops deploying below them. The blackness of the night had given way to a barely discernible dawn. It was as if the day was reluctant to show itself. Content instead to cower behind the heaving clouds and relinquish its control of the heavens to the darker, portentous haze still dominant in the churning sky.

Lausard looked up as he fastened the girth strap of his saddle, shivering like his companions and every other man of *La Grande Armée*. Some shuddered because of the bone-chilling cold, others because they felt a touch of fear and foreboding more icy than even the severest of frosts. As the men prepared themselves for what now looked like an inevitable battle, their breath clouded around them before it was blasted away by the ever more savage wind. Horses, already skittish because of hunger and cold, struggled as cavalrymen all along the French lines saddled them or slipped bits into their hungry mouths.

Lausard patted his mount constantly, as if to reassure it. The horse pawed the iron-hard earth, sending up geysers of snow, which was more than a foot deep in some places. In others, the wind that had gusted constantly throughout the night had caused it to drift. It hammered down on to the men now, blinding them.

Many stopped to wipe their eyes as they prepared themselves. Lausard glanced around and found that he could see less than ten yards when the blizzard was at its height. He stamped his feet hard on the ground in a vain attempt to restore some circulation. When the wind changed direction briefly, he caught sight of the massed French ranks stretching away to his left as far as Eylau itself and to his right in the direction of the village of Rothenen. Between the deploying troops were hundreds of cannon, all trained on the Russians occupying the far side of the valley. Lausard had no doubt that the enemy artillery was also preparing to unleash its own barrage. Soon, the air would be filled not only with snow but with four-, six-, eight-, nine- and twelve-pound solid roundshot flying backwards and forwards as the opposing gunners did their best to pulverise the enemy troops before them. The Russians, he knew, had howitzers and mortars, too. Death could come from aerial blasts that would send red-hot shrapnel raining down as well as the devastating impact of canister and roundshot.

The dragoons moved in virtual silence, even the jingle of so many harnesses muffled by the blizzard. Infantry marching into position seemed to be doing so soundlessly, disturbing the covering of snow with their frozen feet as they moved towards their appointed places. So dense was the snow that many could not even see their officers. Shouted orders were lost on the screaming wind. Despite the bellowing of officers and NCOs, many men could do little except imitate the actions of a colleague ahead of them. Artillerymen huddled closer to their guns. Lausard saw more than one of them break layers of ice on the buckets of water to be used for swabbing out cannon barrels. Others turned portfires constantly in the air to prevent the slow-burning flame from going out. Gunners constantly readjusted the position of the cannon as if the very act of physical movement would bring at least momentary warmth to their freezing bodies. Some carried roundshot from the caissons parked behind the batteries and piled them close to the guns. Within minutes, the roundshot had a thin covering of snow. The horses that dragged the limbers neighed and whinnied protestingly as they stood waiting. A battery of four-pounders galloped into position thirty yards to Lausard's left, close to Eylau itself. He watched as the crew unlimbered the guns and rolled them manually into position.

'At least someone will be warm today,' Rocheteau said, nodding in the direction of the battery.

'Once the battle begins, I fear we will all find the temperature increases,' Lausard muttered.

'How the hell does Bonaparte expect us to fight when we cannot even see the enemy?' Delacor wanted to know, wiping snow from his face.

'We will see them soon enough,' Lausard assured him. He glanced at Rocheteau. 'What time is it?'

The corporal dug in his pocket and pulled out his watch, checking that the mechanism had not frozen during the night.

'Almost eight o'clock,' he said, his voice momentarily lost on the keening wind. A particularly vehement blast of icy air and snow gusted into the face of Lausard and his companions and many ducked their heads to avoid the prickling flakes that dug into their flesh like crystal shrapnel.

Erebus bounded back and forth barking in the direction of the Russians but even the great black dog's exhortations were lost to the wind.

Moreau crossed himself as he finished fastening his saddle in place then he touched his sword, his carbine and his helmet and blessed those, too. Delacor checked that his axe was firmly wedged inside his portmanteau, within easy reach should he need it. Bonet pulled a telescope from his saddle and trained it on the opposite side of the valley but he could see very little through the snowstorm. However, when the wind blew even more powerfully than before he was presented with a clear though fleeting view of the enemy dispositions.

'How many do you think there are?' asked Tabor.

'Twenty, twenty-five thousand,' Bonet murmured. 'Probably more.'

'Many more,' Roussard added flatly.

'I've never seen so many cannon,' Bonet continued. 'There are huge batteries all along their front.'

He studied the Russians for a moment longer until the

blizzard returned with renewed vigour and blotted everything beyond twenty yards from his view. He snapped the telescope shut and replaced it in his portmanteau.

Sonnier and Baumar were busily checking the firing mechanisms of their carbines. Both men had wrapped the weapons in oilskin to prevent the barrels from freezing and both now rewrapped the Charlevilles before slipping them into the boots on their saddles.

Varcon, Rostov and Kruger were sharpening their swords, passing a small flat stone between them, grinding it hard along the cutting edges of the three-foot-long blades before sliding the weapons back into their scabbards. Karim did likewise with his scimitar, spinning the lethally sharp curved blade in his hand before securing it more tightly to his belt.

Laubardemont and Carbonne were checking their cartridges, ensuring that the waxed paper had not come undone or become damp. Satisfied, they closed their cartouches, wiping snow from the black leather pouch.

Delbene was using his *epinglotte* to clean the touchhole of one of his pistols but the freezing conditions meant that he had difficulty even holding the long needle-like implement and he replaced it in his portmanteau before he dropped it in the snow and lost it for good.

Lausard looked around at all these activities, his attention caught suddenly by the approach of a horseman. It was impossible to identify the rider until he was within ten yards but then the sergeant recognised Lieutenant Royere. The officer nodded a greeting and swung himself out of the saddle, standing beside the sergeant and glancing in the general direction of the Russians who had once again vanished from sight as the blizzard momentarily intensified in ferocity.

'The regiment is to remain here, to the south of Eylau, until otherwise ordered,' the officer said, shivering. 'Captain Milliere has just received his orders. We are to act as support for Marshal Augereau's infantry or join the cavalry reserve to the rear, dependent upon what happens.'

'Better to advance than sit helplessly like fairground puppets,' Lausard said.

Royere did not answer.

'Do you not agree, Lieutenant?' the sergeant persisted.

'Sergeant, we have known each other for how long? Ten years? Longer? We have been through many battles together, have we not? Suffered many deprivations.'

'What are you saying, Lieutenant?'

'That I hope you will not think less of me for what I am about to say, but I look around me and I am afraid. Does that make me a coward?'

'If being afraid before a battle makes you a coward, my friend, then you are in good company.'

Royere tried to smile but it was as if the muscles of his face were frozen in the grimace he presented.

'We have been outnumbered before,' he said. 'Sometimes by greater odds than those we face today. But it is the nature of these conditions that frightens me. The field offers little cover anywhere. Except in Eylau itself and the village will make too easy a target for the Russian artillery. I have never seen guns massed with such purpose before. It is as if they mean to blow us off the face of the earth before we advance fifty paces.'

'Bonet also expressed concern at the strength of the Russian artillery.'

'And I fear his concern is well founded.'

From the other side of the valley there was a dull thud. Both Lausard and the others turned in that direction. The sound was followed by another, then another. The noise gradually built until it reminded the sergeant of waves breaking against rocks. A tumult that rolled from one end of the Russian line to the other. And yet, the normal din of roaring cannon was greatly muffled by the blizzard. The unearthly quiet that had reigned over the battlefield since the previous evening showed no sign of being broken, despite the obvious ferocity of the opening enemy fusillades. The smoke from the cannon was quickly blown away by the wind but the barrage began to grow in intensity.

'It begins,' murmured Lausard.

Napoleon trained his telescope on the dark masses of French troops moving towards the right of the Russian line, muttering under his breath when his view was occasionally obscured by thick flurries of snow. All around him, aides dashed back and forth carrying orders that were being hastily scribbled by Berthier. The Chief of Staff was surrounded by six dismounted chausseurs who were doing their best to shelter his makeshift desk from the wind as he wrote, wondering more than once if the ink on his quill would freeze.

Along the full length of both lines, artillery were pouring shot and shell incessantly at their enemies. Napoleon glanced briefly across to a battery of eight-pounders near him and saw the gunners moving with effortless expertise and incredible speed as they loaded, fired then reloaded. The smoke from more than six hundred cannon made it seem as if the already heavy clouds had finally descended on to the field itself. Muzzle flashes brought vivid, blinding seconds of fire in the gloom as the guns roared. They continued to blast away with unceasing fury and, as the Corsican swept his telescope along his lines, he saw that the main fury of the Russian barrage was being directed at Eylau itself. Against the dark sky and within the noxious clouds of smoke, it was difficult to see the rain of cannonballs crashing into Eylau itself but their impact was only too visible. Houses were holed by the roundshot. Shattered timber spun into the air as the wooden structures were obliterated by the weight of shells sent against them. The French troops sheltering within the village had a modicum of shelter from the furious barrage but it seemed to the Emperor only a matter of time before Eylau was simply blasted from the face of the earth by the concentrated Russian fire. He watched as a dozen mortar shells exploded above the village, momentarily lighting the sky with their orange-red detonations.

An aide galloped up and swung himself from the saddle, slipping on the snowy ground in his haste to reach the Emperor. He saluted, blinking hard to keep the snow out of his eyes.

'General Friant's division is approaching from the south, sire,' said the aide breathlessly.

'How long before they reach the field?' Napoleon wanted to know.

'Another hour, sire.'

'What of the rest of Davout's corps? How far behind Friant are they?'

'They will not reach the battlefield before noon, sire.'

Napoleon gritted his teeth angrily.

'Then ride back to Davout and tell him to march faster,' he hissed. 'I need those men.'

'Sire, General Friant is already faced with a substantial number of enemy cavalry, preparing to attack.'

'Tell him to deal with them as quickly as he can.'

The aide nodded, saluted and clambered back on to his horse. He put spurs to the mount and hurtled off as fast as the animal could carry him.

'Soult's advance against the Russian right should cause Bennigsen to weaken his left flank,' the Corsican said, pointing with his telescope in the direction of the dark mass of the French Fourth Corps. 'He will think we intend to turn him there and weaken his left.'

'I hope you are right, sire,' General Rapp said, holding his feather-trimmed bicorn with one hand to prevent the wind from blowing it off. 'But none of that will matter if Marshal Davout does not bring his men up in time.'

'Did you expect the Russians to move against Friant so quickly, sire?' Berthier wanted to know.

Napoleon merely shook his head and fumbled for his pocket watch. He glanced at the time.

The hands seemed to be frozen.

He raised his telescope once more and watched his advancing infantry. Supported on one side by hordes of light cavalry, they strode on towards the Russian lines, eagles held high above their formations. Napoleon winced slightly as he saw the Russian artillery begin to pour even more shot into the men of Soult's corps. Entire files were downed. Blood began to stain the pristine white snow that covered the field. Stray roundshot struck the iron-hard earth, spun up and hurtled onwards into the French ranks, killing and maiming anyone in their path. Howitzer and mortar shells dropped among the men, sending out scything showers of hot metal to bring down yet more of them. Others erupted above their heads with similarly lethal results.

And all the time, the French artillery kept up its own fire, doing similar damage to the Russians.

'They are in tighter formations,' Napoleon said quietly, looking at the green-clad troops formed up across the valley from him. 'We have an inferior number of guns but our targets are clearer.'

'Sire, look,' said Berthier, directing the Corsican's gaze back towards the slightly rising ground now swarming with Soult's men. 'Bennigsen is committing the first of his forces.'

'As I said he would,' Napoleon smiled briefly. He watched as wave after wave of Russian infantry marched forward to meet Soult's men. Again the Emperor looked at his watch, concern etched on his face. He turned to his right and scanned the southern reaches of the battlefield, hoping for some sign of French troops advancing from that direction. 'Where is Friant?' he murmured, his words heard only by Berthier who was certain the tone that coloured them was one of anxiety.

Parts of Eylau were already on fire.

Lausard stood beside his horse, holding its bridle and watching as clouds of smoke rose from the village. The barrage that the Russians had directed against the clutch of buildings had now radiated outwards and roundshot were hurtling towards all parts of the French line. Lausard heard one of the deadly nine-pound missiles scream past him, no more than ten paces to his left. It was followed by countless others. Many ploughed into the infantry who were formed up ahead of the dragoons. Lausard saw men cut in half by roundshot. The eagle bearer of the regiment was hit, his upper torso pulverised by the solid lead ball. Men lost limbs, some of which spiralled heavenward, spraying blood. The ground all around was turning crimson and Lausard could see a fog of condensation rising from the lifeblood that was pouring on to the snow in such profusion. Geysers of snow erupted into the air as shells exploded.

Close by, three dragoons were hit by a single roundshot. A horse was also killed by the same missile. Men stood more stiffly beside their mounts. It seemed just a matter of time before one of the deadly projectiles hit them. From one end of the line to the other, flames erupted from cannon barrels as both sides kept up an unceasing fire.

An eight-pounder was hit and two of its crew killed. Lausard saw one man crawling away, his leg taken off at the knee. Another of his companions sat splay-legged on the ground staring down at the steaming mass of intestines that had spilled from the gaping rent in his stomach. With deliberate movements he tried to push his entrails back into the yawning maw before toppling backwards, motionless, in the bloodied snow. The remaining gunners left the wrecked carriage of the eight-pounder and moved along to help their comrades who were working like demons to keep up the furious barrage.

The sky was still a mosaic of dark cloud, smoke and snow. Lausard glanced up: it was like a night battle, he thought, so bad was the visibility, so intense the gloom that covered the field.

'How long are we to stand here?' Delacor snapped, ducking involuntarily as another roundshot hurtled by.

'Until we are ordered to do otherwise,' Lausard told him.

A howitzer shell burst high in the air above them and Joubert hissed in pain as a metal splinter cut through his left forearm, narrowly missing the bone. Bonet pulled some bandages from his portmanteau and hurriedly bound the wound, gently pressing the big man's arm from shoulder to wrist to ensure that no further damage had been done. Two more horses went down, one dead as soon as it hit the snow, the other squealing and bolting, blood spouting from a wound in its neck as it dashed away. Its rider, who had been holding its reins, was yanked off his feet as the terrified beast galloped madly off in the direction of the Russian lines. It was felled a second later by a roundshot.

'As I said,' Lieutenant Royere mused. 'No cover.'

Several more roundshot came screaming into the waiting dragoons. One bounced up only feet in front of Lausard and he ducked, feeling the air part close to his face as it spun past him. The deadly missile continued on, felling two more men in the second line and taking the front legs from a horse. The roundshot were followed by more mortar and howitzer shells and the familiar acrid stench of powder and sulphur began to fill the men's nostrils. It was becoming difficult to breathe despite the savage north wind. Smoke from the batteries of French guns enveloped everything within twenty yards and the dragoons found themselves standing in what amounted to a foul-smelling man-made fog. Lausard waved his hands before his eyes in an effort to clear the air somewhat. He coughed and spat. His mouth was already dry. He quickly ducked down and snatched up some snow which he pushed into his mouth. It tasted faintly of blood but he did not care. Other men, also parched, followed his example.

'Nine thirty,' said Royere, glancing at his pocket watch.

The cannon continued to roar unabated but now, off to the left, Lausard and his companions could hear the crackle of musket fire, too. The sergeant knew that the battle was spreading, that men were facing each other at last. And yet, oblivious to the fact they could be hitting friend and foe alike, both sets of artillery continued to pound away without respite.

'Has there ever been a battle where *everyone* was killed?' Rocheteau asked, keeping his head down slightly as if that simple gesture would protect him.

'Not yet,' Lausard told him cryptically.

Roundshot pulverised more men. The sky darkened. The snow continued to blind the waiting troops. The artillery thundered on.

TWENTY-ONE

Napoleon paced back and forth agitatedly, stopping only occasionally either to peer through his telescope or to consult his pocket watch. The continuous cannon barrage from both sides had left the battlefield heavily shrouded in smoke and even the Corsican himself coughed occasionally, so rank was the air. Every breath was tinged with the suffocating stench of gunpowder and sulphur. A noxious plume of smoke rose like a black flag over Eylau itself as parts of the village continued to burn, set ablaze by Russian incendiary shells.

'Soult is being pushed back,' Berthier murmured, his telescope pressed to his eye.

'I am aware of that,' Napoleon snapped. 'I am also aware of the fact that Friant's division is under attack. Both of our flanks would appear to be in danger. But it is Eylau itself that Bennigsen covets. If he can take control of the village then he will be able to strike at our centre.'

'How can you be sure, sire?' Rapp asked.

'It is obvious,' the Corsican said. 'He has sent huge numbers of men against Soult's corps in an effort to push him back in the direction of Eylau. He means to swing his main weight against the village.'

The Emperor strode to the left and right, his eyes scanning the battlefield spread out before him.

'There are two choices for me,' he muttered. 'I can order an immediate counterattack against the Russian left to ease the pressure on Friant, or I can instruct Soult and his corps to withdraw and trade space for time until Ney and Davout have arrived on the battlefield.'

'But there has been no word from Marshal Ney, sire,' Berthier insisted. 'We have no idea if he is two or twenty miles from the battlefield.'

'Marshal Davout is also a considerable distance from the main battle, sire,' Rapp reminded his commander.

'But the division of General Morand is already in view, sire,' Berthier said, squinting through the smoke and snow towards the right of the French positions.

'Then the choice is made for me,' the Corsican declared, turning towards Berthier. 'Bennigsen will order the troops under Tutchkov to renew their attack against Soult's corps. Send orders to Soult that he is to stand firm.'

'But, sire, Marshal Soult is badly outnumbered,' the Chief of Staff protested. 'His men will be annihilated.'

'There is not time to extricate them. Eylau must *not* fall into enemy hands,' Napoleon snapped. 'Augereau is to advance, without delay, against Tolstoi's position. He is to be accompanied, on his right, by the division of St Hilaire. Instruct that division to link up with Davout's men. It will re-establish a new line to the south-east. It will also relieve some of the pressure on Soult. Bennigsen will be forced to weaken his right to protect his left and his centre.'

Berthier scratched down the orders with his quill while a posse of aides-de-camp, some mounted, others waiting beside their horses, watched the Corsican who merely stood motionless, gazing out over the battlefield. Rapp looked first at his commander then at Berthier who merely shrugged.

'Sire,' Rapp said quietly, taking a step towards the Corsican. 'The orders must be sent if they are to be acted upon.'

Still Napoleon did not speak. After what seemed like an eternity, he turned.

'See that those orders are delivered and executed,' he said flatly.

The aides scrambled on to their horses and galloped off into the blizzard after those of their companions who had already left.

'Is this advance by Marshal Augereau not a little premature, sire?' Berthier asked. 'The Russian centre is still strong.'

'I have no choice, Berthier,' said Napoleon and, yet again, he looked at his pocket watch.

'To horse.'

Captain Milliere roared the order at the top of his voice, anxious to make himself heard in the wind and the tumult of cannon fire.

Lausard and his companions swung themselves into the saddle, watching as the infantry of Marshal Augereau began to advance, eagles flying proudly in the foul weather. The sergeant caught sight of Augereau himself, strapped to his saddle and supported by two staff officers. It seemed as if he would topple from his mount if either of them were to release their grip on his arm. He had a scarf wrapped around his head beneath his bicorn; Lausard could see some of the white silk protruding from beneath the ornately decorated headgear.

The dragoons waited until the infantry had advanced four or five hundred paces then moved off close to them, many of the men still ducking involuntarily as the endless torrent of Russian shells continued to rain down among them.

'Keep your heads up,' roared Milliere, his voice almost lost within the cacophony of jangling harnesses, marching feet, high wind and artillery fire.

Lausard saw the guidon of his regiment fluttering high in the air and he fixed his gaze on it for a second, his heart thumping a little harder against his ribs.

'What the hell are those dog-faces doing?' hissed Delacor, nodding in the direction of the advancing infantry.

Lausard glanced at the blue-clad mass and also wondered.

The leading brigades of each division were advancing in deployed order, while, behind them, the second brigades had already formed squares and were moving forward rather awkwardly in the more unwieldy formation.

'They're too far apart,' Lausard said. 'There isn't sufficient contact between the first and second brigades. Not in these conditions anyway.'

As if to emphasise his remark, the wind seemed to increase to an unbelievable force and the snow, which Lausard had felt was easing slightly, suddenly returned with even greater ferocity. The dragoons continued to advance but, like the infantry, they were finding it increasingly difficult to remain on a steady course. Lausard felt the horse to his right bump into his own mount and, indeed, all through the regiment, men blundered into each other and the dragoons' formation began to become more ragged. Lausard could see Milliere roaring instructions at his men but he could hear nothing. The captain was signalling with his sword, jabbing the point to his right as if to correct the angle of the advance. All around him, men ducked low over their saddles to shield themselves from the murderous storm and also to offer some modicum of protection from the Russian shells that were now starting to fall among them with greater regularity and accuracy.

A man in the line behind Lausard was hit. The roundshot decapitated his horse and cut him in two. Blood sprayed upwards in a wide crimson arc, staining the snow and any other troopers close by. Another horse went down. Then another. A trooper was blasted from his saddle. Another was obliterated by a roundshot, his body merely brushed from the saddle. Just a foot remained in one stirrup before that finally fell to the earth. The smoke from so many guns only made visibility worse and Lausard and his companions were now struggling to breathe in the fetid air. There was a growing heat to their front which the sergeant could only assume was coming from the unceasing fire erupting from the Russian batteries. He realised with horror that they were closer to the Russian guns than they had thought. Another hundred yards or so and the enemy gunners would open up with canister fire.

More men were hit. The remains of a body fell close to Lausard who urged his horse on through the snowstorm. A roundshot came spinning up from behind them.

'Jesus,' hissed Rocheteau. 'That came from *our* artillery.'

Lausard knew he was right.

'They can't see us in the snow,' he hissed.

'We're being murdered by our own men,' shouted Roussard frantically.

Moreau crossed himself.

Tabor jabbed a finger in the direction of the Russian army, squinting through the snow.

Kruger tried his best to prevent himself from shaking. He touched the hilt of his sword as if that would somehow protect him.

Sonnier was mouthing silent prayers as he rode, his head bowed slightly. He was not alone. More than one man offered words to his Maker as he stumbled on, fearing that he might be speaking his own last rites. And every time someone opened his mouth it was filled either with snow or with the sickening taste of smoke.

The dragoons and the infantry they supported slogged on, buffeted by the blizzard, blasted by Russian and French fire alike. Trapped in a fateful no-man's-land where they were the helpless prey of every round fired in either direction. The bodies of men and horses already littered the ground. Some of the wounded tried to crawl away but, in the terrible conditions, none was sure in which direction to crawl. Lausard himself had the numbing realisation that not only the dragoons, but the whole of Augereau's division, in the blinding snowstorm had veered away from their initial objective. They were hopelessly and irretrievably lost in the middle of the most murderous killing ground Lausard had ever seen. Pinned between a savage crossfire of both enemy and friendly fire. A white hell from which there seemed to be no escape. Even horses whinnied with fear as the advance stumbled on over snow that was two feet deep by now. Animals tottered and sometimes fell but their riders forced them upright again and remounted. Men struggled to keep their formations and, all the time, the artillery of both sides blasted them to pieces.

Just then, there was a particularly strong gust of wind that threatened to unhorse those not firmly seated in their saddles. In that moment, the dragoons saw that the smoke and snow had been momentarily cleared away. For fleeting seconds they had their own devastating moment of clarity. A perfect view of the Russian centre. Of the seventy-gun battery drawn up ahead of the enemy hordes. There were no more than fifty yards between them and the yawning barrels of the guns.

'Oh my God,' murmured Delbene.

He could actually see gunners pressing their portfires to touchholes.

It was the last thing he did see.

The guns opened up simultaneously. From point-blank range, the six- and nine-pounders unleashed a storm of canister that merely swept the French away like wheat before a scythe. It was as if the world had begun to move in slow motion. Lausard saw the gunners light their fuses then the barrels flamed, roaring as they unleashed their fearful load. The noise was deafening, the effect devastating. In that split second before the guns opened up, Lausard had but one thought. He was finally going to find the death on a battlefield that he had been seeking for the past eleven years. The second stretched into an eternity and then the gales of canister hit the French.

Three- and six-ounce lead balls tore through the struggling French troops with ease.

Delbene was hit by four of them and pitched backwards from his saddle. One had staved in his sternum. A second had blasted away most of the left side of his face. The other two had sliced effortlessly through his stomach and thigh.

Gaston shouted in agony as one of them shattered his right ankle. Another three killed his horse instantly, the animal flopping heavily to the blood-soaked snow. Karim spurred across to the young trumpeter and extended a hand, dragging him up on to his own saddle. Gaston gritted his teeth and clambered up with difficulty, his shattered ankle leaving a trail of blood both in the snow and also down the flank of Karim's horse.

Many of the guns were double-shotted. After the initial blast of canister, a roundshot followed. Entire lines of men were simply swept away. All around him, Lausard saw men and horses hit the blood-stained ground, some wounded, some already dead. The pommel of his own saddle was ripped away by a lead ball. Part of his shabraque, too, was torn off. He winced in pain as another six-ounce ball caught him on the forearm, tearing open his tunic and the flesh beneath. A fragment of metal from a shell burst sliced off part of his left earlobe. Another ripped away part of his collar. He wheeled his horse, the animal rearing wildly as the Russians prepared to unleash another volley of shot and shell into the stunned Frenchmen. Before it came, there was a massive eruption of musket fire from the Russian lines and the already shredded ranks of dragoons and infantry found themselves raked with the fire of hundreds of .50 calibre bullets.

Gormier was hit in both eyes and toppled from his saddle. Bonet leaped from his own horse to tend to his companion but as he lifted the other man's head he saw that it was hopeless, despite the fact that Gormier's lips were moving slightly as if he were muttering entreaties to his helper. Tabor rode across and dragged Gormier on to his own horse, laying him across the neck of his mount as easily as a child would lay a doll.

'Leave him, he's dead,' shouted Delacor, himself bleeding heavily from a wound in the neck. He was holding his reins in one hand, the other being clapped to the bullet hole just above his collar. The lead ball had caught him just below the jaw and passed through and the fact that the blood was running rather than spouting from the injury was enough to tell Bonet that the projectile had hit a vein and not an artery.

Captain Milliere, his face splashed with blood, grabbed Lieutenant Royere's arm and jabbed a finger back towards the French lines.

'We must retire immediately,' he shouted.

Royere was about to reply when a bullet hit him in the side. The officer let out a pained breath and gritted his teeth. Milliere held him more tightly but Royere waved him away, as if to signal that the wound was not too serious. He pressed one hand to it and brought his gauntlet away smeared with crimson but he shook his head, his breath clouding before him.

'I'm all right,' he gasped, turning his horse.

Sonnier and Baumar, both firing from the saddle, swung their carbines up to their shoulders and squeezed off shots at the mass of green-clad troops facing them. Other dragoons were also trying to follow their example, as were a sizable number of the infantry, those not already blasted to oblivion by the combined effects of cannon and musket fire. Baumar was attempting to reload when a bullet blasted off his little finger; it was severed at the third joint and spun uselessly into the air before being swallowed by the snow. Snow that was now little more than a red slush where so many had fallen.

'Retreat,' roared Milliere, trying to make himself heard above the incessant din of gunfire.

Lausard heard the order and saw the officer waving madly with his sword but few of the dragoons were aware of the officer's shouts. Still deafened by the howling wind and the monstrous roar of cannon, they remained facing the Russians, helpless in the face of such concentrated point-blank fire. Lausard saw half a dozen men and horses brought down at once as he galloped towards Karim and Gaston. The trumpeter was clinging to the Circassian, trying not to slip off the horse. Occasionally he glanced down at his ankle, from which blood was still streaming.

'Sound the recall,' Lausard bellowed, watching as Gaston lifted the trumpet to his lips and began to blow for all he was worth. The strident notes climbed into the boiling sky like the last prayers of a dying man. All along the line, the dragoons began to turn their mounts. Even riderless horses bolted back towards the French lines. One almost crashed into Lausard. He tugged hard on his reins and managed to guide his horse around the terrified animal. Seconds later, the riderless mount was hit by a roundshot that took off one of its hind legs and sent it sprawling on the snow.

Away to his right, the sergeant saw that most of the infantry were running, too. There was no orderly retreat. No covering fire. These men, like him and his companions, were merely running for their lives. Still cannon fire ploughed into them from both sides of the valley. Some of the foot soldiers made for Eylau itself; others merely dropped their equipment and dashed headlong across terrain they had already crossed. Some, dazed and confused, deafened and blinded, stumbled towards the gaping muzzles of the Russian cannon which were continuing to send volley after volley of canister into the ragged French lines.

'Russian cavalry,' roared Lausard, spotting a mass of enemy horsemen bearing down on the already decimated infantry.

Big men on big powerful horses, the Russian cuirassiers and

dragoons smashed into the fleeing Frenchmen with the force of a farrier's hammer. Some men were simply ridden down, others cut to the ground as they tried to stand and protect either themselves or wounded comrades. Cossacks hurtled among the heavier Russian cavalry, some driving their long lances into the French infantrymen, others content to pick them off with swords or pistols. Several of the light cavalrymen came thundering towards the fleeing dragoons. Lausard caught the first one across the throat with a powerful backhand stroke before felling another with a downward cut that practically cleaved the man's skull in two.

Rocheteau, sporting several dents in his brass helmet and a bullet wound in his shoulder, brought his sword upwards into the belly of a Cossack, tearing it free with a shout of triumph and rage. Entrails were scattered across the snow as the Cossack fell from his saddle. A bullet caught Rocheteau's horse in the head and it dropped like a stone, pinning him beneath it.

Lausard immediately pulled hard on his reins and leaped from his horse, running across to the corporal in an effort to try and free him from the dead weight that held him helpless. Rocheteau kicked at the carcass in an attempt to move it but it was useless. Joubert also dismounted and added his considerable strength to the efforts and, gradually, Rocheteau managed to pull his foot free. He grabbed at the reins of a riderless horse, swung himself into the saddle and joined Lausard and Joubert as they continued their flight back across the shell-blasted landscape.

The guidon of the regiment was still fluttering high in the air, the oiled silk smeared with blood, smoke and gunpowder. Lausard heard a Russian bullet strike the brass eagle that topped the staff but it sang off, merely chipping away a small portion of the precious figurehead. The bearer was not so lucky. A howitzer shell exploded just ahead of him and a piece of hot metal the size of a man's fist punched its way through his chest, tore through his lungs and erupted from his back, spraying those behind with gouts of blood and gobbets of pinkish grey matter. He fell forward in the saddle, the guidon slipping from his hand, but Lausard put spurs to his mount and rode up alongside the bearer, taking the staff from him, thrusting it high into the air once more. As if he had been holding a lighted beacon, the dragoons followed him in the direction of Eylau. The buildings would at least offer *some* cover from the savage fire still pouring into them.

Led by Lausard, the dragoons hurtled towards the village, the leading troopers hurdling the walls around the besieged clutch of buildings, immediately reining in their mounts as they landed among their own infantry. Some of the remaining horsemen headed back towards their own lines. Lausard could see horses, many riderless, running exhaustedly through the bloodied snow. A battery of eight-pounders set up in the cemetery of Eylau opened up immediately to cover the returning French troops and the exhausted dragoons watched blankly as their Russian pursuers were blasted to oblivion in much the same way as so many of their own comrades had been such a short time earlier. Lausard helped Royere from his horse then passed among the men nearest him, most of whom had pulled their carbines free and were already firing back at the Russians from the relative cover of the walls surrounding the cemetery.

'Get the wounded to the surgeons immediately,' Milliere snapped.

'Those who can still fight, get into the church,' Lausard roared.

He locked eyes with the officer for fleeting seconds then Milliere nodded and slapped him on the shoulder.

Those dragoons who could hear the instruction scuttled towards the embattled building, bursting in to join the French infantry already there. The wounded were carried, dragged or helped inside the church. Immediately the men took up positions at the windows. Pews had been overturned and piled up to form firing platforms and Lausard saw Sonnier and Baumar scramble up on to the nearest. Parts of the east wall had been holed by Russian artillery fire. Lausard saw several spent nine-pound cannonballs lying close to the font. The entire building was full of smoke from muskets and from the fire that had broken out on a section of the church roof. The high vaulted ceiling made every discharge seem louder. The screams and shouts of men both outside and in reverberated in Lausard's eardrums.

Bonet laid Gormier gently on the ground and pressed two fingers against his throat, feeling for a pulse. There was none. The former schoolmaster looked briefly at Lausard and shook his head.

Charvet was frantically bandaging Gaston's ankle, not even attempting to remove the boot first. He feared that, if he did, the trumpeter's foot would simply come away with it. Blood soaked through the gauze but Gaston merely gritted his teeth and sat back against the wall as Charvet worked.

'Pull it tight,' he grunted, clenching his fists as Charvet did as he was instructed. 'Where is Erebus?' he wanted to know.

'Gone to hell, where he belongs,' Delacor said, his own wound now bleeding fitfully. It too was bandaged by Bonet.

'That black devil will have survived somehow,' Giresse said, sucking in deep, polluted breaths of air and wiping blood from his face. Outside, the entire cemetery smelled of gunpowder and sulphur. It was shrouded in the fog of cannon and musket smoke, all mingling with the condensed breath of the cursing, groaning men defending it. Lausard stuck his head out of the door, urging more of his companions inside. The sergeant glanced towards the rear of the necropolis and saw a familiar figure standing motionless on a slight rise, surrounded by staff officers and aides.

'*Vive l'Empereur*,' he said breathlessly, through gritted teeth.

It is the 14th Line regiment, sire,' said Rapp, peering through his telescope.

All the officers and their commander had their lenses fixed on the single French unit still cut off in the valley. Formed into a ragged square, they were surrounded by infantry, cavalry and Cossacks who were swarming around them like carrion feeders over a stricken animal.

'Marshal Augereau has already sent two officers forward to give them the order to retire but they have been killed,' Marshal Murat offered. The big Gascon took off his fur hat briefly and swept one hand through his dark curly hair. 'It is only a matter of time before the entire regiment is wiped out.'

Napoleon did not speak; he merely kept his telescope trained on the ever dwindling group of French troops, watching helplessly as it was gradually swallowed up by the enemy hordes.

'They die with pride for *you*, sire,' Murat said.

'I do not want them to *die* for me,' Napoleon snapped. 'Not them or any other man on this field today. I wanted them to see a glorious victory, not fall here in this place.' He snapped his telescope shut and lowered his eyes slightly. 'It is the same all along the line. The initiative *and* the advantage are now with the Russians.' He flipped open his pocket watch and glanced at it as if willing the hands to move faster. 'Where is Ney?' he snarled. 'Where is Davout?' The volume of his exhortations was rising. 'Must I do everything myself? Can I trust no one else? We will be overrun before they drag themselves on to the field.'

Several bullets cut through the air close to the Corsican and Berthier and Murat moved closer to their Emperor as if to shield him. Several of the mounted chausseurs nearby spurred their horses forward to form a barrier but two of them were hit almost immediately.

'The Russians are in the churchyard,' shouted Rapp, pointing madly.

Several hundred French troops were spilling from the cemetery into the streets of Eylau, and those who had survived the initial onslaught were fleeing in an attempt to save themselves. They were pursued by wave after wave of green-clad enemy infantry, all with fixed bayonets, led by bellowing officers who urged them on into the very heart of the French positions.

'You must get away from here, sire,' Rapp said, grabbing the reins of the Emperor's white horse. 'Now.' He and Duroc practically pushed the Corsican on to his saddle while two or three dozen mounted chausseurs and five or six staff officers hurtled madly towards the head of the advancing Russian formation, sabres already drawn. Shouts of *'Vive l'Empereur'* filled the air as the small band of personal guards crashed into the far superior enemy forces. Napoleon, flanked by Murat and Berthier, guided his horse back through the streets of the village as quickly as he could, past more French infantry who were still defending buildings, many of which were either ablaze or had been all but obliterated by the continuous Russian cannon fire. Several detachments of Imperial Guard grenadiers marched briskly into Eylau, their faces set in expressions of grim determination. Napoleon turned in the saddle to watch as they increased their pace and began attacking the Russians with their bayonets in a furious display of something bordering on rage. The Russians fell back immediately, overcome by the sheer ferocity of the Guard's attack. They staggered back through the cemetery and, as they did, both French infantry and also some of Lausard's companions came pouring out the church to reoccupy the graveyard. Laubardemont ran towards one of the eight-pounders, calling colleagues to him.

'Help me,' he roared, reaching for the rammer dropped by one of the dead French gunners.

Lausard and several of the other dragoons hurried to his aid, watching as he pushed the sponge end of the rammer into the barrel, swabbing it clean of excess powder. Lausard realised what the former artilleryman was doing and grabbed a canister of shot while Tabor and Joubert used their considerable strength to adjust the position of the gun slightly. Rocheteau joined them, grabbing the handspike and tugging as Laubardemont instructed. Giresse retrieved the glowing portfire and stood ready.

'Damn it,' snarled Laubardemont, 'there are no cartridges. We will have to use loose powder as a charge.' Tabor lifted a barrel effortlessly and began pouring the reeking black powder into the barrel. 'Enough,' Laubardemont said finally. 'Put the canister in,' he said, stepping back as Lausard shoved the metal container into the mouth of the barrel. He took the rammer from Laubardemont and pushed it down. 'Put some of that in, too,' the former artilleryman said, gesturing towards some straw that was scattered around the wheels of the gun. Lausard did as he was instructed then stood back, watching as Laubardemont ducked close to the rear end of the barrel and adjusted the quoin beneath it, twisting the chock until the barrel was pointing almost horizontally. 'It's sighted,' he said, stepping back. 'Light the fuse.'

Giresse pressed the portfire to the touchhole and stepped back. There was a massive blast as the canister exploded from the barrel, the eight-pounder recoiling several feet, narrowly missing Tabor's foot. A cloud of choking smoke enveloped the men but it cleared rapidly as a gust of wind blew across the cemetery. Dozens of the retiring Russians had been simply blown away by the discharge and some of the dragoons shook triumphant fists in the direction of their slaughtered foe. Lausard slapped Laubardemont on the shoulder and Rocheteau smiled broadly at him, his face darkened by powder and blood. Laubardemont smiled back, accepting the congratulations of some of his other companions, too.

French infantry were now spilling back into the cemetery, taking up the positions they had been in before the Russians had burst through them. Milliere called as many men as possible around him and waved them back towards the streets of Eylau itself.

'Remount,' he shouted. 'The regiment will join the cavalry reserve.'

'Are they our orders, Captain?' Lausard asked, his breath still coming in gasps. His long brown hair was hanging like tendrils around his bloodied face.

'They are *my* orders, Sergeant,' said the officer flatly. 'This regiment has spent enough time out of the saddle already today.'

A slight smile touched Lausard's lips as he followed Royere and some more of his companions towards the streets of Eylau.

Napoleon stood motionless on the small rise to the rear of the village, hands clasped behind his back, his eyes fixed on the smoke-shrouded inferno that was Eylau. All along the French line it was a similar sight. The snow was falling more sporadically now but, whipped by the chill wind, it still drove across the battlefield, as if competing for domination of the skies with the choking smoke belching from so many weapons or from the blazing houses and buildings of Eylau and Rothenen.

'Sire.'

The voice was Berthier's but Napoleon seemed at first not to hear it.

'Sire,' the Chief of Staff repeated, more urgently. 'Your commanders are awaiting orders. The situation is growing critical.

Marshal Davout has still not arrived in sufficient numbers on the right. Marshal Ney is too far away on our left to alter the course of the battle at this moment. The corps of Marshal Soult has been repulsed, that of Marshal Augereau all but destroyed. What is your next command to be?'

Napoleon finally turned and calmly motioned to Murat.

The marshal strode towards his brother-in-law, slapping a riding crop against his thigh.

'It is eleven thirty,' Napoleon said. 'It is time to retrieve what has been lost. I have no reserves left to commit other than my Imperial Guard and your own cavalry. Our centre is lost, possibly the entire army, unless you lead your men forward now. Use them all. All eighty squadrons. All ten thousand men under your command. Take them and attack the Russian centre. You are the bravest man I know, Murat. Never before has France needed your courage so desperately.'

Murat smiled and sucked in a deep breath.

'Bessiéres will support you with the cavalry of the Guard,' Napoleon added. 'Ten thousand and seven hundred men against an army, my brother-in-law.'

'I am honoured that you should choose me, sire,' Murat said, swinging himself into the saddle. 'I will not fail you.' He turned his horse and galloped towards the rear, towards the mass of horsemen waiting patiently there. His aides, their glittering uniforms like beacons in the smoke, followed.

'The situation is desperate, sire,' Berthier said, his face pale.

'I am aware of that,' Napoleon told him, gazing out once more over the battlefield. 'If Murat fails now, we will be destroyed. I have left the fate of France in his hands.'

TWENTY-TWO

Lausard sat wearily on his horse, glancing alternately up at the sky then around at his companions and backwards towards the endless lines of French cavalry that stretched away almost as far as the eye could see. Ahead, Lausard could see six squadrons of chausseurs in their green jackets and red pelisses. He recognised their commander, Dahlmann, moving among them. Countless dragoons like himself in their familiar green surtouts. Cuirassiers, their heavy steel breastplates and helmets making them look like men of steel on their powerful black mounts, sat to the rear of his own regiment. Their commanding officers, d'Hautpol and Milhaud, sat side by side, occasionally pointing in the direction of the Russian lines. Behind them were more dragoons then mounted grenadiers of the Guard, their huge bearskins nodding as they sat motionless. Further back, resplendent in their multi-coloured uniforms sat six squadrons of Mamelukes and more chausseurs. It was as if every single horseman in the French army had been drawn together in this one place. But all they could do was sit helplessly as Russian artillery continued to pound the French lines, many shells falling among them.

Lausard had heard shouts from officers, insisting that the men keep their heads up, despite the ferocity of the bombardment, but he had noticed that many troopers were ducked low in their saddles to avoid the hail of lead constantly flying towards them. Horses pawed the snowy ground and snorted their own impatience. The smell of dung was almost as powerful as that of gunpowder with so many animals, many of them nervous, being crammed together in such a relatively small area. A haze of condensation surrounded the mounted horde as steam rose from horses and men as they breathed.

Lausard had no idea how long he and his regiment had been sitting in orderly lines waiting. It may have been half an hour, it could have been longer. Since leaving the hell of Eylau, the sergeant had not looked at his watch. Time, as ever, had lost its meaning but for different reasons. To Lausard, it seemed that this battle had been going on for as long as he could remember and it would continue until he was dead. It was a simple, but plausible, flight of fancy. He took off a glove and pushed one index finger into his right ear. His hearing was slightly muffled and he was not surprised to see blood on the tip of his finger when he withdrew it. The constant exposure to such a thunderous artillery duel had probably damaged his eardrum. If the snow had not been falling so thickly earlier in the day, he reasoned, then he and all his companions might have been stone deaf by now. He replaced his brass helmet, noticing that it was dented and scratched in half a dozen places. Several chinscales had been torn away and part of the horsehair mane had been singed. He refastened it and looked across at Gaston. The young trumpeter was sitting slightly slumped in his saddle, his shattered ankle trailing bloodied bandages, his foot wedged into one stirrup and secured there by several pieces of leather that he had cut from the gauntlet of a dead companion. Many of the other men also carried wounds of varying degrees of severity. Lausard was beginning to wonder how many more would be hit before the day was over. Would he himself fall to a roundshot, canister, musket fire, a lance or a sword? He looked in the direction of the Russian lines and wondered.

Captain Milliere walked his horse slowly backwards and forwards across the front of the leading rank of dragoons and looked at each of them in turn, stopping beside wounded men, checking with them that they were able to remain in the saddle. Nearly all had attested that they were perfectly able to ride. Less than half a dozen had been forced to seek the help of the surgeons in the grossly overworked field hospitals in the barns to the rear of Eylau.

It was Rocheteau who first spotted the group of horsemen thundering down the slight rise to the left. At their head was the unmistakable figure of Marshal Joachim Murat. He was dressed in a green overcoat, trimmed with fur at the collar, cuffs and hem. There were several huge white ostrich feathers waving from his fur bonnet and he wore gold leather boots. Slung over his saddle was a leopard-skin shabraque. The entire outfit was striking and typical of the flamboyant Gascon.

'It could only be Murat,' said Rocheteau, smiling.

'He acts like some overstuffed peacock because he is Bonaparte's brother-in-law,' Delacor hissed, touching the wound in his neck. It had been dressed again and the bleeding had stopped.

'He is a brave man,' Bonet said. 'A good leader.'

Lausard saw the Marshal gathering Dahlmann, d'Hautpol, Klein, Grouchy and Milhaud around him. They spoke briefly then each of the commanders rode back to rejoin his unit. Almost at once, the chausseurs at the front of the massive French column moved off at a walk.

'Now what?' Roussard murmured.

The dragoons followed after them, then the rest of the French cavalry. Lausard glanced behind him to see that the entire massive formation was on the move. The sound of ten thousand advancing horsemen momentarily eclipsed everything else on the battlefield. The vast formation moved rapidly from the one hundred and twenty paces of the walk to the two hundred and forty of the trot.

Lausard felt his heart pounding hard. So did others around him but perhaps for other reasons. Russian shot and shell began to fall more frequently among the cavalry. Several aerial bursts detonated above them and Lausard heard men scream as they were hit by pieces of flying metal. But he kept his eyes ahead, aware that the pace was increasing still further to the four hundred and eighty paces a minute that constituted a gallop. In perfectly synchronised files, the French cavalry swept forward, the distance between themselves and the centre of the Russian army closing by the second. Lausard guessed they were now less than a thousand yards from the leading enemy units. He could see nothing but those ahead of him, could hear nothing but the thundering of hooves and the almost deafening jingle of ten thousand harnesses. And among all that was the shriek of round-shot as it ploughed into the mass of French horsemen bringing down more and more riders; as each fell another spurred forward to fill the gap and maintain an unbroken front as the entire might of the French cavalry drew nearer its target. And now, as several trumpeters at the front of the massive formation began to blast out the unmistakable notes Lausard recognised so well, he knew what was happening. Over ten thousand men, led by their fearless commander, upped their speed to the six hundred paces a minute of the charge. Lausard felt the adrenalin coursing through his veins. He, and thousands like him, drew their swords and sabres in a deafening hiss of steel.

'Charge,' roared Milliere and the shout was echoed ten thousand times over as the French cavalry swept forward like a tidal wave. Men bellowed oaths and curses. Others whispered prayers and all the sounds melded together to form one massive cacophony of noise that rose to the heavens and threatened to split them asunder.

So many hooves turned the snow into slush and the horses, seemingly infected with the madness of their riders, whinnied frenziedly as they continued to thunder on towards the Russians.

More and more roundshot began to plough into the French. Some canister, too. But it was as if this only served to drive the riders on to even greater speed. Guidons fluttered in the wind. Swords were pointed at the massed green ranks and the hated cannon ahead of and between them. Russian gunners fired one last volley then either ran or hid under their cannon in the hope that the vengeful French cavalry would not be able to reach them.

To his left, Lausard saw hundreds of Russian troops retreating from Eylau merely ridden down by the mass of French cavalry. Men were reduced to bloody pulp by the hooves of so many horses. Some tried to run but were easily caught by the speeding horsemen and also ridden down. Swords cut to the left and right bringing down more of the enemy.

Another hundred yards and they would be in the heart of the green-clad infantry.

Lausard felt as if he were drunk. Intoxicated with the sheer exhilaration of such a massive cavalry charge. He had known this feeling many times before but it seemed to be amplified by the sheer staggering number of other riders thundering forward with him. The French cavalry were powerful men on powerful horses, all seething with frustration and with anger and intent only on reaching their enemy.

There was a burst of canister from the left. Another from the right.

One of the three-ounce balls cut through the right stirrup leather of Carbonne and the former executioner almost slipped from the saddle. Next to him, Charvet was not so lucky. One of the balls hit him in the chest and sent him tumbling. Horses, unable to avoid him, trampled him. Lausard saw him go down but merely gritted his teeth and rode on.

Tigana's horse was hit. It went forward on to its neck, flinging him from the saddle, but he rolled once and shot out a hand to grab the tail of the mount in front of him. For a few insane seconds, he ran along behind the speeding horse before finally throwing himself behind the carcass of another dead animal. Some horses hurdled the body, others merely rode over it. Tigana laid in the bloodied slush, curled into a foetal position, and prayed as the torrent of horsemen continued to flow over and around him.

The leading squadrons smashed into the Russian lines like a battering ram.

The infantry merely melted away, unable to withstand such an incredible onslaught. Ridden down, sabred and shot, the Russians tried to hold their positions but it was impossible. Few regiments had even formed squares to protect themselves against the onrushing cavalry and now they paid the supreme price. Lausard hacked madly to his left and right, bringing down men with every stroke. His companions did likewise. Karim hacked off the arm of a Russian officer who struck at him with a sword. Then, the Circassian turned in the saddle and caught another man across the back of the head, the scimitar hacking deep into his skull.

Rocheteau, his uniform already spattered with blood, cut at

anything that moved, screaming madly. Others were infected with his lunacy. Varcon brought his sword down so hard on to the head of a Russian grenadier that not only did it cut the mitre in two, it also split the skull as far as the eyebrows. Varcon tugged the blade free and continued with his butchery. The French were like men possessed and still they were moving at incredible speed, tearing through the Russian lines with ease, chopping and cutting their way deeper and deeper into the very heart of their enemy's centre.

Lausard felt something cold driven into his left thigh and realised he'd been bayoneted. More in rage than pain, he roared something unintelligible and caught his attacker across the side of the face with a blow that carved off most of the man's lower jaw. Lausard kicked out at the dying man and rode on, blood flowing freely from the wound in his leg. He saw Royere cut down two artillerymen who were trying to run to safety beneath a caisson. More fleeing Russians were merely ridden down. Everywhere, the snow was stained crimson and the bodies of men and horses were beginning to carpet it in ever greater abundance.

Despite the freezing temperatures, the French cavalrymen were sweating, such was the fury of their attack. Horses were lathered by the charge that showed no signs of abating. Men drove their mounts on with frenzied enthusiasm. Through the melee, Lausard saw Marshal Murat riding back and forth waving nothing more than a riding crop above his head. It was a sight that inspired many more Frenchmen to inflict even greater slaughter. The sergeant also saw General Grouchy's horse hit the ground, its head almost torn off by a roundshot. The general, his uniform soaked with blood, rolled over and grabbed the reins of a riderless horse, pulling himself into the saddle before riding on with his men. Dead and dying horses and men from both sides formed bizarre ramparts but the French cavalry merely drove their mounts on ever deeper into the Russian centre, heedless of anything other than the desire to kill. To cut and stab at everything in their path that represented an enemy.

Lausard, his face a mask of blood, his sword blade dripping crimson, saw woods ahead of him and, finally, as if it could not take another step, his horse slowed then stopped as he tugged hard on its reins. Both animal and rider were exhausted and the same was true of the thousands upon thousands of other French cavalry who had roared across the valley and smashed through the Russian centre.

'Re-form,' shouted Milliere, waving his sword. The officer had been wounded in the left arm by a stray bullet and was having trouble holding his reins. Everywhere, the victorious horsemen were turning, forming, with matchless expertise, into one huge column. Lausard had no idea how far they had charged. The entire episode seemed to have taken place in the blinking of an eye. But he now saw that the Russian troops who had been broken so easily were turning to face their opponents. Rank after rank of green-coated infantry were forming up, presenting a barrier of fifteen-inch-long bayonets, ready to meet the now shattered French cavalry as it tried to return to its own side of the valley. Lausard sucked in deep breaths and looked around him. Hardly a man he saw was not bathed in blood, some of it their own. The ground they had crossed was a sea of crimson slush littered with thousands of dead and dying. Kruger, holding the guidon aloft, brought his horse close to Lausard's. The Bavarian had been cut across the face with a sword. Part of his nose was missing and one cheek had been laid open to the bone. He merely looked at the sergeant and swallowed hard.

'We'll never get back,' Giresse gasped. Even as he spoke, a roundshot struck the ground near him, bounced up and took his horse's head off. The animal, the stump of its neck spouting blood, stood motionless for long seconds then went down in a heap, legs twitching madly as the muscles gave way. Giresse rolled over, looking around for another mount. He grabbed one that had belonged to a cuirassier. The man's foot was still in the left stirrup. Giresse kicked it free as he mounted, gripping the reins of the great black animal.

Already, thousands of French cavalry were hurtling back towards their own lines and Lausard saw the head of the massive column thundering towards the stoic lines of Russian infantry. The foot soldiers unleashed a devastating volley of fire and hundreds of men and horses were hit. A bullet caught Charvet just below the right eye. He toppled backwards, his foot still caught in the right stirrup. His horse thundered on, dragging him with it. Lausard raced after it, watching as Charvet's body bounced madly over the ground, his arms trailing out behind him. He put spurs to his exhausted mount, guiding the animal up alongside Charvet's horse. Lausard tried to catch the reins, anything to stop the animal's dash. Anything to stop it dragging Charvet's body. Finally he swung his sword and cut the stirrup leather. Charvet's body rolled free and the horse careered on. For fleeting seconds, Lausard thought about reining his own mount in and going back for his companion but the momentum of those riders behind him carried him forward. On towards the Russian infantry and artillerymen who were still trying to hide from the vengeful swords of the French. One huge corporal suddenly sprang out from beneath an artillery caisson and swung a rammer like a club. He caught Lausard in the midriff with it. The impact winded the sergeant and lifted him from his saddle. He hit the ground hard, still wheezing, his sword flying from his grip, but he had the presence of mind to roll out of the path of the nearest horses, only too aware that he was now unarmed. However, there were so many bodies lying around it would only be a matter of snatching up another sword. Before he could, the artillery corporal struck at him again with the rammer, this time slamming it into his injured leg. Lausard shouted in pain and dropped to his knees as the corporal advanced upon him, pulling a knife from his belt. He snarled something in Russian and threw himself at Lausard who ducked under his lunge and kicked out at him. The corporal overbalanced and Lausard was on him, hands reaching for his throat, thumbs digging deeply into the big man's bull-like neck. Lausard broke off momentarily to drive a powerful fist into the corporal's face. Three more times he struck him, grabbing at the hand that held the knife. Still the corporal cursed him, his voice cracking, spittle dribbling over his lips.

Lausard had no choice. He sank his teeth into the man's throat and gripped him like a fox would grip a rabbit. Not even releasing the pressure when he tasted the blood that filled his mouth. He tore his head back, ripping away a portion of the corporal's windpipe with it. The big man was making gurgling noises now, blood spouting from his throat. Lausard, his uniform soaked with crimson, staggered backwards, away from his dying enemy. He snatched up a discarded sword and looked around for a riderless horse.

The first one he saw was brought down in a hail of bullets, one of which sang off the sergeant's helmet. Another tore off the knee cuff of his right boot. He grabbed at another mount and pulled himself up into the saddle, dashing on with the rest of the French cavalry. He spat blood as he rode, urging the horse on to even greater speed, but it was blown, its strength gone. Exhausted by the charge across the valley and handicapped by a bayonet wound in its side, the animal could barely muster a gallop. Lausard felt it stumble and, as it hit the ground, he rolled over in the red slush.

'Sergeant.'

He heard the voice and looked around in time to see Gaston thundering towards him. The young trumpeter could not stop but he slowed his horse down as best he could. Lausard shot out a desperate hand and managed to grab one of Gaston's stirrups. Gritting his teeth he hung on, using all his strength, trying to prevent his arms being torn from the sockets as the horse thundered on. Lausard felt his boots dragging over the earth, occasionally bumping over the countless bodies on the battlefield, but he held on, the wind rushing into his face and into his open mouth as he roared. How easy it would have been simply to have released his grip. To have rolled away from the horse and allowed himself to be ridden over. How easy the death he had sought would find him then. But something forced him to cling on. Some instinct he had acquired over the last ten or eleven years. An instinct as precious as any gem. The determination to survive. He felt as if his arms and shoulders were on fire but still he held on and he sensed that Gaston was at last slowing the horse down.

From somewhere ahead he heard the pounding of more horses' hooves, more shouts and curses and shouts of '*Vive l'Empereur*'. As he glanced up, wave after wave of Guard cavalry charged past, slamming into some Russian cavalry that had pursued the retiring French. The chausseurs and Mamelukes brushed the Russians aside then ploughed on towards the already scattered enemy infantry and the dazed gunners. Lausard released his hold on the stirrup he had been gripping. He fell forward, face first into the freezing mud, and lay still for a second as more horses rode past him. Every muscle in his body ached. There was pain with every movement but, somehow, he forced himself to stand up, almost falling again as he tried to put weight on his injured leg. He slapped a hand to the wound then quickly inspected it. The bayonet had not penetrated deeply but it had gouged his thigh badly. Gaston, his face pale, looked down at the sergeant and nodded almost imperceptibly. He swayed uncertainly for a moment longer then fell sideways into the mud. Lausard knelt beside him, cradling his head in his hands.

'Don't let me die,' Gaston whispered, his eyes never leaving Lausard's. He gripped the sergeant's hand tightly and Lausard responded.

Close to him, Tabor and Rocheteau reined in their mounts and hurried across to him.

'Get him to a surgeon now,' Lausard snapped.

Tabor bent and picked Gaston up as if he were a child, cradling him in his huge, powerful arms.

'You should go with him, Alain,' Rocheteau insisted, seeing the blood that had soaked the sergeant's uniform. 'Get that wound attended to.'

Lausard ignored the remark and looked around at the returning French cavalry. Without exception, they looked exhausted beyond endurance, some of their mounts collapsing as they finally reached the safety of their own lines once again. The men who rolled away from fallen horses barely had the strength to move. Many were wounded. Riderless horses dashed in all directions. Kruger rode over, the guidon still gripped in his hand. His eyes were bulging wide and the knot of muscles at the side of his jaw pulsed madly. The Bavarian looked down at Lausard and the sergeant saw that there were tears in his eyes. Bonet too looked as if he were about to lose control. He was sobbing uncontrollably. In his right hand he held what remained of his sword. It was shattered. Broken just above the hilt, but still he held it. Moreau put out a comforting arm and pulled the former schoolmaster closer to him.

All around them, the remains of the French cavalry were forming up into their squadrons once more, using their own guidons as rallying points while NCOs and officers checked numbers or noted those who had not returned.

Only by a monumental effort of will did Lausard prevent himself from dropping to his knees. The mental and physical exertion he and his companions had endured so far had been almost intolerable but, somehow, he sucked in a breath of tainted air and took the reins of a horse that Rocheteau handed to him. The sergeant mounted and walked the animal towards Milliere and Royere. The captain had lost his eyepatch during the charge. He sat stiffly on his horse, occasionally muttering words of encouragement to Royere who was looking at his wound and nodding, as if to assure his superior that the bullet had not done too much damage.

'Form up,' Milliere shouted and the dragoons did as they were ordered.

Lausard took off his helmet and ran a hand through his matted, blood-soaked hair before replacing the brass casque. As he began to count the dragoons who had returned, several roundshot struck the ground nearby as if to remind the French that the battle was still raging.

Napoleon sucked in a deep breath and surveyed the carnage before him. He paced back and forth for a moment, his eyes never leaving the battlefield, his gaze constantly travelling from the burning hell of Eylau, south-east to the Russian centre and then down to Rothenen which also seemed to be ablaze.

'Sire,' said Berthier quietly, almost reluctant to disturb the Emperor's thoughts. 'Your orders have been carried out. Marshal Davout's Third Corps has been ordered to attack Tolstoi's open flank. They have had considerable success against them. Marshal Murat's cavalry and what remains of Marshal Augereau's corps are holding the centre and Marshal Soult's men continue to maintain their position on our left. If you should see fit to release the Guard then the Russians may well be defeated . . .'

Napoleon suddenly turned and cut him short.

'And use up my last reserves,' he snapped. 'I have not conquered half of Europe by showing that kind of recklessness, Berthier. You, more than anyone, should know that.'

'But, sire, as the positions stand, Bennigsen has lost the initiative. Marshal Murat's charge gave fresh heart to the entire army. The Guard are standing idly by when they could be the instrument of the victory you so badly desire.'

'And what of Lestocq and his Prussians? If I send in the Guard now and the Prussians arrive on our left. What then? If he somehow manages to elude Ney and succeeds in bringing his forces to the field to reinforce the Russians, what am I to do to combat that if my only reserves have already been committed?' He returned his attention to the battlefield before him. 'Why has Ney not marched to the sound of the guns? How can a man not hear more than six hundred cannon?'

'The weather does not favour him, sire,' said the Chief of Staff.

'Then why has he not simply obeyed his orders and marched here from Kreuzberg? What time was the order sent?'

'Eight this morning, sire.'

'Then where is he?' rasped the Corsican. 'He has fourteen thousand of my men under his command. More than enough to turn this day in our favour once and for all.'

Not for the first time that day, Napoleon looked agitatedly at his pocket watch.

'More than half our strength killed, wounded or missing,' said Royere softly.

'Do not expect to see those who are missing again, Lieutenant,' Lausard exhaled wearily.

'What of Charvet?' Rocheteau wanted to know.

'And Tigana?' Karim added.

'Delacor. Carbonne. Delbene. Collard.'

Voices called from all along the line.

'I saw Charvet die,' Lausard said flatly. 'As for the others . . .' He allowed the sentence to trail off.

'Then they are lost to us for ever,' Rocheteau murmured.

'If they are dead they will be buried in mass graves,' said

Moreau, crossing himself. 'They will lie where they lost their lives.'

'No,' Lausard exclaimed. 'I will not allow that to happen. I will not let men who I knew, who I respected and *loved*, to be buried like diseased cattle. Hurled into some pit and covered with snow. I will not allow it.'

'How will we find their bodies, Alain?' Rocheteau wanted to know.

'We may well be sharing a grave with them if night does not soon fall,' Roussard offered, glancing up at the overcast sky. 'Is there to be no end to this battle?'

Lausard snapped the reins of his horse and guided it towards a small rise a few yards ahead of where the dragoons were drawn up in open order. Rocheteau followed him. Both of the men sat astride their mounts gazing at the battle still raging all around them.

'If they are not dead, then they are prisoners or they are wounded and already freezing to death in this place,' Rocheteau said. 'I feel their loss as keenly as you, Alain. I too loved them.'

'Then do not abandon them, Rocheteau,' the sergeant said, looking at his companion. 'When your wife died of smallpox, what did they do with her body? Do you remember telling me that story? Tell me again what they did with her.'

'They buried her in a mass grave just outside Paris.'

'And what did you do? Tell me again, Rocheteau.'

The corporal did not speak; he merely lowered his gaze.

'You went back to her grave,' Lausard breathed. 'You removed her body and you buried her in a place of *your* choosing. Didn't you?'

The corporal nodded.

'Those who are dead we will find,' Lausard told him. 'Those who are wounded we will help. Those taken prisoner we will free.'

Rocheteau swallowed hard and nodded. Lausard rested one hand on his companion's shoulder and gently squeezed it.

'Whatever you do,' Rocheteau told him, 'I am with you. I and every man in this squadron.'

Twenty-Three

The young aide-de-camp who galloped through the line of Imperial Guard grenadiers towards Napoleon and his staff tugged hard on his reins as he neared the Corsican. His grey horse, spattered with mud and blood and as exhausted as its rider, pawed at the ground as the aide scurried across in the direction of Napoleon who had already turned to face him. He saluted and handed a crumpled piece of paper to his Emperor who took it and read it before passing it to Rapp.

'The Prussians have forced Davout out of Kutschitten *and* Anklappen,' said Napoleon flatly. 'What was won three hours ago is lost again.'

'Not if the remainder of Marshal Ney's corps can take the field within the hour, sire,' Rapp said, doing his best to inject a note of optimism into his voice. 'They have already recaptured Schloditten on our left flank. Their appearance has galvanised the troops of Marshal Soult. The Russians can make no more moves against us now.'

Napoleon looked at the young aide.

'How old are you, boy?' he asked.

'Twenty-one, sire.'

'Then pray that you never see another day like this one if you live to be a hundred.'

He turned his back on the aide and wandered away alone, gazing to the north where the sky was the colour of wet steel. Smoke and dense banks of low cloud scudded across the heavens and, every so often, snow flurries would fall, as they had done all day.

'What do I tell Marshal Davout, sire?' the aide called.

'Tell him I have no troops left to send him,' Napoleon replied without turning round. 'Tell him to hold his position as best he can.'

The aide looked at Berthier as if hoping the Chief of Staff would issue some kind of order himself but Berthier merely walked across to join his commander.

'We are in possession of the field, sire,' the Chief of Staff said. 'Surely it is a victory?'

'Bennigsen's army is damaged, not destroyed,' the Corsican said. 'It still holds its positions on the field. We are faced with the possibility of renewing the battle come dawn despite the fact that our own army has been crippled, possibly beyond recovery.'

'With inferior numbers we prevailed, sire,' Berthier persisted. 'Is that alone not reason for celebration?'

Napoleon did not answer.

Lausard sat motionless in his saddle as a roundshot came hurtling from the direction of the Russian lines. He was not sure of its origin or its nationality. There seemed to be as many dark-coated Prussian troops on the field now as there were green-clad Russians. The lethal projectile struck the earth a few yards away and rolled harmlessly away into a shallow depression where several men had been sheltering earlier in the day. All of them were dead, huddled together in one single bloodied mass. All over the battlefield, the firing of both cannons and muskets was gradually fading. As the north wind began to blow, the only sound that rose with any clarity was the moaning of the thousands of wounded. Hidden by the darkness, they were like disembodied souls, their howls of pain and despair rising as if from the depths of hell itself.

'What time is it?' Lausard asked.

Rocheteau squinted at his pocket watch, finding it difficult to pick out the position of the hands in the funereal blackness.

'Ten, no, eleven o'clock,' he said, his voice cracking. Like all of his companions, like every single man in *La Grande Armée*, he was exhausted, tortured by the worst thirst he had ever known, starving, soaked with blood and water and freezing cold.

'We have been in the saddle since eight this morning,' Lausard murmured. 'And for what? What have we gained?'

'If the Emperor had used his Guard then it might have been different, but he treats them like toys. He should keep them in a damned box. It seems he is reluctant to use them. Perhaps he thinks the rest of us are less useful. Meanwhile, those bastards are the only ones within twenty miles with anything to eat or drink. I heard that Jews had brought them brandy from Warsaw and they were selling it for six francs a time. And what do we have? Melted snow and horsemeat, if we can get it.'

'You dare to question our Emperor,' Lausard said, his voice full of scorn. 'You complain about his methods?'

'What do I have to thank him for?'

'Not much, Corporal.'

Both men turned as they heard Lieutenant Royere's voice.

'I could not help but overhear your conversation,' he said, almost apologetically.

'And do you disagree with our words? Are we wrong to question the usefulness of such a conflict, Lieutenant?'

'No, my friend, you are not and I fear that something else has died here today, along with thousands of our countrymen. I fear that the love the Emperor basked in has been diminished. A man so profligate with the lives of those he rules must be prepared to lose the devotion of some of their surviving colleagues.'

'Did *you* lose your idealism out there, Lieutenant?' Lausard wanted to know. 'Where others spilled their blood, was the only thing to drain from you those ideals you always held so dear?'

'Those you sought to mock me for, my friend?' Royere asked, attempting a smile. 'No. I still believe in the Emperor. I still cling to the ethics of the revolution.'

'How many lying out there in the snow, starving, dying of thirst and cold, robbed by scavengers, would agree with you, Lieutenant?'

'None, Sergeant, and I would not blame them. But the men of this squadron who died today were more than just troopers to *me* as well as to you. Do not presume to claim sole right to despair, my friend. We all have a right to share *that*.'

'Quite so, Lieutenant,' said Lausard, turning his horse. 'And I have no doubt that we will all continue to share it for a long time to come. Courtesy of Bonaparte.'

He rode off slowly into the blackness.

'Alain,' called Rocheteau. 'Where are you going?'

Lausard did not answer.

The barn that stood in a hollow just behind Eylau had been cleared of wounded. All that remained inside it were the blood-soaked tables where French surgeons, in freezing conditions, had amputated limbs and attempted to patch up wounds as best they could. In one corner of the darkened building there was a large wooden tub. It was filled to overflowing with amputated arms and legs. Next to it lay a pile of torn and holed jackets, boots and helmets. The interior of the building stank of death. A small fire had been built and Napoleon studied the maps by its sickly yellow light. The pieces of paper had been laid out on a hastily scrubbed operating table. Beneath it, the Corsican noticed, lay several spent bullets, taken from wounds, and several teeth. He took off his bicorn and ran a hand through his close-cropped hair. Outside, the wind whipped snow ever more vehemently around the draughty building. One of the shutters creaked and slammed continuously with every gust of wind.

On the other side of the table, Soult, Murat, Augereau and Berthier stood, also glancing down at the maps. Augereau's left elbow was heavily bandaged and, more than once, he had to lean against the table as if to prevent himself from overbalancing.

'The truth of what happened here today must never be revealed to the French people,' said the Corsican finally. 'The official bulletin of the army will reveal that the losses of *La Grand Armée* were one thousand nine hundred killed and close to six thousand wounded.'

'Sire, that is nowhere near the truth,' Augereau said quietly. 'My division alone suffered more than five thousand casualties in twenty minutes during our attack this morning. I lost one man in every three.'

'I am well aware of the true nature of our losses, Augereau,' the Corsican snapped. 'But why burden the population at large with such considerations? All they will be concerned with is that the Russian army has been beaten.'

'But it has *not* been beaten, sire,' Augereau insisted. 'Both Russian troops *and* their Prussian allies still occupy ground no more than a thousand yards from our own front lines.'

'They are in no position to claim victory,' Murat interjected. 'If they cannot boast of victory then surely it is we who must take the laurels for this day.'

'You would claim a victory if we had two men alive and they just one, Murat,' Augereau said dismissively.

'Where is your loyalty, Augereau?' the Gascon sneered. 'Would you have us crow from the rooftops that we were beaten here by the Muscovites?'

'I would expect nothing less than such mindless bravado from a mountebank such as yourself,' said the older man.

'How dare you insult me,' Murat snapped.

'You are a tightrope dancer,' Augereau continued. 'A dancing dog. A scoundrel in fancy dress and plumes.'

'And you are perhaps too old to hold the position you now occupy. Perhaps the advancing years have clouded your judgement. At least I did not lead my men into the very jaws of the Russian cannon *in error*.'

'Enough,' Napoleon rasped. 'You squabble like children over mere words.'

'Words like victory are not to be treated lightly, are they, sire?' Augereau continued.

'What is the true extent of our loss?' Soult wanted to know.

'Twenty thousand,' said Berthier. 'Perhaps more.'

'The Russians have done us great harm,' Napoleon admitted.

'And we them,' said Soult indignantly. 'Our bullets were not made of cotton.

'Russian casualties are estimated at around fifteen thousand,' Berthier offered. 'It is hard to put a figure on the true numbers of dead and wounded at the moment. That task will become more pressing with the coming of dawn.'

'Word will be spread that great damage has been done to the

Russian army,' Napoleon said. 'That the Russian army demands peace. Two thousand copies of the official account of what happened here will be circulated among the Hanse towns. I myself will instruct Fouché to spread news of the reports first in the salons of Paris and then to the newspapers.'

'You would lie to your own people, sire?' Soult said quietly.

'It is no lie, Soult,' the Corsican snarled. 'The Russians *have* suffered greatly today. You said as much yourself.'

'But not as greatly as our own army, sire,' Soult offered. 'We are not even in a position to pursue them should they decide to retire.'

'My cavalry will pursue them, when the time comes,' Murat said haughtily.

'Your cavalry will *follow* them,' Augereau hissed. 'Not pursue them. You could not pursue a train of crippled mules at the moment. This is not the aftermath of Jena. You are not riding to glory this time. We have not enjoyed a shattering victory over our foes today. We have barely survived the fight *ourselves*.'

'More sedition,' Murat sneered. 'Why do you not return to your sick bed, old man? You would be more use there than commanding troops.'

'Damn you to hell, Murat,' Augereau said, stifling a cough. 'You and all your pantomime outfits. You belong in a circus, not on a battlefield.'

Napoleon brought his fist crashing down on the table top.

Silence greeted the gesture. The Corsican looked at each of his marshals in turn, his eyes glowing yellow in the light of the fire and the waning candles.

'Return to your men,' he said quietly. 'All of you. Our discussion is over for now.'

He looked at his pocket watch.

It was 3.05 a.m.

Lausard guided his horse along the Bartenstein road, the wail of thousands of wounded men assailing his ears throughout his journey. The entire valley was covered with dead and dying men and horses. All of them leaking their lifeblood into the snow that still covered the field. In some places, Lausard knew that the dead lay more thickly than others. On the small knoll where the French 14th Line regiment had been slaughtered. On the ground just outside Eylau where thousands of Russians had been annihilated as they reeled back from the buildings. And on the far side of the valley where the worst of the hand-to-hand fighting had taken place during the massive French cavalry charge.

On both sides of him, injured men were still being helped into the barns that had served as makeshift field hospitals all day. Torches burned outside the barns, attracting the wounded like moths. Those who had no help attempted to crawl towards the refuges, some of them on limbs that had been crushed or shattered. Many merely lay where they were and waited for death in the freezing temperatures. In the gloom, scavengers from both sides moved among the dead, stealing boots, clothes and valuables from them. Once they had gone, the wolves and other carrion creatures would descend from the woods that surrounded the battlefield to enjoy a feast the like of which they would never see again.

Lausard was about to stop at the closest of the hospitals when he heard hooves thundering towards him from the opposite direction. A single horseman, dressed in the uniform of a French hussar, was galloping along the muddy road as fast as his mount could carry him. He slowed his pace slightly as he reached Lausard.

'The Russians are retreating,' he said triumphantly, then rode on, his voice echoing on the wind.

Lausard glanced in the general direction of the enemy lines then dismounted. He tethered his horse and stepped inside the first of the field hospitals. It was like walking into hell. Screams, moans and wails of the wounded. The high-pitched rasp of saw on bone as shattered limbs were hacked off with as much speed as the overworked surgeons could muster. Assistants did not even bother to remove them; they left them to lie where they fell on the hard ground. The floor of the hospital was awash with blood, the operating tables soaked in it. As each patient was removed an orderly would throw a bucket of water over the surface to remove the worst of the gore then the next poor wretch would be lifted on, given a piece of wood to bite on and the amputation would begin. The surgeon would make a deep incision with a scalpel then set to work immediately with his saw. The stump would be cauterised with either hot metal or, in some cases, tar. Lausard could see several tubs of the black liquid bubbling over small fires. Flesh wounds were ignored. Deeper ones bound tightly with bandages, some of which had been taken from dead men earlier in the day. Bullets were probed for with long metal hooks and tugged out if possible. If not they were cut free with scalpels or merely left inside the wound. As Lausard watched he noticed that many of the surgeons' assistants' hands were so cold they could barely hold the instruments. The floor was littered with bloodied instruments, crimson-soaked gauze, pieces of flesh and hacke-off limbs. The stench was incredible. The overpowering coppery odour of blood, the more pungent odour of excrement and the all-pervading stink of tar and smoke.

The sergeant passed among the wounded, checking their faces – those among them that still had faces. He saw uniforms of all colours but the one he sought was red. He was looking for the familiar crimson tunic worn by Gaston. He had no idea which of the field hospitals Tabor had carried the young trumpeter to but assumed it would be one of those close to Eylau. Lausard moved almost robotically through the rows of wounded, many now tended to, hundreds still waiting their turn, his eyes ever alert for faces he recognised. For while his primary target was Gaston, he knew only too well that dozens of other men from his squadron could also be in this place.

As he moved among them, both the treated and the untreated, the wounded capable of movement reached out to him imploringly. Those that were able to speak asked him for water but all Lausard could do was shake his head. Like them, he was desperate for something to drink but had nothing. He noticed that several of the wounded were supping from the puddles of icy, bloodied water that had been used to swill down the operating tables. They lay on their bellies, faces in the foul liquid, ignoring the taste in their desperation to slake the thirst that was raging within them. Lausard thought how he would have found this almost bestial display abhorrent twenty years earlier but, in those, very different times, he had never known the kind of deprivation and suffering that had become second nature to him ever since he had first pulled on the uniform of a dragoon.

He continued with his search, occasionally stopping beside a wounded man to check his identity but finally, after what seemed like an eternity, he wandered out of the hospital, swung himself back into the saddle and guided his tired mount down the road in the direction of the next charnel house. As he stopped the horse at the second, and larger, barn, he saw a surgeon sitting outside on some bales of straw, his head in his hands. The man's apron and trousers were soaked with blood and, as Lausard drew nearer, he saw that the man was sobbing uncontrollably. A burial party were loading corpses on to a flat horse-drawn wagon, ready to transport them away to the massive pits that would be dug the next morning to accommodate the dead. The bodies were frozen into macabre shapes by rigor mortis and the bone-chilling weather.

The sergeant paused for a moment then passed into the field hospital. Again he was confronted by the same vision of purgatory he had seen earlier but, if anything, there were even more amputated limbs piled up against the walls. He passed one operating table where two surgeons were hopelessly attempting to staunch the geysers of blood spouting from the severed femoral artery of an artilleryman. The wounded man was lying quite still while his life fluid spurted madly into the air, every jet taking him closer to death. An infantryman sat close to the door, his face creased with pain. He was holding his stomach and, as Lausard passed him, he saw that he was vainly attempting to hold his intestines in. His attempts to prevent his entrails from spilling from the savage wound in his belly seemed hopeless.

The sergeant saw a red jacket and hurried across to the man wearing it. He knelt beside the occupant and attempted to turn him over.

'Gaston,' he whispered.

The body rolled over and Lausard saw that the man wore the pelisse of a chausseur. He looked blankly at Lausard, wondering if *he* could perhaps help to remove the metal splinter that had punctured his right lung and left him close to death. The dragoon sergeant got to his feet and moved on. Past the infantryman with two smashed feet, beyond the cuirassier with part of his brain bulging through a rent in his skull.

'Sergeant.'

The shout made him turn. He recognised the voice immediately.

Propped up against the far wall was the huge frame of Tabor.

Lausard hurried across to him, embracing the big man warmly.

'I thought it was you,' Tabor said. 'I knew you would not leave us here.' He coughed. As he did, blood spilled over his lips. Lausard wiped it away with one gauntlet.

'Is Gaston here?' the NCO wanted to know.

'Yes. I brought him here, as you ordered. I was close to the hospital when a howitzer shell exploded. I was hit in the stomach. Gaston was wounded again.'

'Where is he?'

'He is here, next to me. I would not let him out of my sight. I would not let him die.'

Lausard touched the big man's face with one hand. Then he looked down as Tabor pulled back the thick green cloak covering the figure beside him. Beneath it lay the young trumpeter. His eyes were already closed. Lausard pressed an index finger to the younger man's throat and felt for a pulse. He saw the blood on Gaston's face as he leaned closer.

'I tried to do as you instructed, Sergeant,' Tabor said, blood spilling again from his mouth. 'Is Gaston dead?'

Lausard shook his head slowly. The pulse in the trumpeter's neck was very faint.

'We have been lying here for more than six hours,' Tabor said. 'The surgeons are doing their best.'

Lausard gritted his teeth and got to his feet. He looked around and saw a medical orderly nearby.

'I need a surgeon to look at these men now,' the sergeant hissed.

'They are all too busy,' the orderly said, trying to push past.

Lausard drew his sword in one fluid movement and pressed the tip against the orderly's throat.

'Get me a surgeon now or even Larrey himself will not be able to help *you*,' snarled the NCO. He pushed the man away and watched as he muttered something in the ear of a surgeon who had just finished removing an infantryman's leg an inch above the knee. The orderly pointed in Lausard's direction and, moments later, the surgeon made his way over.

'They need your help now,' Lausard said.

'So does every man in this building, Sergeant,' said the surgeon without looking at him.

'I don't care about the other men in this building. I *do* about these two men.'

The surgeon inspected Tabor's stomach wound first, pulling his already torn tunic further open. He took a probe from his pocket and began poking around inside the wound.

'There's a piece of metal in there,' he announced, oblivious to Tabor's groans of pain. 'If it is removed he should survive.'

'Then remove it,' snarled Lausard threateningly.

The surgeon looked at him with an untroubled expression then turned his attention to Gaston.

'He'll lose that foot,' he murmured. 'It's the other wound . . .' He allowed the sentence to trail off, then pointed at a hole in the trumpeter's chest large enough to push a fist into. 'He isn't strong enough for me to amputate his foot and the other wound is too close to his heart.'

'Can you save him?' Lausard wanted to know.

'No,' said the surgeon. 'I'm surprised he's lasted as long as he has.'

Lausard held the man's gaze.

'Thank you for your honesty, Doctor,' he said.

'It doesn't benefit a surgeon to be on friendly terms with deception, Sergeant.' He patted Lausard gently on the arm. 'Was he in your squadron?'

'Both men are.'

'Let me see what I can do for you, big fellow,' said the surgeon and he motioned to three orderlies who hurried over and helped Tabor to his feet. They supported him as best they could over to one of the many operating tables where they helped him to lie down. Lausard stayed with Gaston. As he looked down, the younger man's eyes suddenly opened. For fleeting seconds they remained open and Lausard was sure he saw the glimmer of recognition there. Gaston tried to speak but his lips merely fluttered soundlessly and he reached for Lausard's hand, momentarily squeezing it hard in his own. A single tear rolled from the trumpeter's left eye but his mouth turned upwards slightly as Lausard gripped his hand even more tightly. The pressure was not reciprocated.

'I'm sorry,' the sergeant whispered.

He reached out gently and closed Gaston's eyes.

'Another one for the burial party, eh?' said an orderly who was passing by.

'No. I'll take him,' said Lausard. He knelt, then carefully lifted the trumpeter on to his shoulder before straightening up, carrying the weight effortlessly. He headed towards the hospital doors, passing the operating table where Tabor lay. The surgeon was about to begin his work. Lausard looked at the big man and nodded.

'I'll be waiting,' he said quietly.

Tabor managed a smile.

Lausard made his way towards the doors then out into the freezing night. He laid Gaston's body over his own saddle and took the reins in one hand. He patted the horse's neck to calm it and led it slowly along the road towards the next field hospital. He walked with his head down, barely noticing that it had begun to snow again.

TWENTY-FOUR

Rocheteau prodded the remains of the fire with the end of a discarded sword and men huddled closer to it, seeking warmth from the meagre blaze. Black smoke rose into the grey dawn sky and, from the north, heavy clouds drifted menacingly across the heavens spilling a steady dusting of snow over the battlefield. All over the valley and the low slopes, the remains of *La Grande Armée* stirred, like an animal waking from hibernation, but there was very little sound from the thousands of troops gathered in the frozen wasteland. Hundreds wandered about looking for food or drink. Others carried bundles of wood taken from the flattened buildings of Eylau and Rothenen with which to feed their fires. Very few seemed to want to move from the temporary warmth. A few moved among the dead of both sides removing clothes and rifling pockets but the events of the last two blood-soaked days seemed to have dulled the acquisitive appetites of even the most determined thieves. Money, gold, rings and watches were nowhere near as valuable now as potatoes and crusts of bread or half-drunk bottles of brandy or vodka.

Clothing that had not been stolen during the night was being collected for future use. Lausard saw an enormous pile of cuirasses close by. Just beyond them was a similar stock of muskets and carbines. Sappers inspected them all to see if they were still in working order. Those of use were loaded on to the many flat wagons that trundled across the snowy field. Swords and sabres by the hundreds were also packed on to the wagons and transported back towards the French depots.

Burial details tried their best to dig pits in the rock-hard ground, some aided by local peasants who had also emerged on to the field in search of food. Others merely contented themselves with taking boots or other clothing from the huge piles that littered the field. Farriers and veterinarians from every cavalry regiment passed among the horses inspecting them for wounds. Those that could still be ridden were led away; those beyond help were shot. The carcasses were being burned in a massive pyre just south of Eylau itself. Lausard and his companions could smell the stench of cooking horseflesh as it drifted through the snowy air.

Few words were spoken. The men had, once again, had little or no sleep during the hours of darkness and Lausard could not remember the last time he had enjoyed more than three hours' sleep in one night during the past week. Every single man he looked at was as pale as a ghost, exhausted both physically and mentally by what he had gone through.

To the rear of the dragoons' bivouac, now partially covered by a light dusting of snow, were a number of bodies. They were covered by blankets, cloaks or greatcoats. The corpses of those companions they had been able to find during the hours of darkness. Lausard himself had laid the body of Gaston with the others just two hours earlier before riding off across the valley with Rocheteau and Karim, all of them bearing torches, to sift through the masses of dead and wounded, trying to find familiar faces. Those they had recovered had been brought back to where they lay now. Of Tigana, Delacor and Collard there was still no sign. Whether they were dead, alive or prisoners no one knew. Lausard was sure that if any or all of them had been wounded and spent the night on the field without medical attention, they would now most definitely be dead. Temperatures had fallen again during the night and he did not expect any poor wretch to survive a combination of wounds and such murderous conditions.

Lausard looked up as he heard the jingling of harnesses. A group of horsemen were riding across the field, the leading figure wearing the uniform of a marshal of the empire. As the man removed his feathered bicorn, Lausard saw his shock of red hair and realised that the man was Marshal Michel Ney. He slowed his mount to a walk, his staff officers doing likewise. As the marshal drew nearer, Lausard and the other dragoons drew themselves erect and saluted.

'At ease,' Ney said quietly, looking around at the carnage. The dragoons relaxed from their positions.

'You suffered heavily during the fighting?' he said. It came out more as a statement than a question.

'The whole army suffered, sir,' Lausard told him.

'Quite so,' Ney agreed. He drew in a weary breath and shook his head, once more looking around at the piles of dead, the scattered weapons, the dead and dying horses and the blank faces of those who had survived. 'It is a massacre without result,' he said finally, then turned his horse and rode off followed by his aides.

The dragoons watched him heading off in the direction of Ziegelhof.

A voice nearby shouted *'Vive la France'*.

Another called *'Vive la paix'*.

'I fear the Emperor would not rejoice to hear such exhortations,' said Bonet. 'I have not heard those words spoken on a battlefield for more than ten years.'

'Perhaps the time for praising Bonaparte is at an end,' Lausard mused. 'There will not be many men left alive today who would pay him the respect he craves so fervently. And who would blame them?'

A heavy silence settled over the men, finally broken by Varcon.

'Where is the marshal going, do you think?' he asked.

'To see the Emperor,' Bonet suggested.

'Perhaps to eat a hearty breakfast,' Joubert added, his own stomach rumbling loudly.

Lausard ignored the ramblings of his companions.

'We have work to do,' he announced. He reached for the shovel that lay on the ground nearby. The others followed his example. They wandered across towards the line of bodies to their rear. Moreau looked at them again and crossed himself. Despite the unforgiving earth, the dragoons began to dig.

*

'The reports were correct, sire,' said Berthier, sweeping his telescope over the snow-flecked ridges on the far side of the valley. 'The Russians and their allies have retreated.'

Napoleon nodded almost imperceptibly, his own telescope trained on the shadowy groups of Cossacks arranged along the ridge and the outskirts of the forest beyond.

'Just as well,' the Corsican murmured. 'I am not sure we could have faced a third day's fighting and prevailed. Three or four more battles such as this and I shall no longer have an army.'

He snapped his telescope shut and turned back to the huge fire that had been built for him by the men of his Imperial Guard. A huge sergeant with several scars on his grizzled face was feeding pieces of wood into the blaze as the Emperor warmed his hands.

'What are your plans, sire, if I may ask?' Berthier enquired.

'Plans? My plans are the same as they were when this campaign first began, Berthier. To destroy the Russian army and secure a lasting peace with the Tsar. How long that will take remains to be seen.' He inhaled deeply. 'Bennigsen's men fought us to a standstill, Berthier. Only in Paris will this be seen as a victory and only then because *I* have ensured there is no other way to view the events of the past two days. But the men who fought here know the truth. And when I ask them to continue this war, what will they do? Will they throw away their lives with such wantonness again?'

'They will do whatever you order, sire, because they love you.'

The Corsican managed a smile but it did not touch his eyes.

'Marshal Murat will begin his pursuit of the enemy later today, sire,' Berthier offered.

'Augereau was right in what he said last night,' the Corsican muttered. 'It will not be a pursuit. Murat will *follow* the enemy because his cavalry are in no state to do otherwise.' Napoleon turned and looked out once again over the body-strewn field. 'The Russians have retreated, Berthier. They have left the field. Normally a commander and his army would rejoice at such an occurrence, but this time they have left me not with a field of glory but with a slaughterhouse.'

*

Lausard had no idea how long it took to dig the graves. Time, as had happened so often before, lost its meaning once again. All that any of the dragoons were aware of was how unyielding the iron-hard soil was to their shovels. Nonetheless, they battled against it, cutting through it until they had created enough shallow resting places for their fallen comrades. Then, the bodies were laid carefully in each one, still shrouded by the blankets, cloaks or overcoats. While the other men refilled the holes, Baumar and Rostov fashioned rough crosses for each grave, binding two pieces of wood together with pieces of harness or strips of discarded stirrup leather. On the horizontal part of each cross they wrote the names of the dead men with pieces of burned wood. When the task was completed, Lausard tossed his shovel contemptuously to one side.

'They have need of your God now, Moreau,' he said quietly. 'And they have a need for you. Speak His words. Bless them. Do whatever you feel He demands.'

Moreau nodded and stepped forward. The other dragoons gathered around the graves. Some bowed their heads. Lausard stood bolt upright, his eyes open. He gazed unblinking at the rudimentary crosses, driven into the ground with difficulty. Each one bore the name of its occupant.

Carbonne.

Charvet.

Gormier.

Delbene.

Gaston.

The only reminder that the men had ever existed. The flimsy nature of that last monument was curiously appropriate to the fragility of the life whose passing it marked, Lausard thought.

'Merciful Father,' Moreau began, somewhat falteringly. 'We ask your blessing for these men.' He looked at Lausard who nodded, encouraging him to continue.

The sergeant remained upright, his arms at his sides, his eyes fixed ahead.

Beside him he saw that Bonet had his eyes closed.

Joubert's hands were clasped before him.

Even the lips of Giresse were moving silently as if he were whispering his own prayers.

'Take them into your arms, Lord,' Moreau continued, his breath clouding before him. 'Take them into heaven where they may dwell with you for eternity. Free of the pain and suffering of their earthly lives. May they find peace.'

Lausard was surprised to find that tears were rolling down both his cheeks. He made no attempt to wipe them away.

'We ask you, Lord, to protect them and also to protect *us*,' Moreau continued. 'We who continue to serve you, as these men we now pass to your keeping served you.'

Rocheteau had his head bowed.

'We ask this as we ask your forgiveness, Lord,' Moreau said, his voice cracking slightly. 'Do not despise us because we are sinners. Instead, when the time comes, welcome us too into your kingdom as you now welcome these men we called comrades, citizens and friends.' He genuflected over the grave of each man in turn then crossed himself.

Bonet and several of the other men did likewise.

'Take them unto paradise,' murmured Karim. 'In the name of Allah, all praise to Him.'

Lausard finally wiped the tears from his face and nodded at Moreau.

'Amen,' said Moreau loudly.

'Amen,' Lausard whispered.

The sound echoed from the other men.

It echoed upwards into the overcast sky, carried by the souls of those who now lay in three feet of icy Polish soil. A gunshot rang across the valley as a farrier put another wounded horse out of its misery.

'I thought you didn't believe in God, Alain,' said Bonet.

Lausard almost smiled.

'After what you've seen these past two days, Bonet, you still question my faith,' said the sergeant. 'How could any man believe after what has happened here? I spoke one word. One word that those who believe claim as their own. But what are words? They are empty. Meaningless. Like what happened here. Like our lives.'

He turned and walked away.

Rocheteau strode across to join him.

'What of those who are missing, Alain?' he wanted to know.

'I told you before; if they are dead we will find them and bury them with the dignity they deserve. If they are prisoners we will free them when the time is right.'

'And when will that time be?'

'We will know it when it comes.'

'Looking at those graves, I thought how lucky I was still to be alive. What did you feel, Alain?'

'A sense of helplessness. An anger that I could do nothing to prevent any of those men from ending up where they are now.'

'Moreau says they are with God.'

'Let him cling to his beliefs, Rocheteau. Every man must believe in *something*. Be it God, the Empire, his country or Bonaparte.'

'And what do *you* believe in?'

'The one thing I can trust.'

He patted the hilt of his sword gently.

The snow was beginning to fall more thickly.